Dear Reader,

Who would ever have dreamed what could happen that fine spring day that Boone and his hired hand picked me up hitchhiking in the Sawtooth Valley? For starters, I thought I had them fooled, dressed as a boy!

Boone didn't have much time for me then and I can't say I blamed him. He took me on as a cook, and I'd never even grilled a cheese sandwich before. It didn't take his cowboys long to find out, but Boone never gave up on me.

Let's see, where should I start? With dear, dear Mattie, Boone's grandma, who became the grandmother I'd never had? With Ho, his foreman, who never let me down—ever? With my friend Bonnie, who helped me when I needed help most? If only I hadn't told that great big fat lie right at the start....

Oh, heavens! Why don't you just read our story....

Love,

Lucie

Please address questions and book requests to: Silhouette Reader Service
U.S.: 3010 Walden Ave., P.O. Box 1325, Buffalo, NY 14269
Canadian: P.O. Box 609, Fort Erie, Ont. L2A 5X3

WESTERN *Lovers*™

JUDITH BOWEN

A HOME ON THE RANGE

Published by Silhouette Books
America's Publisher of Contemporary Romance

SILHOUETTE BOOKS

ISBN 0-373-30168-5

A HOME ON THE RANGE

To my parents, Dick and Dorothy Corser, with thanks.

For moose meat and wild blueberries,
For fresh air and freedom.

Prologue

The dream—if it was a dream—was always the same: the pretty face smelling of roses and sunshine bending down toward her, the love in those blue, blue smiling eyes as she came closer...closer. And then the soft sweet kiss, and the giggle as the woman's loose braid fell forward over her shoulder to tickle the baby's cheek. Who had giggled? Herself, the child in the cot, or the woman she knew to be her mother?

And then the other dream—if it was a dream: she was perhaps three, pudgy legs churning on the old red tricycle, its bell rusted and broken, one back wheel wiggling ominously. But it worked, it worked...and it belonged to her. Oh, the joy of that day! She felt it still in her dreams. Oh, the cleverness, the thrill of pedaling furiously on, keeping just ahead of the laughing girl who chased her round and round on the cracked pavement.

Or was the girl only pretending to chase her? For she was

older, her hair in braids, her legs thin and long under her cotton dress. And there, in the distance, in the back of her dream, was their mother—for she knew with a knowledge that defied everything she'd ever been told, that this *was* her mother and this *was* her sister—their mother laughing, sitting on the top step of the sagging veranda, her hair shining, her face sad and happy at the same time.

And that always made Lucie cry, and she'd wake up, her fist in her mouth to stop from crying out in the thick, frightening black of the night, because the people she called Mother and Father now didn't believe in leaving a light on. They thought it was a weakness in Lucie's character that she wanted it, and they told her so. They said it wasted electricity and money, and Lucie didn't know which they disapproved of most.

But that was before she was twelve, before she found the old letter in the library, stuffed into one of her father's leather-bound books. She'd been sent there to wait for him to come and administer punishment for some childish sin, now long-forgotten. There were so many, it seemed. *Spare the rod, spoil the child.* And while she waited, to keep her fear from smothering her, she leafed through some of the forbidden books. Another transgression, if they only discovered it.

There it was, staring up at her...an envelope with no name on the outside, and inside, a small piece of paper— faded, stained, creased, precious...a lifeline to the past. She had a middle name...it was Crane. *Crane.* And where had that funny name come from? A father she'd never known? A father to go with the woman in her dreams? And her mother wasn't named Myrta at all, her mother's name was Eve...Eve Douglass. And her father's name was...

"Lucinda?"

Lucie held her breath, hearing slow, heavy footsteps on the second landing. Desperate, she looked around for somewhere to hide the piece of paper. Then she saw a big leather-bound book on the second shelf and quickly stuffed it inside, her heart pounding with fear. She'd remember that...*David Copperfield*. And she'd sneak back up here later and retrieve the paper and hide it in the old chestnut tree in the garden where no one but her would ever know. It belonged to her, not them.

Shaking then, knowing her face was pale, she turned to face the man she'd always called Father. She lifted her chin slightly, her Douglass eyes defiant, her New England blood stiffening her spine, her secret new knowledge thrilling her very soul. *You can't hurt me anymore. You're not my father.* She heard the words tumble inside her head, she felt the power of the words, felt the strength they gave her. *Not my real father.*

But her child's heart trembled. Who was she? Where did she really belong?

Chapter One

"Aw, *heck*, Boone! Can't ya even stop to give a lady a lift? I mean, the whole valley knows how you feel about women, ever since that business with yer brother and Becky McNeill, but that was going on two years ago. Whatcha got against a lady hitchhiker? Ya better stop and pick her up before somethin' happens to her."

Lady? D. Boone Harlow glanced in the rearview mirror in surprise and took his foot off the gas. Hitchhiker?

"I mean, sure this is the great state of Idaho, and there ain't no finer place, but even here folks ain't the same as they once was. These days, who knows what could happen? Ya hears all kinds of stories. Why, I remember when I got that first job driving for the Rideout outfit over t' Shoshone Falls, back in '58—"

"You think that's a woman, Ho?" Boone interjected, pressing his foot on the brake. Lord, it was hot! And this monkey suit he had on didn't help. Nor did Ho's dig about how Carson had pulled out of the Double H when the girl he'd been courting since high school informed him that no way had she grown up on one backwoods Idaho spread just to end up spending the rest of her life on another one. Boone sighed. Women. Hell. You couldn't really blame them for wanting out....

He ripped off the string tie he was wearing and tossed it behind the seat, where his jacket had landed earlier. Then he rolled down his window and gave his passenger a quick sideways look, a look that might have been read by anyone who knew him well as amusement, maybe even affection. Boone Harlow might be known in the Sawtooth Valley for his views on women, but Holcomb Pickens had quite a reputation, too—for his views on anything and everything, and plenty more where they came from, too.

Usually Boone didn't mind. Usually, like today, he tuned out his garrulous old friend and neighbor and concentrated on what was on his own mind. Just now he'd been thinking of what that new banker in Ketchum had had to say about giving him credit for buying this year's feeder steers. He had to have it if he was going to pull Beaver Creek Ranch out of the red this year instead of next. Maybe. Carson's defection hadn't helped.

Boone sighed. Land rich, cash poor. It was the story of his life, and you'd think he'd be used to it by now. But money troubles never seemed to get any easier, not when your entire family depended on you to make the ranch pay, and a dozen men counted on you for seasonal work. Right now, with the cook gone again, the third one in a month...

"Well, heck, Boone. I ain't no good-lookin' young buckaroo like you are anymore, but I guess these old eyes can still tell the difference between a woman and a fence post, and where I come from, *that there's a woman!*"

Holcomb actually sounded a little offended. Boone grinned, then turned and stretched his right arm along the faded vinyl of the pickup's bench seat, expertly steering with one hand as the truck lurched backward toward where the hitchhiker was standing. She—if it was a she, and Boone had serious doubts about that, no matter what Holcomb had said—was standing there waiting patiently. Why didn't the kid run to meet the truck, like most people hitching a ride did?

Boone frowned, the grimace giving his tanned and handsome face a sternness familiar to all who knew him. The Harlow eyes, warm, rich and tawny brown in some lights, were hard and cold and alert now, as he quickly sized up the figure at the side of the road. A woman? Perhaps. His gaze, more practised lately at sizing up horseflesh or a good market steer than a woman—and by his own preference, too—narrowed, and he drummed callused fingers on the steering wheel. Damn! First Holcomb managed to catch up with him in Ketchum, now this. He was late getting back to the ranch as it was. He'd promised Mattie he'd be home by suppertime.

The truck squealed to a halt at the side of the road in a swirl of summer dust. Boone waited, watching in the rear-view mirror. He had to admit…whoever this was, had piqued his curiosity. He'd never seen a hitchhiker walk up with such containment, such tense preoccupation, such… such detachment. Not a smile, not a wave…nothing. And she—for he was beginning to think Holcomb was right, this was a girl after all, not a teenage boy—slung her backpack off so slowly and so carefully that Boone could tell instantly that she was hurting. She was stiff, or sore, or maybe it was just her way of moving through life…skirting the edges, keeping still, pretending she was invisible.

Boone snorted. Fanciful! What was he thinking? She was just some hard-luck kid, looking for a free ride and he wished she'd hurry up and get in and he could be on his way again. Then he felt his jaw clench, hard and angry.

What kind of parents did she have that let her do such a damn-fool stupid thing anyway? Hitchhike by herself through one of the loneliest stretches of backwoods highway in the entire state? Hell, even with a partner it was down-right dangerous. Boone felt his shoulders tense, then he took a deep breath. Kids today! he didn't know the whys and the wherefores; he didn't *want* to know.

"So! Where y'all headed?" Holcomb obviously didn't have the same reservations. He'd gotten out of the truck and was holding the door wide, giving the kid one of his friend-liest, toothiest bewhiskered smiles. Boone knew the smile—he and Mattie referred to it as Ho's Sears Roebuck Spe-cial—and smiled a little to himself, hand resting lightly, impatiently, on the gearshift.

The hitchhiker barely nodded, just climbed into the cab with a quick glance at Boone. He knew she couldn't see him clearly: she'd come in from the brightness and the sun was in the window behind him. And his Stetson was pulled extralow to shade his eyes. But he could see her, just a flash of her. A flash of wide eyes, pale skin, wisps of honey-red hair sticking out from the cap she'd obviously stuffed it into, the slenderness of her hand as she leaned on the seat then hiked herself across, the way she folded those soft white hands on her lap, not touching either him or Holcomb. Boone noted that. He noted the care she'd taken, the wari-ness, the endless patience in the gesture of folding her hands like that, just so, and his eyes narrowed again as he shifted into first and let out the clutch. He didn't look at her again, but he could feel her beside him, could feel her with every atom, every fiber of his own body...and he wondered at that.

Thank God he didn't have to make conversation. He could leave that up to Holcomb.

"Nice day, ain't it?"

"Mmm."

"Where'd ya say ya was headed?"

"Didn't say."

Boone wanted to laugh. But he just gripped the steering wheel a little tighter and shifted into high. Sounded as if his nosy neighbor had his work cut out.

"Well, now, ya oughta think about it. Keep on this Star Route here, bear right at the junction and ya might end up in Montana! Hot damn! Ya wouldn't want to do that now, would ya?" Holcomb hooted at his own joke and slapped his knee, and Boone found his gaze wandering from the asphalt in front of him to see how the hitchhiker took it. He couldn't see her face for the big billed cap she'd squashed over her hair and he quickly wrenched his eyes back to the road. He'd had a sudden image of what that hair might be like, loosened, shining....

But he heard her soft reply. "Maybe I would, maybe I wouldn't." He frowned. She wasn't from the valley. She wasn't a Westerner. Where had he heard that soft, flat accent before?

"Come on now, honey. Me 'n' Boone here—we're a coupla good guys, cross my heart 'n' hope to die." Boone saw Holcomb draw a big *X* on his cleanest going-to-town shirt and catch himself, with a quick guilty look at Boone, just before he spit on the floor to emphasize his sincerity. "Darn lucky we picked ya up, that's the truth. Didn't yer mama and daddy ever tell ya not to hitchhike? Why there's no telling who might have come along. Now, my name's Holcomb, Holcomb Pickens—folks call me Ho—and this here's Boone Harlow. We both got spreads over t' Redfish Lake way. What's your name, honey?"

The girl in the middle hesitated for a few seconds and Boone had made up his mind she wouldn't tell them. But then she surprised him. "Lucie. Lucie Crane."

"Glad ta meet ya, Miss Lucie," Holcomb said putting two fingers to the brim of his greasy Stetson and giving the girl an odd formal little nod. Boone had to hide a smile again. What was the old badger up to now? "That's a real nice name. Lucie. Yessirree, real nice. Why, I had a dog once, one of them blue tick hounds—ya ever seen one? Well—"

Boone tuned out again, but it wasn't the same as before they'd picked up the girl. He couldn't forget that she was sitting beside him like that, so straight, so…so prim. He was curious about her, and annoyed at his curiosity, and he wondered why he couldn't just relax and concentrate on his driving and his money problems and the rest of the stuff he had on his mind—had had on his mind for years, it seemed—and just forget about her. Should he take her on to the junction? Or just drop her off at Holcomb's corner?

He hated to do that, hated to leave her to find another ride. Holcomb was right: hitching wasn't safe. He stole another glance at her and this time surprised a shadow of a smile on her face. But she was turned away slightly, listening to some fool story of Holcomb's and he couldn't see her that clearly. Something in her face reminded him of something.…

She seemed so…well, defenseless, under that grim exterior. And so young. She couldn't be more than…he'd guess about seventeen or eighteen. A runaway, probably. Not much younger than J.J.

J.J. The thought of his youngest brother had Boone frowning again. J.J.'s college fees were due in another two months and how was he going to scrape up the money this year? Somehow he and Mattie had always managed to come up with it. And if this year was different? Boone shrugged mentally. Hell, J.J.'d just have to take a semester or two off and earn some money on the ranch and go back again next year. He could think of worse things that could happen to a young fellow who thought he wanted to be a poet. Do him good.

"Say, Boone—" Holcomb's voice broke into his thoughts. "I was just tellin' Lucie here maybe you could give her a job?"

Boone swung sharply to look at his neighbor. What the—? Holcomb had a silly grin on his face, and that, Boone knew, could spell trouble.

"What kind of a job?" he said, hoping his voice sounded as bored and indifferent as he wished he felt. He didn't dare look at the hitchhiker.

"Well, cookin', mebbe. Tom tells me Mattie's on the warpath again and he says yer crew's ready to quit on ya over the grub they're gettin' at the Double H and this here young lady might be just the ticket. Eh?" Holcomb removed his hat and scratched his grizzled crown, wearing an exaggerated look of innocence that made Boone want to slam on the brakes and kick the old codger out on the Star Route right there. Let *him* hitch a ride home.

But it was true. He needed a cook. Mattie had run off three in the past month and the men had told Boone that they weren't going to take much more of his cooking. Damn! Holcomb was right. He needed a cook—badly. But was this any kind of a cook? He shot a glance at the girl and caught her looking at him for the first time.

For a moment, probably only a few seconds or so, their eyes held, and when Boone wrenched his away, he knew that he was going to offer her a job and he knew that offering her a job was probably one of the dumbest moves he'd made in a long, long time. What he'd felt just now weren't the vibrations from the shimmy in the U-joint that needed replacing on the pickup. And she wasn't seventeen or eighteen, either. She was a woman, with a woman's eyes.

"All I can offer is room and board and the going wage," he said gruffly, his gaze steady on the road ahead, cursing himself for the weakness in his heart, telling himself that he felt sorry for her—as anyone would, that it was just that she looked as if she could use a good meal herself. "And only for the summer. Can you cook?"

She hesitated, and she looked away, and he sent up a quick plea to the Almighty that she couldn't, that she had other plans, that someone, a man even, was waiting for her just around the bend, maybe in Boise, or Missoula, someone who'd look after her, who'd take care of her as he knew she needed taking care of. But he'd made the offer and he wouldn't take it back now. A Harlow's word was his bond. It was his honor. It meant more, a lot more, than cold, hard cash had ever done in this part of the world. Still—

"I can."

Holcomb crowed, and slapped his knee with his hat.

Boone looked at her and she met his gaze again, her eyes big and blue-gray and serious as hell. "I'd be proud to work for you, Mr. Harlow. Thank you very much for your kindness. I appreciate it."

Kindness? He let out his breath, and the whole blue Idaho sky and the snow-capped Sawtooth mountain range and the windswept wild hills of the valley he loved came crashing down around him, in one big jumble of mixed-up sensations. *Now* what?

Not even caring that the old truck couldn't take much more of the kind of treatment he was giving it, he ground down to third gear, then second, to slow for a schoolbus ahead, flashing its lights. Then he took a deep breath to steady himself, his hand still on the gearshift, only an inch or so from the knee of the girl beside him, her legs pressed together carefully, he knew, so as not to touch him.

She knew. She'd felt it, too.

I don't need this, Boone told himself. *I don't need this, not on top of everything else.* Then he looked out the window to the west at the jagged mountains that rimmed his home and saw that the Sawtooths had landed right-side up after all, despite his crazy sensation of a moment ago.

Oh, well, Boone thought, grimacing and slowly pulling one large callused hand over his face, he supposed it could be worse. At least he had a cook lined up for a couple of days. He gave Lucie a quick, indifferent sideways glance. With any luck, Mattie'd have this little snip of a thing run off inside of a week and he could stop kicking himself for letting himself get into this in the first place.

Damn Holcomb Pickens, anyway. He glared at the old rancher over the girl's head. Holcomb grinned back.

He owed that old buzzard. He owed him good.

The ranch house, appearing suddenly around a bend after nearly two miles of bouncing over a pitted, gravel road, a road on which she hadn't even seen a sign of another ranch or house, was a surprise, although Lucie didn't really know what she'd been expecting, maybe some newer, ranch-style bungalow, vinyl siding and a picture window.

It was a solid, two-story structure, of frame-and-log construction, and it looked as if the builder had started out with one idea and then had changed his mind—maybe over a couple of generations—and had added wings and extensions lovingly and haphazardly as time and necessity and circumstances permitted. It could have used a coat of paint, Lucie noted, but more than anything, she realized, feeling her heart swell with pleasure, it looked as if it belonged to someone. Someone who cared.

There were lilacs planted along the east side, worn wooden swings in the yard and tumbling, rambling roses climbing all over the veranda. Big shade trees had been planted near the house by some thoughtful pioneer, to provide relief from the hot Idaho summer sun for his unknown great grandchildren someday. It was someone's home. It looked loved and lived in and as though it had been there forever and intended to go on being there forever.

She stole a glance at the grim-faced cowboy beside her

as the truck rumbled over the cattle guard under the big open gates that supported a weathered sign high above. It read Beaver Creek Ranch, and had a simple brand burned into the wood crosspieces above it. Double H. Were Boone's children the great-grandchildren some long-ago ancestor had dreamed of having one day? That thought, oddly, hurt her somewhere just below her heart. She hadn't seen a wedding ring on his hand—she had to confess that, yes, she had looked—but that didn't mean anything. Lots of men were married without rings. And she was pretty sure this man was. He had that air of sobriety, of responsibility, of deep weariness, that married men usually had. And that, she told herself firmly, sitting a little straighter, was a good thing.

He was apparently the strong, silent type too, she mused, shooting him another quick glance. He hadn't said a word since they'd dropped off the other rancher at his place. She'd kind of liked that old guy, and he sure could make her smile with those crazy stories he told. It felt good to smile again. Life, Lucie thought with a sigh, had been way too serious for way too long.

Ho. She tried the word out mentally on her tongue a couple of times. Holcomb Pickens. And Boone. She stole another look at the frowning man beside her. The names these farmers out here had! That brand on the gate…just like in the movies! Lucie wanted to hug herself at her good fortune. Things were looking up, and about time. This was perfect. She had the chance to live here, work here for the rest of the summer, until she turned twenty-five and…

She hesitated and chewed her lip worriedly for a few seconds as she thought of what she'd taken on. Cooking for a crew of cowboys… How many? Three? Five? Seventeen! Well, she hadn't lied, she *had* learned to cook. It was one of the domestic skills she'd had drilled into her at the fancy school in Lucerne Jack had sent her to before college.

Her blue eyes clouded. There's no way she wanted to think about all *that* now, not when her prayers had finally been answered. That morning, when she started walking out of Ketchum, she'd shut her eyes and hoped with all her heart that today would be the day she'd find someplace safe to hole up in for the next couple of months, someplace where she could be alone, finally, someplace where no one would dream of looking for her. It had been ten days since she'd stolen away from Concord in the middle of the night—ten long, weary, nerve-racking days—and she'd prayed fervently that the next ride would be the magical ride she was looking for, the magical ride that would take her to where she wanted to be.

And it had been. She looked around at the intricately connected corrals, the cattle sheds, the buildings that housed strange looking machinery, the big barn, the hay sheds scattered around—their workings all a mystery to her. She saw horses grazing in the distance, some with foals by their sides. And a couple of dogs suddenly rushed out from the shade to bark at the pickup, tails wagging, pink tongues lolling. The truck stopped.

"This is it. Welcome to the Double H." But the man beside her didn't look welcoming. He was still frowning and he barely glanced at her, just pulled on the emergency brake with one hand and and reached for the door handle with the other. "Come in and I'll show you your room. I've got a couple of things I've got to do before supper and that'll give you a chance to rest and clean up. I'll fix supper for the crew tonight and you can give me a hand. That way you'll know where everything is. Tomorrow you're on your own." Then he got out of the truck and slammed the door.

Lucie stared at the closed door, thunderstruck. Well! Looked as if she'd just gotten her first orders from her first boss, and it didn't look as though he were tongue-tied after all.

She stood quietly by the truck, gazing around while Boone carried some boxes out of the back of the pickup into what she presumed was the kitchen, judging by the labels on the boxes he carried. Idly she looked up at the second floor and saw the flutter of white lace curtains at the half-opened windows. She wanted to cry; the homey sight of those curtains made her heart ache so.

But she didn't, of course. And when Boone returned from the kitchen a second time, he frowned at her, as though he expected her to do something, and she lifted her chin a little and clasped her hands together. She didn't have a clue what he wanted. She met his lowered gaze with one eyebrow lifted slightly, and he made some kind of a rude sound and strode over to the truck to haul out her pack.

"Oh!" she said, realizing that she should have carried the backpack herself. "Here. Let me take that—"

"Never mind," he growled, and pushed past her to the door. She walked up as he held open the screen door and, acutely conscious of his nearness, of the unfamiliar male scent of his body so near her, of the nervousness that his glare of irritation caused in her middle, she pushed past him awkwardly, pretending to herself as she brushed by that she hadn't actually touched him at all.

"Thank you," she murmured politely, and moved into the room. He swore and held back the spring-loaded door with one hand and maneuvered aggressively through the doorway with her heavy pack in the other.

"Through here," he said, with a black look, and stalked ahead of her, through a roomy kitchen, a hallway, into a foyer, dark and cool in the late afternoon, blinds pulled down to shut out the glare and the heat, and to a stairway. She had caught up and was right behind Boone, and although she tried not to look at him, at those strong, lean legs in the tailored Western-style dress pants, at the rhythmic movement of hard muscle under his sweat-stained shirt, his hand angled to balance her pack on one broad shoulder— Although she tried not to look, there really wasn't much else to look at, except the faded wallpaper above the dark wainscoting, and the sight of her own fingers trailing up the handcarved railing. She took a deep breath, grateful when they reached the top and stood in an airy, bright landing.

Boone hesitated outside one of the rooms, glancing at her, then seemed to change his mind and strode down the hall to the next one. He pushed the door open and tossed her pack onto an old-fashioned brass-and-iron bed made up with a white cotton bedspread that had a gaily colored quilt draped over the footboard. Lucie's gaze took in the rest of the room. There was a walnut dresser, an old mirror, speckled and tarnished and filled with silvery ghosts—

It was one of the rooms with the dormer windows half open and the lace curtains blowing in the wind.

"Oh!" Lucie said softly, unable to help herself, and went to the window, the man she'd been so conscious of a moment before quickly forgotten. She pushed back the curtains and stood, taking a deep breath and holding it. The White Clouds on the other side of the valley, a gentler range than the rugged Sawtooths behind them, rose in the distance. In between there were dry rolling hills, the broad, broad valley and all around her, in every direction, such space, such peace, such...such freedom as she'd never believed was possible.

She heard his footsteps as he came up to stand just at her shoulder.

"Like it?" His voice was gruff and hesitant.

She turned and looked up at him, hearing only the soft lazy sigh of the wind in the cottonwoods, the distant bawl of a hungry calf, the insistent buzz of insects in the long grass. She wasn't sure if she could speak, or should even try. "It's beautiful," she breathed, finally. "It's—it's the most beautiful thing I've ever seen...."

He looked down at her for a moment, and she thought she could see his eyes change from that hard black indifference to something else, a warm, rich, tawny gold, the kind of eyes you could dream in. Then he cleared his throat.

"Yeah. Well. Come down to the kitchen in about an hour. Mealtime is eight o'clock on a day like this, sun shining. We're trying to get the first hay crop in and the crew doesn't come in until they have to."

Make hay while the sun shines, Lucie thought to herself, absolutely thrilled that it had occurred to her.

"Where's...where's everybody else? Where's Mattie?" she asked, sure that she'd heard Holcomb mention that name.

"Who?" He looked at her, suddenly alert.

"Your wife."

"I don't have a wife."

"But..." she felt her face go pale, then hot, as her veins flooded with acute embarrassment and something else... something that sang so high and so sweet in her blood that it scared her. "I—I thought Mattie was—"

"You'll meet Mattie soon enough," he said, with a strange look that went straight to her heart. "Mattie's my grandmother."

Chapter Two

Live free or die. That was the slogan on the license plates of New Hampshire, her home state, and that was exactly what Lucinda Crane Douglass intended to do. *Live free or die.*

And this was exactly the place to do it. Lucie leaned out the window and breathed deeply and tried, in a few seconds, to replace all the hurt of the past twenty-four years with the fresh pure cool breeze of the Idaho hills and the clean soft heat of the Idaho sun. Sometimes she had to pinch herself to realize that, yes, this time she really had escaped. Her uncle, Charles Douglass, was her guardian, according to her adoptive parents' will, until the day she turned twenty-five. He held the purse strings, he controlled her life. And ever since they'd died five years ago, he'd made her life a living hell. Every moment of every day she'd been under the watchful eye of one or another of his hired goons. It was for her own good, he'd said. Rich young women were a target for every weirdo who came along, he'd said, every gold digger, every crackpot with a scheme to sell. The watching had driven her wild; it had bruised her spirit and brought her near despair.

No longer...no more. She felt like a caged bird that suddenly discovers that the wire door is open, perhaps has been open for a while. She was free. Really free, for the first time in her life. She looked around her, at the faded wallpaper, at the worn pine floorboards, waxed and mellowed with age. For the first time in her life, she was accountable to no one. No one knew where she was, or where to look. For the first time in her life, she had a chance to find out who Lucie Crane really was. She knew she could do it, now that she had the chance; she knew it in her bones. Standing at the window with her eyes closed, Lucie breathed deeply, again and again, and then, feeling a little light-headed, she turned and faced her room once more.

There was no way she could rest. She was too excited. Maybe she'd unpack her things and then have a quick shower and change before going to help Boone with supper. Lucie pulled off her cap, the man's cap she'd hoped would help disguise her looks as she traveled, and her braid fell over her shoulder, thick and soft and red-gold in the old mirror. She pushed back the wisps of hair that had sprung free and curled around her face, leaned forward and stuck out her tongue at herself.

"You're a cook, Lucie Crane," she whispered to her image in the glass. "Can you believe it? You've got a job!" Then she grinned and threw her arms into the air and flopped onto the big white bed. The springs protested gently, rhythmically, for a few moments, and then she lay there, still spread-eagle, looking up at the tongue-in-groove painted ceiling, the plain, no-nonsense light fixture in the center.

Beaver Creek Ranch. Her home for the next couple of

months. Nothing could have been more different from Four Elms, the place she'd had to call home for as long as she could remember. There were no anxious servants here, no polished mahogany heirlooms that children mustn't touch, no priceless Oriental carpets that children mustn't play on, no manicured lawns, no flower borders filled with stiff, worried-looking tulips and sly, beckoning daffodils that children mustn't pick.

This room, Lucie decided, with its white-painted woodwork, its faded hand-braided rug on the bare pine floor, its mismatched but lovingly cared-for furniture, its scarred old bed with a soft-springed mattress—this room was heaven.

And before she got up, she sent a quick heartfelt thanks to Saint Christopher, the old patron saint of travelers, that she'd managed to get to heaven after all. She'd relied on Saint Christopher rather heavily over the past ten days, ever since she'd left Concord on a westbound midnight freight train. He hadn't let her down.

She unpacked her few items of clothing and put her wallet and personal things away in the dresser drawer. She double-checked, although she knew the contents as well as her own name: there was some cash most of which she stashed under her mattress on sudden inspiration, but nothing to identify her as a Douglass. For the next few months, she'd be Lucie Crane, plain Lucie Crane. Then, clean underwear in hand, she opened her door and peeked down the hall.

All was quiet and dim and cool. Where was the mysterious Mattie, she wondered? Her curiosity about this family she'd stumbled upon was in full flood. The fact that Boone had said he wasn't married had been a shock, but when she'd recovered from her first surprise, she'd told herself that it made no difference, no difference at all. Married or not, a man like Boone—her boss—was strictly off-limits. Besides, romance was not what she was after. She hadn't left behind all the suitors thrust at her by Uncle Charles in his efforts to marry her off to the right man—his choice—just to get mixed up with some other man out west. Some cowboy.

Lucie blushed and mentally scolded herself for her over-active imagination. She crept down the hall, looking at the various doors that opened onto the passage and trying to guess which one might be the bathroom. She pushed open one that was half ajar, the door Boone had hesitated at before he'd led her to the room she was in. It was larger than hers, furnished with matching heavy old-fashioned furniture. And it, too, had windows half open with curtains blowing in the wind. There was nothing personal in the room, just a few bright spots on the faded wallpaper that showed her that pictures of some kind had once hung there.

Hmm. The room opposite that one was open, too, but Lucie instantly realized whose room it was when she paused on the threshold. And then Boone's earlier hesitation at assigning her the opposite one began to make sense. It was clearly a man's room and the room, with a window that looked out on the Sawtooths, matched the man. Oversize handmade furniture, a huge bed, bookshelves along one wall jammed haphazardly with books and magazines, a leather-covered armchair and ottoman and a massive carved chest under the window filled the room. And thrown across the bed was a jacket that obviously matched the trousers Boone had been wearing, and over one chair was thrown those very trousers. And a shirt. Lucie gasped and stepped back. There were dress boots, kicked off beside the chair, one on its side, the tooled leather gleaming in the sunshine. A towel was lying rumpled on the floorboards.

Lucie took another step backward, a sudden image of him standing there, naked, the muscles in his broad tanned back shifting in the bright light, the look on his face as he would slowly turn toward her....

Heart hammering, she continued down the hall. Obviously, if she'd been a few moments earlier, she might have caught him changing. Didn't anyone close doors around here?

Finally, there it was, the bathroom, and Lucie stepped in. Knowing that Boone had been in this very bathroom so recently didn't help her attack of nerves. Determined not to let her imagination run away with her again, she stripped and stepped into the shower cubicle, and, while she soaped and scrubbed, recited the old familiar lines of *The Song of Hiawatha* under her breath. A favorite nanny had taught her the Longfellow poem as a child, and she'd said it a thousand times in an effort to focus her mind away from things she didn't want to think about.

It had never failed her. By the time she stepped out, clean and shining, she had recited a hundred lines and hadn't thought of Boone Harlow once.

Half an hour later, dressed in clean jeans and a T-shirt, her hair still damp but loosely braided, Lucie walked down the stairs. She reached the bottom and paused, her hand on the newel post, feeling the glassy smoothness that came, not from a bottle of lemon oil and the paid elbow grease of a servant, she knew, but from the caresses of a thousand hands over the years.

"Boone? That you?"

The thin querulous voice came from the room to the right and, hesitantly Lucie walked in that direction. This must be Mattie. Her heart pounded. Maybe she should wait until Boone got here…wait until he introduced them properly.

"Oh, for Pete's sake, boy. Come in here. How's an old woman supposed to get a cup of tea for herself if you don't leave that blasted contraption where a body can get hold of it— Who the dickens are you?"

Lucie had slipped through the half-open door to a room that looked as if it might once have been called a parlor many years ago. A very old woman was half lying, half sitting on the sofa opposite the window, a multicolored afghan over her legs. As Lucie walked in, the woman hoisted herself a little higher and jammed the glasses, which had been dangling from a piece of string, onto her nose.

"Lucie, ma'am. Lucie Crane." Lucie stood straight, her hands behind her back. So this was Boone's grandmother!

"Well, who in heck is Lucie Crane when she's home, that's what I'd like to know? You that teacher he goes down to see in Twin Falls once in a while?" The old woman glared at her suspiciously for a moment, then mumbled something to herself as she took her glasses off and turned them around twice to untangle the string around her neck, then jammed them back on her nose again. "One of Boone's women, I suppose," she grumbled. Then, amazingly, the old woman heaved a big sigh and fixed Lucie with another glassy stare. "Oh, don't I just wish."

She continued. "Well, don't just stand there, Lucie Crane, give me a hand. No, never mind. Just bring me that danged-fool contraption over there—"

Lucie saw an aluminum walker in the corner. She brought the walker over to the old woman, then stood there while she tried to pull herself to her feet, mumbling and muttering what sounded an awful lot like curses to Lucie's shocked ears.

"Here—" she reached for the old woman's elbow "—let me give you a hand—"

"Leave me alone, dang it!" Mattie made a sudden irritated gesture with one hand and grabbed fiercely onto the walker with the other. "I can manage myself. Done it for eighty-six, near eighty-seven years countin' the fifty-three I was married to Harlow, and I guess I can still manage myself."

Lucie thought she'd better start again. "I guess you must be Mattie—"

"Hmph! What business is it of yours, young lady? What'd that grandson of mine tell you anyway?"

She'd somehow managed to heave herself to her feet and stood peering suspiciously up at Lucie, a little bit of a woman in a pair of old-fashioned cat's eye glasses, complete with rhinestones in the corners. Somehow Lucie didn't think they dated from the current sixties' revival, either. Her blue-veined hands with shiny, papery skin gripped the walker tightly. The aid was obviously the sole key to her remaining freedom on the ranch, Lucie suspected, and the hated reminder at the same time that she couldn't manage like she used to, couldn't manage at all.

"He told me he had a grandmother living here with him and he said her name was Mattie, and since you're the only other person I've seen around here, I just figured you must be Mattie. Pretty dumb, huh?" Lucie looked at her, trying not to smile, keeping her eyes as round and innocent as she could.

The old woman stared at her, her mouth slack, her eyes bright, her body absolutely still. Then, to Lucie's delight, she began to wheeze with laughter. She grabbed Lucie's arm and squeezed it so hard, Lucie almost winced, and Mattie leaned a little closer.

"I don't know who the dickens you are, dear, but I don't much care. I like a woman with a quick answer. Reminds me of myself," she confided with a sly wink and a nod. "Say, why don't you stay for supper, dear? I'll get Boone to set another place for you. I'm just about to start cookin' now. The men will be comin' in soon and they're always awful hungry in hayin' season."

Lucie realized that things were suddenly getting pretty confusing. Maybe she should have said she was the new cook right off the bat. Mattie seemed to think she was some special friend of Boone's—but she didn't seem too clear about that, either. The teacher from Twin Falls? Why did that thought send her blood pounding—

"Ah, there's Boone now."

Lucie listened; she hadn't heard anything. But sure enough, a second or two later she heard the heavy sound of riding boots on the hard wooden floor just outside the door. And suddenly Boone was there—tall, dark, bringing all the Idaho outdoors inside with him, dressed exactly—Lucie swallowed a lump in her throat—exactly like the quintessential American cowboy she'd seen a million times on billboards. All he was missing were the riding chaps and the cigarette.

He stared at the two women for a moment, brow stern, dark eyes moving quickly from Lucie to his grandmother, back to Lucie again. Then he smiled and, with a single expert easy gesture, tossed his hat onto the floor lamp standing by an overstuffed armchair. Lucie swallowed again.

She hadn't seen him smile before, and it did unexpected things to her insides. His face softened, his eyes gleamed with love and pleasure and he suddenly looked...handsome, relaxed, sexy—everything she'd ever thought a man could ever look like in her dreams. The smile, of course, was for Mattie.

"I see you've met the new cook," he said, and walked toward his grandmother, still smiling.

Lucie felt something swell and hurt in her chest. This woman was this man's family. His grandmother. *Family.* She, who had never had a grandmother, felt the ache of loss all over again. She'd never had a grandmother that she'd known, or a grandfather...maybe not even a sister, although her dreams told her she did, and if it were true, she swore she'd find her someday. The woman who'd raised her, whom she had had to call Mother, was not her mother. Her real mother was dead...and she didn't know why or how, or even where. Jack and Myrta, her mother's distant cousins, had adopted Lucie before she'd turned three. And her father...there'd never been a father in her life, not a real father, she thought bitterly. Only Jack, and, of course, she'd had to call him Father, whether she liked it or not....

And yet this crotchety old bit of a woman meant the world to someone. She was Boone's grandmother, and it was clear that he cared about her deeply. He loved her. Lucie felt an ache swell inside her until she thought it would spill over in tears, but she beat back the pain, as she'd done so many times before, and she smiled brightly at her new employer and his grandmother, and hoped that the smile she'd practised most of her life would be all they saw.

"*Cook?*" It was a squawk of outrage. "What do you mean, 'cook'? Don't tell me you've gone and hired somebody again, Boone. You know dang well I've always done the cookin' around here. Haven't I?" She glared at him. "Your mama never amounted to any kind of ranch cook, although she did turn out an awful nice blancmange, and I told her that plenty of times. Lord knows your poor mama never amounted to much of anything, not that she had much of a chance hitched up with that no-good son of mine."

Lucie glanced at Boone and saw his jaw tighten as he glanced at her then back to his grandmother. She was embarrassed. Mattie was obviously going on about something private, something between them, something meant for none but family ears.

"Come on now, Mattie." Boone's tone was deep and conciliatory, cajoling. "Sure, I know you're the cook around here, but I just think you ought to have a little help. I don't want you to work too hard. Right?"

He grinned at his grandmother and Lucie knew that if he smiled at her like that, she'd probably faint dead away.

"Well—" Mattie shot a grudging look at Lucie. "Well, all right. I suppose I could use a little help. And I wanted to tell you I kind of like this one, Boone," she whispered, looking up at her grandson. When she spoke again, a little louder, her voice had an odd hopeful note in it. "I took her for one of your women, Boone, at first. A right nice little thing, she is."

Lucie felt the heat flood her face. Mattie was talking as though Lucie wasn't in the room, and… *One of his women.* What in the world did that mean? How many women did the man have? She didn't dare meet Boone's eyes.

"Aw, hell, Mattie. You know I've got no time for women. Too damn busy patching things together on the Double H. Besides, I've got you." He grinned at his grandmother and she cackled with laughter.

Lucie knew he was just teasing the old woman. She was quite sure a man like him would have time for plenty of women. Just not her. She wished Mattie would get that straight once and for all. But it seemed Mattie had quite a bit of trouble keeping things straight. She seemed to think she was still doing the ranch cooking, too.

Lucie frowned. Maybe that particular delusion had contributed to the fact that three cooks had left the Double H that month, as Holcomb had mentioned as he'd filled her in on local gossip on the ride from Ketchum. Strangely, she felt herself wanting to defend the old woman. After all, Mattie was nearly ninety. A woman of her age was entitled to a few eccentricities….

"Tell you what, Mattie." Boone glanced quickly at his watch, then, with a warning look, at Lucie. "I'll take you to the other room and Miss Crane, here, will bring you a cup of tea. How's that?"

Lucie nodded, realizing that Boone was trying to distract his grandmother. Before Mattie could protest, he stepped forward, took her walker from her and swept her into his arms. Then he strode from the room, and all Lucie could hear was the deep rumble of his laughter and the old lady giggling. She was actually giggling! Lucie picked up the walker and followed them into what looked like some kind of a family room, less formal, with more comfortable clutter. She set the walker within easy reach of Mattie's chair, something she suspected Boone was not too good at remembering to do. Boone adjusted the television set and they left Mattie watching one of her favorite programs, happily chipping in with her own thoughts and opinions of the action on the small screen.

Boone's gaze met Lucie's as they stood in the shadow of the doorway, and she thought she saw a deep silent plea for understanding in the dark depths of his eyes. But he said nothing. He held the door for her, as he'd done earlier that day—although this time she realized he actually meant for her to precede him—and she walked ahead of him, down the hall and into the kitchen.

The kitchen was huge, and Boone ushered her to large doors that opened into a sort of outbuilding that adjoined the kitchen, a room with its own door to the outside. "There is where the men eat," Boone said.

Lucie walked in, conscious that he'd followed her and was standing at her shoulder. She looked around. There were big screened windows along both sides, and right now they were wide open, with the soft summer breeze drifting through. Lucie could smell freshly cut grass and a pungent scent that she realized might be a combination of sage, and the faint background scent of horses and saddle leather. But perhaps that was only her imagination.

She moved away from Boone, too aware of his nearness, of the male scent he brought with him, of the heat of his body standing so near hers. She looked at the long tables, permanently set with salt, pepper, mustard, catsup, sugar bowls, napkins, jam tins.

"Why—" She stopped, shocked. There must be room for twenty men to eat here! She whirled to face Boone. "How many am I cooking for?"

Boone laughed, a short burst of deep laughter. He sounded genuinely amused. "Don't worry, Miss Crane—"

"I'd like it if you called me Lucie."

He paused, regarding her levelly, those dark eyes warming to buckwheat just for a few seconds. "Don't worry, Lucie—" the sound of her name on his tongue warmed her clear to her toes "—you'll only be cooking for a crew of eight this week—" Eight! "—plus me and Mattie, of course."

Lucie shifted her weight from one foot to the other and chewed her bottom lip apprehensively. It was beginning to dawn on her that she'd have to do some fancy footwork and some darn creative thinking between now and tomorrow morning when he'd said she'd be on her own. Then she met Boone's steady glance.

"You've cooked before?" Was there a note of skepticism in that honey-soft Idaho drawl?

"Well, not actually for a lot of people, but—" She hated to lie. Nervously she rubbed one toe of her canvas sneakers over the other one, then stopped when she noted Boone's lazy interest in her action. His gaze returned slowly, too slowly, to her face. Did passing her mixed hors d'oeuvres course at the finishing school in Switzerland by coming up with a barely acceptable tray of fancy canapés count?

"You'll do fine," he said reassuringly, gesturing her toward the main kitchen. They walked through the double doors together. "Ranch hands generally aren't too fussy, as long as it's hot and there's plenty of it."

He glanced at her and a wry smile twisted his lips. Lucie found herself drawn to the movement, eyes on that handsome male mouth…watching, wondering, despite herself. "I can tell you, after putting up with my cooking for a week, I reckon they'll eat anything."

For a split second their eyes held. Boone suddenly frowned and seemed to remember that he was giving her a tour of the kitchen where she'd be working. He briskly started opening cupboard doors, showing her an array of massive pots, pans, mixers, spatulas—all the accoutrements of a well-equipped commercial kitchen. In the pantry were shelves stacked high with all kinds of canned goods—she gulped in dismay when she saw the gallon tins of pie filling—and sugar and tea and flour and other necessities. Pies!

"We can't be going to town every time we run out of something. That's why we keep a good supply ahead. You'll have to keep a running list so that when I do make a trip into Ketchum I can pick up what you need." Then, casually, too casually, he went on, "You a country girl, Lucie?"

"No—yes, well actually I—I've lived kind of all over the place," she stammered, surprised at the unexpected question. It was true, she had lived all over the place, but she felt guilty because she knew that was not what Boone was asking.

"Well, you need anything, just ask. Mattie can…" His voice trailed off and he frowned blackly at nothing in particular, his gaze distant. Lucie watched as he slowly unbuttoned his cuffs and began to roll up his sleeves. Then she wrenched her eyes away from the sight of his tanned, strong forearms, lightly dusted with fine dark hair, and remembered that she was to take a cup of tea to Mattie. She hurried over to where she'd seen an electric kettle, took it and filled it at the sink, then plugged it in with a flourish, feeling a little ridiculous that the simple task gave her so much satisfaction. Tea! She could handle that, all right.

"I don't know how you feel about Mattie…" Boone began again thoughtfully, staring at her. But she knew he didn't really see her, he was still thinking about something else. He sighed, and turned away and went over to a drawer and pulled out a couple of can openers. He seemed to have made his mind up about something.

"Mattie's eighty-six. She had a stroke last year and she

can barely get around with her walker—you saw how she is—'' Lucie nodded. ''She's got a weak heart, high blood pressure and her memory's going, although she has her good days and her bad ones.''

Boone met her eyes, and she could feel the pain she saw reflected there. ''Today's one of her bad days, I'm afraid. Sometimes she forgets she's not in charge anymore and, well, she can be pretty hard to handle.'' He grinned ruefully, and Lucie felt herself smile back. For a moment, the smile hung between them in the air, trembling, tensile.

Then Boone turned away abruptly and strode over to the pantry. When he returned he was carrying a flat cardboard box, which he put down heavily on the scrubbed wooden kitchen table. ''I guess none of the Harlows are too easy to handle—at least none I've every met.

''I'm telling you this, Lucie, because, frankly, Mattie has a tendency to drive a person nuts. Most of the cooks I've hired can't put up with her for more than a week or two, not when she gets into one of her spells and starts interfering in the kitchen. She's hard on women and she ran off the last man I had cooking because she found out he was going through a lot more vanilla extract than accounted for the number of cakes he baked.'' Boone gave her a pointed look, and she realized that what he meant was that the cook had a drinking problem. Vanilla extract, she knew, had a lot of alcohol in it.

''Vanilla?'' She wanted to giggle, but realized that this wasn't exactly a laughing matter.

''Yeah. Sometimes they prefer lemon extract and we've even had one or two who go for after-shave—''

''You're not serious!''

''Hell, when a drunk falls off the wagon on a job in some backwoods outfit where he can't get his hands on his preference, he'll drink anything he can get. I've seen a man drink shoe polish! Some of them strain it through a loaf of bread to take the color out. Some of them don't. With that kind of thirst, there's not much a man can do about it, Lucie. You must know that.'' Boone looked at her curiously, as though he couldn't believe that she'd never heard of such a thing. As if, what kind of a country girl was she anyway?

"Still—'' He frowned at the box he'd brought to the table, then went over to the cupboard to return with a large plastic bowl. "I kinda wish Mattie hadn't found out, because he was a pretty good cook. But she can't abide a drunk. Never could.''

Lucie went over to the counter to unplug the kettle and pour boiling water over a tea bag. Then she got down a tray she saw hanging on the wall, folded a tea towel carefully to put on the bottom of the tray, then set the teapot on it and a cup and saucer and—

She turned to find Boone staring curiously at her. "Does Mattie take her tea clear?''

"Cream and sugar. One lump.''

Humming a little to herself, Lucie turned back and put a spoon and couple of lumps of sugar on a saucer on the tray. She then went to the big refrigerator to find the milk.

"How about a cookie or something to go with that? Does Mattie like cookies?''

Boone smiled that easy, slow smile that she'd seen when he'd smiled at his grandmother. She felt her heart do a little flip-flop. He didn't answer, just walked over to a cupboard and reached for a cookie tin on the top shelf. He handed it to her, and their fingers touched accidentally. Lucie felt her skin tingle.

"I keep them up high where she can't reach them. Yeah,'' he said, still smiling, "you could say she likes cookies.''

Smiling, too, and wondering why she felt so breathless, so nervous all of a sudden, Lucie picked up the tray and sailed off down the hall.

When she got back a few minutes later, Boone had brought out another box from the pantry and had arranged two neat lines of a dozen or so cans on the table, one on each side. She walked over and looked curiously at what he was doing.

"Can I help?"

"Sure," he said, and handed her a can opener. "You start at that end. Just dump it in here." He gestured to the plastic bowl, with another vague wave toward the microwave she'd seen earlier.

Lucie picked up a can. Canned spaghetti. Canned *alphabet* spaghetti. The other row of cans looked to be green beans.

"What are we, uh...what are we doing here, Mr. Harlow?"

"Boone." Boone didn't look up as he dumped a tube-shaped congealed orange-and-white mass into the bowl from the can he'd just opened.

"Boone." She tested the word on her tongue, felt its unfamiliarity, but found she liked it just the same. As she said his name, he glanced up with an intent, indecipherable look. She cleared her throat. "Uh, what are we doing, Boone?"

He grinned suddenly and saluted her with a half-opened can.

"We're fixing supper."

Chapter Three

After that meal, Lucie figured her success was guaranteed. It didn't matter what she served; anything beat microwaved green beans and alphabet spaghetti. At least, Lucie thought with a grin, he hadn't tried to save on dishes to wash and dumped the beans and spaghetti into the same pot. Judging from the groans when she helped Boone carry the meal into the mess hall just after eight o'clock, it hadn't been the first time the ranch hands had seen that particular menu.

"Hey, what are you guys complaining about? We didn't have the same thing last night." Boone pretended to glare at the men who'd come in, hot and dusty and tired after a long day in the fields. But Lucie could see the gleam in his eye.

"Last night we had peas, damn it. Tonight we've got beans. And we had ice cream last night, too. Chocolate, as I recall." Boone looked around with an injured air as the table erupted in hoots and guffaws. "And tonight we're having canned strawberries. You guys don't watch it, you're going to hurt the cook's feelings.''

''Might be dangerous on some other outfit,'' growled one cowboy. ''Can't see what difference it'd make to the grub on this one.''

The crew laughed. Then Boone introduced Lucie, very formally and politely, and each ranch hand sat up on the long benches, straight and curious. She saw the bald speculation in their eyes as they looked from her to Boone and back again and prayed she wouldn't end up blushing in front of them.

''Say, where'd you cook before, Miss Lucie?'' It was the same dour ranch hand who'd challenged Boone.

''Oh...uh. Here and there,'' Lucie said breathlessly, giving Boone a quick stricken look.

''Miss Lucie's not from the valley,'' he said, stepping in smoothly to answer for her, as though he sensed her agitation. Beneath her wave of relief, she thought, *he must know.* He must know that she was no cook, but he hadn't exactly asked for references, had he? Maybe he didn't really care, as long as he managed to get out of the kitchen himself. But she was grateful to him for speaking up for her. She wasn't ready to handle the easy gibes and tomfoolery of these rough-edged Western men.

Thank goodness there were no more questions, just a lot of good wishes that Lucie knew were one hundred and ten per cent heartfelt. As she walked back into the kitchen, she made a mental note *never* to serve the poor crew canned spaghetti again.

Pancakes. Pancakes had to be dead easy.

Lucie got up at five o'clock and quietly pulled on her clothes. She hesitated, not wanting to take the time to rebraid her hair, but decided she'd better. If she was going to be the ranch cook, it was important that she look the part.

Then she pinned the braid neatly at her nape and double-tied it with a ribbon. Hygiene had been emphasized at the finishing school, but the main focus, she remembered ruefully, had been on vetting prospective employees for the wealthy households most of the students would be heading one day. As wives, not as housekeepers.

She tiptoed down the hall, wincing as the old floorboards squeaked in a few places. She didn't want to awaken anyone this early; she wanted an hour to herself in the kitchen to practise. She'd seen big sacks of pancake mix on the pantry shelves and figured the instructions would be written on the outside and, after all, anyone could follow a set of instructions. She wondered if Boone had ever made pancakes, or if that was beyond his aspirations in the kitchen—even from a mix. She knew a lot of people made them from scratch—Mrs. Pip, the cook at Four Elms, had—and so would she one day, when she figured out how to do it. Flapjacks—was that what they called them out West? Hotcakes?

A floorboard groaned in loud protest just as she stepped extra lightly outside Boone's half-opened bedroom door, and the resolve she'd had to stare straight ahead as she went by flew out the window as she cringed and automatically looked to see if she'd woken him. Then she held her breath, her throat suddenly desert dry, her heart thumping in her chest—but, of course, that was because she'd scared herself stepping on the loose board like that.

She hadn't woken him; at least she didn't think she had. His face was turned away, one arm flung over his head, the other flung out to the side, the sheet pushed down and draped loosely over his hips. She could see the dark shadow of morning beard on the angle of his jaw and throat. She could see the slow, even rise and fall of a tanned, muscular chest, lightly shadowed with dark hair, hair that thinned over his lean, flat midriff…he obviously wasn't wearing a stitch.

Lucie swallowed, with difficulty, and let her breath out

slowly, painfully. She could hear her heart pounding. The room was half in shadow, half in sun; Boone was half in shadow, his face hidden, his lower body bright with the contrast between white linen and tanned skin. She dragged her eyes from the man on the bed. Through the window, the Sawtooths looked hard and bright and dangerous against the blue of the early morning sky. No curtains.

Figures, Lucie thought, then took a quick deep breath and dashed down the hall on tiptoe, her heart hammering, her cheeks hot. She flew down the stairs, not caring anymore if she did wake him. She just wanted to put distance between them. Her careful plans for getting a head start on breakfast, for figuring out how to make pancakes ahead of time so she didn't embarrass herself at seven when the men came in for breakfast, everything she'd set up so carefully in her mind for this morning had scrambled. All she'd wanted to do for one brief blinding second, she realized, horrified at the image that had burned itself into her brain, was to slip out of her clothes again and slide quietly under the covers next to the man sleeping upstairs.

And nothing—*nothing*—like that had ever crossed her mind before. Never. Not in twenty-four years; not once in the last five painful years of being constantly in the company of urbane, sophisticated men, a never-ending parade of Uncle Charles's hand-picked suitors, some of the best-looking, smartest, wealthiest, most up-and-coming young men from Bangor to Boston. No one had ever made her heart trip over in crazy double time like this man had, this dark, brooding cowboy with the lines of care on his sun-tanned face and the love in his eyes for that cranky old grandma of his....

"*What the hell—?*"

Boone couldn't believe his eyes. Heaps of soapsuds covered the kitchen floor, mounds, piles—*mountains*—of fluffy white soapsuds. And there, in the middle of it all, was Lucie on her hands and knees, with soapsuds up to her elbows and beyond, with the roundest, trimmest, most delectable female bottom he'd seen in a long time, high in the air. She had a bucket beside her and was obviously trying to clean up the mess.

"Oh!" She sat on her heels and looked over one shoulder. "Boone." Her voice trembled through the bright smile she put on for him. He knew she was ready to burst into tears. And if he laughed—which was what he suddenly wanted to do—she probably would. "I—I'm sorry. I don't know what I did wrong. I just—" She bit her lip.

Boone highstepped it through the suds, trying to skirt the shallow lakes of water on the floor and not get his boots too wet. Then he reached down and grabbed Lucie's hand and hauled her to her feet. Her hand felt small in his, and slippery and soft and all wrinkled from being in the soapy water, and for a moment he didn't let go. Then he did, and grinned at her. He couldn't help it.

"What the hell's going on around here?" He said it softly this time.

"Oh, Boone! I—I don't really know what happened...." Her bottom lip quivered and her eyes were wide and bright with tears, and at that moment, he realized he wanted nothing more than to take her in his arms and kiss her silly and tell her he didn't really care what had happened. Kiss the soapsuds from the end of her nose, her eyebrows, kiss those trembling rosy lips that had put his hormones into overdrive the moment he'd first laid eyes on her. Everything was happening way too fast. It scared the hell out of him. And remembering that made him stiffen and step back and frown again as he surveyed the shambles in the kitchen. Hormones, that's all it was. He'd been too long—way too long—without a woman in his life. It was something he just had to get used to.

"I just thought I'd wash the breakfast dishes and—and I can't understand what I did wrong." Her words tripped over each other in her hurry to tell him, and she wiped the back of her hand against her nose in agitation, leaving another blob of quivering rainbow-white on one cheek. "I stacked all the plates and cutlery in the dishwasher, just like the diagram said to do—" Her eyes, earnest now, sought his. He frowned. Surely she knew how to stack a dishwasher without looking at a diagram?

"And I put soap in the little thing in the door. You know, that little sort of bucket thing? Both places, just like it said. And then—" She looked accusingly at the machine in the corner, quiet now. At least she'd had the sense to shut it off.

"Then it worked for a little while and then—then when I turned around there was this!" She waved one hand weakly at the kitchen floor and turned to him again.

"And it just kept coming out!" she wailed. "And everything—breakfast and everything, had been going so good up until then!"

Well, just how good was debatable, Miss Lucie, but he wasn't about to bring *that* up right now. One of the men had told him the pancakes were great but she'd forgotten to make coffee and then had brought them tea instead. Hot tea! The cowboy had looked at Boone in utter shock. *In a teapot!* And the bacon coming in burnt and curled up ten minutes after the pancakes were all gone wasn't exactly what they'd been hoping for from the new cook. "But I ain't complainin', Boone—don't get me wrong. I ain't complainin' about Miss Lucie atall, atall," he finished up with a wink and a grin. That wink had irritated Boone, but he didn't want to think about that, either. Maybe all Hank had been referring to was that a new cook meant a welcome change from Boone's cooking.

Boone strode over to the utility closet and pulled out a

mop. "Here." He tossed it to Lucie and she caught it. He tried not to look at her damp shirt, where the soapsuds had soaked here and there so that it stuck to her in some interesting places, revealing her soft roundnesses, her modest feminine curves. He could tell that she wasn't wearing a bra and wrenched his eyes away guiltily. He hoped none of the other hands had been in here offering to help clean up! "That should pick up the water a little faster than that rag you've got."

Then he strode over to the dishwasher. He pulled open the door. It was filled almost to the brim with suds.

"Lucie?"

"Yes?" She was industriously scrubbing at the lakes of soapy water, wringing the mop into the bucket beside her.

"Tell me again what happened."

"You mean about the dishwasher?"

"Yeah. Tell me again, exactly what you did."

"Well." She frowned and reached up to push back the damp red-gold curls that had escaped from her braid. "Let's see... I loaded the dishwasher, just the way it said to." She smiled at him, a brilliant smile that hit him somewhere, hit him hard. She looked so darned pleased with herself.... "And then I put some soap in that little holder thing inside the door—"

"Hold it." It was dawning on Boone that maybe this was the first time Lucie Crane had ever loaded a dishwasher by herself. "You put soap in—what kind of soap?"

"Dishwashing soap, of course." She looked at him like he was maybe a little slow, or hard of hearing. "The dishwashing soap that's under the sink—"

Boone strode over to the sink and pulled open the cupboard door. "This stuff?" He held up a clear bottle of green dish detergent for her to see.

"Yeah," she said slowly, still frowning. "Isn't that—?"

"Well, hell's bells, Lucie Crane, that's the problem. This

isn't the soap you use for a dishwasher." He pulled out a box and held it up high, waving it around in disgust. Lord! "*This* is what you use for a dishwasher. See—it says 'For automatic dishwashers.'" He stopped. Maybe he was being too hard on her.

But she was just staring at him, her mouth open, her eyes wide. Then suddenly she covered her mouth and began to giggle. He stared. She giggled louder. Finally she took her hand from her mouth and leaned on the mop and laughed out loud, her knees sagging. It was the most delightful, delicious sound he had ever heard.

"Thank goodness—" she gasped, her eyes brimming over with tears, but of merriment this time, not worry. "Thank goodness the floor needed a good wash anyway—you should have seen it before!"

Then Boone laughed, too, and for a minute or so he felt a connection between himself and this bedraggled imp of a woman, this mystery hitchhiker that he'd picked up yesterday on the road to nowhere, a connection as strong and true as fresh-forged steel that bound him to her although she was a good fifteen feet away. Mostly, though, he realized how long it had been since he'd let himself laugh. And it felt good. It felt real good.

Lucie couldn't believe how quickly the day seemed to fly by. After she'd gotten the mess in the kitchen cleaned up, she looked at the clock and realized she'd better get busy on the masses of sandwiches Boone had said he'd take out to the men for lunch. They usually stayed in the fields when the weather was fine, and ate their lunch under a tree somewhere in the shade. One of these days she was going to do that, Lucie told herself, humming as she slapped peanut butter and jam onto presliced bread lined up on the table. She admired her rows as she went along—strawberry jam on top, peanut butter on the bottom. Nothing to it—all this job took was a little organization. One day she'd make a little picnic lunch just for Mattie and her and they'd eat under the trees somewhere.

Now, coffee. She had to make coffee and find some kind of container to put that in. No one had said a word when she'd forgotten to make coffee this morning, but she'd seen the disbelief on several of the hands' faces when she'd brought in the teapot. Maybe they didn't drink much tea out West. No problem, she thought, smiling gaily to herself and looking at the big coffee urn, hands on hips. Miss Lucie was flexible. Now…how the heck did this thing work?

When Boone came in an hour later, she had everything packed and ready. She'd even made a big jar of lemonade, jingling and tinkling with ice, but she didn't tell him about that. She wanted the men to have at least one surprise when they unpacked their lunch.

Afterward, she wandered outside to watch while Boone strapped the load behind his saddle. She kept a healthy distance from his horse, a big rawboned bay gelding that kept stepping from side to side and snapping at flies with his long tail. Balzac, one of the collie-shepherd-blue heeler crosses, sat at her feet, staring up at her with adoring liquid eyes. She murmured the kind of silly little things she knew dogs liked and scratched his ears and ruffled the fur on his head, and he leaned against her knee, eyes closed in bliss.

Lucie noticed that Boone glanced at the dog once or twice and at her, but he didn't say anything. Talk about strong, silent-types, these cowboys, Lucie thought, with an exasperated blast of breath at a lock of hair hanging in her eyes. Lord, it was hot! Her braid that had been so neat and tidy this morning was becoming messier by the hour. Sometimes she wished her new boss talked more. She wasn't used to all the silence there seemed to be room for in these wide Idaho spaces.

She watched Boone slowly and deliberately test the leather straps securing the lunch and wondered how many hours he could spend with her without saying anything. One day, she thought with a little smile to herself, one day she'd find out. Now she was content just to watch. In what she called his cowboy clothes, he was everything she'd ever thought a cowboy should be—strong, tall, lean, slim in the hip, broad in the shoulder, with a sun-lined face and a worn-looking black cowboy hat jammed low over narrowed eyes. His jeans were faded, his boots were scuffed and dusty and his shirt was creased.

With a sudden graceful movement, he swung himself up into the saddle and the horse danced sideways, startling her. She straightened, shading her eyes to look up.

"Whoa, Bogart...whoa," he murmured soothingly, and Lucie felt the tenderness in his voice clutch at her chest.

"Bogart?"

The horse tossed his head toward her and pulled a couple of times at the bit. Boone patted the horse's shoulder and grinned, and Lucie felt her heart lift a little.

"See? He knows his name."

For a half a minute, perhaps less, Boone looked down at her, their eyes holding even as the horse continued to side-step, bit and bridle jangling.

"Miss Lucie?"

His voice was deep and rough and his eyes held hers, and she tried to swallow but found she couldn't. "Yes?" she finally managed to squeak out faintly.

He tipped his hat and smiled, the very smile that she thought yesterday would probably make her faint dead away. It didn't and for that she was hugely grateful.

"You're doing a great job, Miss Lucie." He nodded again, a brief manly salute with his leather-gloved hand just touching the brim of his hat. "Thanks." Then he wheeled the big bay and cantered away, the faithless Balzac loping along behind him. She watched Boone go, until he was just a speck of dust in the distance, and treasured his words, her eyes swimming. No one had ever told her she'd done a good job before. Nothing she'd ever done had ever counted for anything—only who she was, a Douglass, had counted.

But the day wasn't over yet. By the time ten o'clock rolled around that night, Lucie was beginning to wonder if she'd be able to make it up the stairs. She left the dishwasher running in the kitchen, too tired to wait until its cycle was completed, too tired to wait to put the dishes away. This time she'd used the right soap. This time—she crossed her fingers, just in case—the machine had better deliver.

She yawned as she dragged herself up the stairs, one foot slowly following the other. At this rate she'd be napping in the afternoon, like Mattie did. Mattie, in fact, told her she was plumb crazy not to take a nap.

"With the men hayin' and comin' in at all hours, you got to be ready to put supper on the table anytime. And you still have to get up early in the morning. Don't I know it! I done it plenty of times." She'd fixed Lucie with her glassy stare and leaned toward her, looking as if she dared Lucie to challenge her words.

Lucie didn't have either the energy or the inclination. She just pushed over the cookie tin and poured the old lady another cup of tea and replenished her own cup. Mattie cackled, and started in on a story about the time she'd had to feed a haying crew of twenty-seven, back in the days before all the newfangled machinery, balers and the like, came in and took jobs away from men who needed them.

Lucie had listened, fascinated. There was no end to Mattie's stories. Sometimes, before she'd finished one story, her eyes would kind of glaze over for a minute and then she'd seem to remember another one, just as good, and off she'd go on that one. Some of Mattie's stories, Lucie suspected, weren't entirely the truth and nothing but the truth. But who cared? They were tales of the West, of settling in the Sawtooth Valley many years before, of church suppers and rustlers caught and brought to frontier justice, and young brides from the East setting up house in the middle of nowhere. Mattie loved to talk and Lucie loved to listen. Lucie thought they were going to get along just fine.

Where was Boone? Had he come in yet? She'd seen him go out after supper with a couple of the men and hadn't seen him come back. There was no end, it seemed, to the things that needed doing, or that needed Boone's attention, on the Double H.

Double H. She tried it again, just as she reached the top of the stairs. Why, it practically rolled off her tongue, smooth as silver. Lucie grinned to herself. Yesterday she didn't know where she was headed, only that she needed to find somewhere safe to hole up for a couple of months. Now she was practically feeling like a native.

Well, maybe not quite. She pushed her hands into the small of her back to relieve the stiffness. These Westerners seemed to be made of pretty stern stuff.

"Lucie?"

"Oh!" It was Boone. He'd startled her, coming out of one of the rooms at the end of the corridor as he had.

"Can I see you a minute?"

She hobbled down the hall to the door he'd stepped out of, entered the room and gingerly sat on a chair in front of a big scarred oak desk. She looked around. This must be his office. Filing cabinets, a computer console, walls of books and periodicals, a red-and-white calfskin covering the chair she was sitting in...

"I moved up here when Mattie got too sick to make it up the stairs anymore." He studied her for a minute. He had obviously come in while she'd been busy in the kitchen, she realized. He'd changed his clothes and had taken a shower. She could see that his hair was still wet, and combed down long and curling over his neck and collar.

"Mattie had the room opposite mine but after her last bout in the hospital, I insisted she move into my office downstairs. This is kind of a—" He made a gesture to include the general contents of the hastily furnished room, the lace curtains showing that it had obviously once been someone's bedroom. Then he sighed. "Well, it's a temporary measure."

Temporary? She stared at him. Did that mean he thought Mattie might move back upstairs sometime? Or that she might die soon? It surprised Lucie how that thought gripped her in the middle. She was just getting to know the old woman— Or did that mean Boone was going to find a nursing home or something for her? He couldn't!

"Are you going to put her in a place for old people?" She immediately regretted blurting it out. It was none of her business. "Oh—sorry, Boone. I didn't mean that. I—"

"Mattie was born on a spread five miles from here, in the middle of a snowstorm without even a midwife to help her into the world." Boone's voice was icy. He held Lucie's gaze, his eyes flaming with some emotion she didn't understand.

"She's been to Boise once, she's been to Twin Falls maybe five or six times, she's never been out of the state and, frankly, Lucie—" His voice lowered and he leaned toward her, his eyes intense and glittering. "I don't know how you do it where you come from, but in the Sawtooth Valley we look after our own. Mattie's not going anywhere. This is where she lives. This is her home."

It was more than Lucie could bear. She stood up. "I never said she should! I never thought she should go—go anywhere! I think it's—" She gripped the back of the chair she'd been sitting in, searching for words to express what she felt. It had hurt her, wounded her terribly to hear Boone accuse her of even thinking that—

"I think it's—it's *wonderful* the way she lives here, the way you look after her, the way—" She waved her hand at him, knowing just about what she looked like, too: hair sticking out in a tangle, her second clean shirt that day grimy and sticking to her ribs, one hand with a clumsily bandaged thumb where she'd slipped with the can opener while opening the endless cans of beef stew she'd guiltily served the men for supper. At least they'd had fresh salad with their meal, not canned green beans. "A nursing home is the *last* place I'd *ever*—"

"Look, Lucie—" Boone interrupted, motioning her to sit again. He looked weary, too, as weary as she felt. "Forget it. I guess I'm just a little—I don't know. On edge for some reason." He drew one hand wearily over his face. "Sit down. That isn't what I asked you in to talk about."

He wheeled his chair to the filing cabinet and bent over an open drawer, flipping through the files, searching for something. Reluctantly, Lucie sat down again.

"Here," he said, pulling a file out of the drawer, and turning back to face her. He slapped the folder on the desk. "Okay. I've got to get a few details from you since you'll be working for me for the summer. Stuff for the government."

He looked up and she hoped he didn't see her hands clench to stop them trembling. She felt herself go pale, then redden, then go pale again. Her heart was pounding. Was this what she thought it was? Just when she thought she'd fooled everyone, including Boone? Just when she thought she was home-free?

"Just a couple of things. Permanent address, Social Security number, next of kin, the usual—hey! *Lucie!*"

He knocked over his chair—he got up so fast—and with one powerful bound he had leapt around his desk.

Lucie Crane had fainted dead away.

Chapter Four

Boone scooped her up into his arms. She hardly weighed a thing—not much more than Mattie did. Just like a bantie hen, he remembered thinking later, all fluffed-up feathers and spirit. Both of them.

Instinctively he held her tighter as he straightened, and then he frowned down at the still form he held in his arms. His own heart was pounding. Figured—she'd given him a hell of a scare, that's all. Fainted. At least he hoped that's all that had happened. He bent to press his cheek against her forehead. It was damp and clammy, and for a moment he caught a drift of the faint sweet perfume of her woman's hair and he stiffened and raised his head abruptly. She was pale, so pale that he could see a few tiny freckles picked out on gold across the bridge of her nose. Seven. But her pulse was throbbing wildly in her temple and he knew he had to get her somewhere where he could lay her down. Get her head between her knees, below her heart, get the blood flowing again.

Lord, what an idiot he was! Boone cursed himself as he strode down the hall with Lucie in his arms. Letting her work like that, that hard, her first day here. Who knew how long she'd been on the road? Whether she'd been eating properly? He should have insisted she rest for a couple of days, take it easy. It's just that he'd been so damned relieved at the prospect of getting out of the kitchen again. Now...

It was his fault that this happened. *His!* Boone kicked open her bedroom door and strode over to the brass-and-iron bed, his jaw tight. But he didn't let go. Not right away. For a couple of long seconds he just held her tightly, relishing the soft feel of her woman's body curved against his, listening to the syncopation of their breathing, seeing the way the red-gold of her loosened braid glowed against the tan of his arm. Then, with a deep breath, he leaned forward and carefully placed her on top of the bed.

He stood staring down at her for a few seconds, then turned on his heel and headed to the bathroom. He had a wet cloth in his hand when he returned a moment later.

"Lucie!" No response. He wiped her face gently with the cloth he'd wrung out in cold water, scrubbed at a smudge on one cheek, then folded the cloth and draped it over her forehead. He shook her, gently at first, then harder. "Lucie...come on, girl. Wake up!" She stirred slightly and frowned and sighed and then her breathing changed tempo, deepened.

Boone saw the color flow slowly back into her cheeks, then, frowning blackly, he bent to untie her laces. She curled her toes automatically when he freed them from the confines of her sneakers and the tiny movement made something flutter madly for a moment inside him. "Bloody voyeur!" he cursed himself, and pulled off her socks roughly, tossing them into the corner of the room, after the shoes.

He hesitated for a few seconds at her belt, then took a deep breath and unfastened it, unsnapped her jeans, and pulled down her zipper. He eased the stiff denim awkwardly under her hips, first one side, then the other, finishing by grabbing both pant legs at the bottom and pulling hard. The jeans came off in one smooth, surprisingly easy movement. He tossed them after her socks and shoes and turned to the dresser against one wall, pretending to himself that all he was doing was following the proper first-aid rules: loosen constricting clothing, apply cold compresses to the victim's face and neck. Wouldn't this be the time for Lucie to come out of it, when he'd half undressed her? Wouldn't she just scream blue murder?

He pulled open a drawer, thinking vaguely that he might find a nightgown or something that he could put on her, when he spotted her wallet. It was well used, but of the finest leather. He picked it up, hefting it lightly in his large hand. He saw the fine letters carved along one edge: Hermès, Paris. *Very* high-class.

It reminded him of something he hadn't thought of in years. His mother's saddle. She'd brought her own saddle with her, a Hermès saddle, when she'd come to the Sawtooth Valley as an eager young bride from Philadelphia, nearly forty years ago. It was an English-style saddle, he remembered, all hand-rubbed leather and delicate polished steel. She'd ridden every day in the early years, before the grit and the poverty and the hopelessness of it all had dragged her down and killed the laughter in her eyes and finally sent her to her grave, still young, still beautiful, just after J.J. was born. She'd wanted to be buried in her wealthy family's plot, back East. But there wasn't the money then, and his father, the man she'd loved and to whom she'd given the joy of her youth, hadn't cared enough to find it. She lay in the windy pioneer cemetery at Beaver Creek, the valley burying ground. Sarah Livingstone Harlow...his beautiful, laughing mother. Dead at thirty-six. That's how old he was now.

Boone took a deep, shaky breath, startled at the thick feelings of loss that had risen in him. Things he hadn't thought of in years. His mother's saddle. Where was it now? In the tack room out in the barn? Had Jane taken it with her to Twin Falls when she moved out?

Deliberately Boone wrenched his mind back to the problem at hand. He knew suddenly what he was going to do. He took one quick calculating look over his shoulder, a look made even swifter as he caught sight of Lucie's long pale legs gleaming in the light from the overhead fixture, her T-shirt rumpled and pushed up to expose a few inches of smooth white skin above the brief pink panties she wore, then...

Boone rifled her wallet. He did, and he'd never, ever before done anything like that in his life. There was money, some, but that was all. He wasn't looking for money, although he was glad to see she wasn't completely broke. That probably meant she'd been eating, at least. But there was no identification of any kind. No driver's license, no credit cards, no birth certificate...no Red Cross blood donor card. Nothing. Why didn't the lack of ID surprise him the way it should have? Boone thought, shoving the wallet into the rear of the drawer and grabbing the first soft, feminine article of clothing that he felt. What he had grabbed looked like an oversize shirt, a nightshirt, that read Hug Me. Boone stared at it for a moment, then, oddly saddened, he tossed it back into the drawer.

He wasn't taking any more of her clothes off. She could sleep in the grubby T-shirt she had on.

He returned to the side of the bed and looked at Lucie, feeling something inside him, something uncomfortable, tighten as he watched the way she slept, her face turned a little to the side, her hands curled slightly, palms exposed. Her color was better now. She'd come out of her faint and was sound asleep. He removed the wet compress from her head, then leaned down and cradled his left arm under her shoulders to raise her slightly, awkwardly, so that he could pull back the bedclothes with his other hand. She didn't awaken, only made a tiny little contented moan, a nuzzling sound, and turned her head against his chest so that he couldn't see her face. Boone pushed her under the covers as fast as he could, not caring if his rough movements woke her, and pulled the quilt, one of Mattie's hand-pieced Star of Bethlehems, up to her chin. Her ragtag braid escaped to lay thick and shining on her shoulder. Slowly, deliberately, almost against his will, Boone reached over and caught one end of the crumpled blue ribbon that had secured the end of her braid and gently pulled it off. He dropped the ribbon onto the nightstand beside her bed and walked out, reaching blindly for the light switch on the wall as he left. Then, when he'd pulled the door closed behind him, he leaned against it for a long moment, his eyes shut.

The house was quiet, the only sound the wind in the eaves. Boone took a deep breath, squared his shoulders and strode back down the hall to his office.

"Well, my, my. Ain't *you* the early bird!"

Mattie's sly sarcasm wasn't lost on Lucie as she burst into the kitchen next morning, cheeks flushed from her hectic rush down the stairs. It was nearly nine o'clock! Mattie was sitting quietly at the small breakfast table in the kitchen, the remains of tea and toast in front of her, a garishly colored half-knit something-or-other on her knees. She looked up brightly at Lucie's sudden entrance, then bent to her knitting needles again with an absent smile, giving a practiced yank to the yarn leading from a half-unraveled sweater that was sitting on the floor.

"Where's Boone?"

"Oh, he's gone out to the bull pasture. He'll be back around ten, he said." Mattie glanced up at the kitchen wall clock, then gestured toward the teapot. "Sit down, dear. Tea's still hot."

"What about breakfast?" Lucie wailed, then realized that obviously breakfast was long past. "Who cooked breakfast for the men?"

"Why, I did." Mattie looked at her in astonishment, then her eyes clouded slightly as she continued, with some confusion in her voice. "'Course, I did. Don't I always?" She hesitated, then added somewhat grudgingly, "Mind you, Boone *did* give me a hand." Mattie frowned severely at her knitting and thrust the needle viciously into the next loop.

"Oh, Lordy!" Lucie flung herself into the chair opposite Mattie. What that meant, Lucie knew, was that Boone had made breakfast for the haying crew. "Now what am I going to do? It's my second day on the job! Boone's going to kill me!"

"Tsk, tsk," Mattie clucked. "Such foolishness! I'm afraid you don't know my grandson or you wouldn't say anything so darn silly. Boone Harlow's got the softest heart in the valley, though he'd be right annoyed if he knew I'd told you. Why, Boone said you should be left to sleep, said you needed your rest...though why a young thing like you should need your rest, *I* have no idea...." She gave Lucie a brief, piercing look, then began muttering into her knitting, more to herself, it seemed, than Lucie, about young people today.

Lucie moaned and rested her head, facedown, on her crossed arms. He'd fire her...he'd probably fire her, and then what was she going to do? She couldn't face hitting the road again, she just couldn't! And she couldn't go home to New Hampshire, not yet, not for another couple of months, not until she turned twenty-five, not until her inheritance was hers, free and clear, no matter *who* she married—

And to think that...Boone had had to put her to bed last night. He'd carried her to her room. He'd undressed her. She blushed fiercely. How could she face him this morning?

Fifteen minutes earlier, Lucie had woken with a start and had known immediately that something was very, very wrong. It was bright outside her window, too bright, and she could hear the slam of truck doors and the whinny of horses. She'd slept in…she'd missed breakfast! Her second day on the job….

She'd leapt out of bed and looked down at herself in amazement. She still had on the filthy T-shirt she'd worn the day before, and—and panties…! Then a faint memory of those last few moments in Boone's office returned, and in an agony of embarrassment she covered her face with her hands. She'd fainted. Right in his office. She'd remembered feeling hot and cold and light in the head and then…nothing. Boone must have brought her in here and put her to bed. Carried her…and—and taken off her clothes, some of them, she thought wildly, looking around. There they were—her socks, her shoes, her jeans, crumpled in a corner.

Frantically Lucie scrabbled in her drawer for some clean clothes. Then, dressed, she dragged a brush through her hair and bolted down the hall to the bathroom. My God! She looked a mess, she thought, splashing cold water into her face and eyeing herself dubiously in the mirror. She was pale, but at least she looked rested. The dark circles under her eyes, circles she'd noted yesterday, were gone. She'd slept like a baby last night…couldn't remember sleeping that soundly in months…years, maybe.

She'd plaited her hair on the run, twisting a covered elastic onto the end just as she reached the bottom of the stairs, then had skidded and nearly fallen on a hooked rug as she tried to make the corner to the hall.

Lucie reached down to rub her ankle where she'd twisted

it slightly. Mattie concentrated on her knitting, lips pursed, counting under her breath, ignoring her.

Well. It couldn't be helped. She'd blown it. Breakfast was over. The sun was shining through the big double hung windows, the counters were wiped and clean. The dishwasher was humming placidly through its rinse cycle—Lucie eyed it balefully for a moment—and everything seemed to be under control. She'd just have to make it up somehow. First thing on her shopping list, first trip to Ketchum, was an alarm clock.

Knowing that there was not much she could do about her situation, at least not until Boone returned, made Lucie feel a little better. She eyed the teapot and reached over to pull it toward her, picking up a cup that had been set out on the table. A delicately flowered cup and saucer. Bone china. She hesitated for a few seconds....

"No, go ahead, dear, help yourself. Boone set that out for you. Most folks around here just use mugs, but Boone said you weren't from around here, said you'd most likely appreciate a cup and saucer for your tea." Mattie looked up again, eyes twinkling. "That so? Proper lady, are we?" She winked, and Lucie tried to smile.

But Mattie's innocent remark shook her. Did Boone know more about her than he was letting on? Surely not. How could he? She was getting paranoid. Sure, the Douglasses were a well-known family in the East, but who'd have heard of them out here? Lucie pushed back the feeling of panic that suddenly rose in her throat and got up to get a bowl from the cupboard and a box of corn flakes from the pantry. When she returned, she smiled brightly at Mattie, determined to change the subject.

"What are you making, Mattie?" She gestured toward the older woman's knitting needles.

"Oh, this old thing." Mattie frowned severely at the half-finished article spilling off her lap. "An afghan...I think.

See how far I get. I told Ho Pickens—he's our neighbor, you'll meet him soon enough—I'd knit him something to cover his knees when he watches TV in the evenings. He's gettin' on, silly old fool, and hasn't got any womenfolk to knit for him, not since his sister passed on three years ago—"

"I met Ho a couple of days ago, with Boone," Lucie said, and poured herself a glass of milk. "Nice old guy." She smiled, ignoring Mattie's "harumph." "He'll like that, Mattie."

"He'd better. I'm using up some of Jane's old things she left here when she moved out, stuff I knit her when she was a teenager. See here?" Mattie yanked at the yarn that, unraveled from the red sweater on the floor, was feeding her current project. "No sense wasting perfectly good yarn, and this is plenty fancy enough for Ho Pickens."

"Who's Jane?" Lucie asked with interest, digging into her bowl of cereal. She was starved! Must be the Idaho air.

"Why, Jane! Don't you know our Jane?" Mattie eyed her skeptically. "Why, Janie's my granddaughter, only one. Boone's the oldest—he's thirty-six this past February, and then there's Carson, he's next to Boone. Oh, Carson's a handsome lad, looks just like his mama, he does. You'll meet him come Thanksgiving—he always comes home for Thanksgiving, wouldn't miss it. Jane's next, and then there's our J.J., my baby. He's twenty-three."

Lucie didn't bother to remind Mattie that she'd be gone long before Thanksgiving. For the next ten minutes, while Lucie finished her breakfast, Mattie filled her in on details of the Harlow family. Jane, it seemed, had left the ranch years before to pursue a career in Twin Falls, then New York, and then back to Twin Falls to start her own business. Carson—Mattie called him a "rock hound," but perhaps she meant he was a geologist—had left only a couple of years previously, in painful circumstances, Lucie gathered.

Something gloomy and complicated that she couldn't quite follow about Carson and a local girl named Becky McNeill and about Carson letting Boone and the Double H down. Then there was J.J., due to start his final year of college....

"A poet!" Mattie snorted. "Did ya ever hear anything so cracky in yer entire life?"

"I don't know, Mattie," Lucie said pleasantly, gathering up her dishes. "I think it's kind of a lovely thing for a man to want to do. Romantic." Lucie suddenly had visions of a handsome, younger version of Boone, with hot lover's eyes that could melt a woman's heart, with eyes that—

"*Romance!*" Mattie snorted. "As if this family hasn't had its fill of romance. As if the Harlows haven't had enough romance to choke a rodeo bull! Romance, young lady, don't pay the bills and don't put beans on the table!"

Lucie glanced up at the clock. Boone, if he was on time, was due back in ten minutes. She rubbed her damp palms against the sides of her jeans, shocked at the wanton image that had floated through her mind. She carried her dishes to the sink and ran some cold water into her bowl. Mattie's vehemence over J.J.'s choice of a career surprised her. Lucie was beginning to realize that the undercurrents that she'd already felt at the Double H ran deep. Somehow she doubted she'd get much on the subject out of her taciturn employer. Mattie, on the other hand, seemed to welcome the chance to talk. Maybe because she, Lucie, was an outsider; maybe an outsider didn't count.

"*Romance!* No good's ever come of romance in this family...none! And if you don't believe me, just ask Boone. Though," she added with a frown and another vicious jab at her knitting, "I don't suppose he'd tell you."

Lucie silently agreed.

"Damn-fool romantic notions killed his mama, wrecked his daddy's life and near buried the rest of us. Boone's daddy's to blame. My own son. Art, poems, romance—all that la-de-da stuff! Where does it get ya?'' Mattie fixed her with her fierce stare. ''Thank heaven for Boone Harlow, that's all I can say. He's the man his granddaddy was. Got the two feet God gave him, on the ground—where they belong!''

Then Lucie did stare at Mattie. Funny...Mattie was right, Boone definitely had the look of a man of care and responsibility and duty—that's why she'd been so sure he was married, at first—and he bore it well, but she wouldn't have thought there was no room for anything else in his life. In fact, those carefully shuttered dark eyes seemed to hide more of himself than they showed; at least that's the impression she had. What did they hide?

Everyone had something to hide—look at her! But what her boss was hiding was none of her business. No question about it. Her curiosity, Lucie thought firmly, would just have to take a pass this time. It had already got her in more trouble than she cared to remember in her twenty-four years.

Boone didn't show up at ten. Lucie discovered with dismay that she'd been counting the minutes. He didn't show up by quarter past, and by half past ten, Lucie wondered if she should mention it to Mattie. Which she did, silly as it seemed. Mattie wasn't the least bit concerned.

''Lordy, girl! You might as well get used to it. Boone said he'd be back at ten and no doubt he intended to, but a hundred and one things probably came up between then and now and we might not see him before suppertime.'' Mattie glanced up with interest, her old eyes sparkling. ''My, my...waiting on menfolk. I've spent most of my life doin' just that, girl. You will, too,'' she added slyly, ''if you stick around.''

There was no chance of that. In a couple of months she'd be gone.

By eleven o'clock, Lucie was too jumpy to sit still anymore, so she dug out some of the stained and torn cookbooks she'd found in a drawer the day before and persuaded Mattie to teach her how to make biscuits. She'd realized, browsing through the cookbooks, that biscuits were a staple of Western cookery, and she'd better try and master them. Mattie was horrified when she confessed her ignorance.

So when Boone finally did arrive, just before noon, she was up to her elbows in flour at the baking counter, giggling as Mattie shouted instructions from the breakfast table.

She thought she'd heard the slam of the outside screen door, but wasn't sure it was Boone until she heard Mattie behind her.

"There you be! Lucie's been looking for you all morning, Boone." Mattie cackled with delight and Lucie knew it was at her sudden rush of color. She forced herself to continue kneading the dough, not facing him. That Mattie!

"She has?" Behind her, Boone sounded mildly amused, and Lucie blushed even hotter. What would he think? That she'd started getting notions about him already? And after last night—

She turned finally, her arms floury to the elbows. Meeting his gaze, Lucie found she couldn't deny Mattie's charge, as she'd intended to do. She didn't trust her voice. He was smiling slightly and she met his eyes gamely across the room, willing the blood to leave her cheeks. He looked dusty and hot, and as she watched, he looked away from her, to his grandmother, his smile for her, then went to the coatrack just inside the kitchen back door and tossed his hat onto it. He shrugged a couple of times, irritably, as though his shoulders were cramped and sore, then reached up and ran his fingers through his hair in a gesture of deep weariness. She could still see the furrow in his thick, dark hair that marked where his Stetson had sat. Then, to her dismay, he wrenched savagely at the buttons on his sweat-darkened shirt and tugged it out of his jeans. He had his back to her, and as she watched, mesmerized, he casually shrugged out of his shirt and tossed it into a basket near the sink that stood just inside the back door.

"How—what do I do next, Mattie?" Her voice was wobbly, she realized, and she turned and attacked the biscuit dough with renewed energy.

"Land sakes! Easy on that dough, young lady. You'll wear it out. Here." Mattie limped over to the counter and leaned against it. "Let me finish that. You look after getting some lunch on the table for Boone. He'll be hungry as a bear after a whole morning of—"

"I can take care of my own lunch," Boone said quietly, and Lucie automatically faced him to say that, no, she was the cook, she would fix lunch. Then she wished she hadn't turned around. Lord, how she wished she hadn't!

Boone looked... Well, she supposed she hadn't seen all that many men with their shirts off, but she could say this: Boone looked absolutely wonderful without his. He was rubbing his hair with a towel—he must have doused his head under the tap—the posture throwing the rock-hard muscles of his arms and shoulders into sharp relief. Then, as she watched, mouth dry, he lowered his arms, giving his face a hard final wipe and when he slowly drew the towel, so white against the dark muscled hardness of his upper body, over the smoothness of his skin, the darkness of the tangled mat of hair on his broad chest, under his arms...their eyes met. For one intense second everything else simply fell away from Lucie's consciousness: the dough, Mattie, her discomfort over facing Boone after last night, the mess that had brought her all the way from New Hampshire to Idaho in the first place. All she saw, all she felt, was that he was man and she was—she was woman. Then Boone broke the tension—thank goodness, Lucie thought, horrified—by casually turning away again to pick a clean shirt off a hook on the wall and shrug into it. When he turned back, slowly, deliberately fastening the buttons, his eyes were hooded and his glance barely skipped over her to rest on his grandmother again.

"Mattie."

"Yes, Boone?" his grandmother said meekly.

"You take your pills this morning?"

"Darn it. No, I haven't. Haven't needed them this morning yet." She looked up and grinned at her grandson. Lucie felt her heart flip-flop at the love she saw pass between them. "Been havin' too much fun showing Miss Lucie how to cook. For someone who's supposed to be a cook, she sure do ask a lot of questions, Boone!"

"Pills?" Lucie gently, quickly, helped the older woman transfer the misshapen rounds of biscuit dough to a baking sheet she'd already prepared, as Mattie had instructed her. Her mind and blood were humming, awhirl with the sensations she'd had when she'd looked at Boone, when he'd looked at her. She was thoroughly annoyed with herself, and couldn't believe she'd had such a sophomoric reaction to seeing a man with his shirt off. Heavens! She'd seen far more than that on Mediterranean beaches. Mind you, Boone Harlow wasn't just *any* man with his shirt off....

"Oh, just some little yellow-and-pink ones the doc says I'm supposed to take," Mattie admitted, shrugging her thin, bent shoulders. "Ticker, y'know. Don't see as it makes too much difference whether I take 'em or whether I don't. I tell the doc, what can a body expect at my age? Boone worries too much."

Mattie grinned up at her grandson, who'd come to stand at Lucie's shoulder. Lucie tried desperately to concentrate on what she was doing, spacing the biscuits carefully the way Mattie had shown her. But she was as acutely conscious of him, of his height, his warmth, his presence, where he was, unseen behind her as she was when she'd faced him across the room. It was unsettling.

"Have you had lunch?" Boone asked. He was talking to Mattie.

"Oh, tea and toast, tea and toast all morning." Mattie's voice suddenly sounded old and querulous. Lucie could almost see her transferring her independence to Boone's broad shoulders. "I think I'll go lie down for a while, Boone. Missed my nap this morning."

"Here. I'll take you. Hold still." Boone effortlessly swept Mattie into his arms and carried her from the room.

He seemed to do a lot of that around here, Lucie thought, with a grimace. She shivered, and carried the pans to the wall oven. It wasn't the slightest bit cold in the big ranch house kitchen, not with the sun shining in and the oven turned up. No, her gooseflesh had to do with something else, something altogether different.

She'd fix lunch, that's what she'd do. Sandwiches. Then, she supposed, they'd eat together, at the breakfast table. Just the two of them.... Lucie wished Mattie hadn't missed her morning nap so she could have stayed in the kitchen with them now. That's pretty silly, she thought, frowning as she got out the bread and peanut butter and grape jelly, you're a grown woman.... Surely you're capable of holding your own with any rough-edged Idaho rancher you might happen to meet.

Lucie cut the sandwiches she'd made and put them on a plate on the table. Then she prepared two place settings and went to the fridge to get the milk. Maybe Boone drank coffee with his meal; it seems most of these Idahoans did.

"Oh! You startled me." Boone was back, standing tall and silent in the doorway to the hall, watching her. "Uh, this okay?" She nervously gestured toward the table and watched as Boone walked over to the table and pulled out a chair. He waited until she came up, his eyes on hers, then, to her surprise, seated her before going around to take a chair himself. So far he hadn't said anything. Which made her even more nervous. She hadn't had a chance yet to explain about last night, to apologize for fainting, or falling asleep or whatever had happened. She hadn't had a chance to apologize for oversleeping this morning and missing breakfast, to give him her word that it wouldn't happen again.

"Milk, all right?" she asked, holding the pitcher over his glass.

"Fine." She knew he was watching her as she poured, and Lucie was thankful that she didn't spill any. She kept her own eyes lowered, watching herself pour, the thought of meeting that clear tawny gaze again this close up, meeting what Mattie called the Harlow eyes, after what had happened by the sink, making her tremble inside. Still, nothing *had* happened, had it? She pushed over the plate of sandwiches.

"Sandwich?"

Boone stared at the plate for what she thought was an inordinately long time for a person to make up his mind about whether or not to have a sandwich. Then he stretched out his hand and took one. He put it on his plate and looked up at her. Nervously Lucie put one on her own plate.

Boone cleared his throat. "Now…uh, I've got a couple of things I'd like to straighten out with you, Miss Lucie," Boone drawled, and she thought she could seen an odd light in his eyes. "Right off the bat. And the first one is this—"

"Yes?" she said breathlessly, her eyes on his, her heart in her mouth. Was he going to fire her after all?

"Cowboys don't eat peanut butter-and-jelly sandwiches."

Chapter Five

Lucie didn't know whether to laugh or to burst into tears. For a few seconds she just stared at Boone, eyes wide, mouth agape.

"You don't—don't..."

"Actually," Boone said, picking up his sandwich and studying it carefully, "I'm not much of a cook—as you might have gathered—and I don't mind them all that much." He took a bite and chewed with satisfaction, his eyes aglimmer with amusement. He swallowed. "I guess you could say I've survived on peanut butter sandwiches more than once. When necessary.

"But," he continued, frowning at the rest of his sandwich, "I can't say the same for the rest of the men, and I believe it is my duty to pass on their sentiments."

"You mean—" The oddity of the situation was beginning to dawn on Lucie. She sat up straighter, eyes on Boone.

"Yeah." Boone regarded her closely, then grinned.

"Let's put it this way—the lemonade you sent out yesterday wasn't the only surprise the men got."

"But—but they never said anything to me," Lucie said earnestly. "No one mentioned it last night at supper—"

"Too scared," Boone interrupted calmly. He smiled again, and Lucie felt her heart skip a beat, then steady itself. "You might have quit and they would have ended up with me in the kitchen again, and I get the feeling it'd take more than a couple of peanut butter-and-jelly sandwiches before they're feeling quite that desperate."

Lucie laughed. She couldn't help herself. Boone didn't laugh, not out loud. He just grinned broadly, watching her, and reached for another sandwich.

"Look—" she gasped, breathless from laughing, automatically reaching out to touch his hand, to stop him. They both froze as their hands made contact, and Lucie snatched hers back as though she'd been burned. "Look, uh, don't eat that if you don't want to—I'll fix something else."

"You will?" Boone regarded her with lazy amusement, another sandwich already in his hand. The arched brow said it all: What else *can* you make, Miss Lucie?

"I'll heat up some soup," she said, thinking quickly. "I'll—I'll make a grilled cheese sandwich." Surely she could handle that; what could be simpler? Toast a couple of slices of bread and stick some cheese in between.

"Not for me. I'm fine," Boone said. "I just thought I'd let you know what the men think, that's all."

"Thanks." Lucie chewed her sandwich in silence for a moment, then raised her head and sniffed loudly.

"Damn!" Boone leapt out of his chair and bounded over to the wall oven. He threw open the door. A faint swirl of smoke drifted lazily out of the oven and the smoke alarm in the kitchen began to wail.

The biscuits! Lucie leapt up and grabbed a couple of pot holders from the counter.

"Give me those before you burn yourself!" Boone growled, and snatched the pot holders from her. He reached into the oven, pulling out two pans of exceedingly brown biscuits and flipped the pans onto the counter, cursing loudly. Several biscuits overturned and Lucie could see that the bottoms were a uniform glossy black.

"Damn it, anyway, Lucie. Can't you do anything right?" Boone said sourly, waving the pot holder in his hand to disperse the smoke. Lucie looked at him. He had a point. She couldn't seem to do anything right. But it wasn't her fault, was it? She'd never made biscuits before! But she was willing to learn, wasn't she? And she'd had—she'd had things on her mind! He knew that. The smoke alarm wailed on; it was loud enough to awaken the dead—or Mattie from her nap.

"Can't you do anything about—about *that?*" she yelled, pointing angrily in the direction of the alarm.

"Nope." Boone looked down at her, almost with distaste, arms folded in challenge. It made Lucie's eyes brim, whether from the smoke or from his attitude, she didn't know, and she turned and ran over to the door.

"How's this for doing something right?" she yelled, and kicked open the door, wedging a chair against it. "And this?" She opened a couple of windows—*slam, slam.* "And what about this?" She raced over to the big kitchen range, noting with satisfaction how the sudden violent action relieved her feelings. She flicked on the switch that triggered the exhaust fan and within a minute or so the smoke had cleared and the alarm had stopped.

Boone hadn't moved. He was regarding her from beneath lowered brows, leaning against the kitchen counter, arms crossed resolutely.

"Well?" She came to a stop in front of him, hands on her hips. She tossed her head to flick her braid onto her back, then blew ineffectively at a couple of flyaway strands that had drifted over her eyes. Lord, it was hot in here!

"Well, what?"

"You said you had a couple of things you wanted to straighten out with me. One—you don't want any more peanut butter sandwiches. Okay. Got it. Two—you think I'm a lousy cook. Got it. Three—I slept in and missed breakfast today—"

"Hey, I didn't say anything about—"

"You didn't have to." Lucie's breast was heaving. She was hopping mad and she was going to say what needed saying. "You cowboy types might be used to all this strong, silent stuff, but I've about had it!" She noted his raised eyebrow and the arrogant gesture of inquiry made her even madder. "I want to know what's going on around here! I think it's high time you said what you meant. Okay?

"So, let's get this clear, for once and for all. Are you telling me you made a big mistake hiring me and you want me to hit the road, or what?"

Boone looked at her so seriously and for such a long time that Lucie nearly lost her nerve and apologized and crept out of the kitchen to nurse her wounded feelings in private. Already she'd amazed herself at what she'd said to him.

"You're right, Lucie. Dead right," he said softly, in that deep gravelly voice that she felt clear through to her bones. "I made a big mistake when I hired you."

She looked at him in dismay. So he *was* going to fire her!

He nodded his head slowly and sighed. "Yeah. A real big mistake. But, no, I'm not going to fire you. In fact, I'd hate like hell for you to quit over this. I'm begging you, Lucie—" she regarded him narrowly, suspiciously "—please, don't quit on me. I'd hate to face that crew of mine if they found out I'd driven you off—"

"You're serious?" He meant it! The wonder that she felt crept into her voice.

"Dead serious. Don't go."

"Well…" Lucie rubbed the toe of one sneaker along a line in the linoleum and looked down. She hadn't expected this. Not at all. Then she straightened and tossed her hair again and said airily, "I guess I could be persuaded." She smiled a little then—couldn't help it—and felt her heart leap once more when she saw the answering softness in his eyes, and something else…something that was very, very male.

"Shake?"

"Shake." She offered him her hand and he took it, and held it. His hand felt so warm, so strong, so…so absolutely right holding hers. "No more cheap shots about my cooking, though."

"Scout's honor."

"After all, you must have figured out by now that I don't know a whole lot about cooking, despite what I said that first day. Although I didn't actually lie to you." Her chin went up marginally as she met his gaze.

He nodded solemnly, his eyes alight with amusement. "As a matter of fact, that had occurred to me."

"But I'm willing to learn. And Mattie said she'd teach me all she knows. I'll do my best, Boone. I promise." It occurred to her that it went without saying that her best, modest though it was, probably outstripped his by a country mile.

Boone nodded again. He still hadn't let go of her hand, and, uneasy at the gleam of growing awareness in his eyes, she pulled her hand free. He let her go immediately, and folded his arms across his chest again.

"And—and I'm sorry about sleeping in this morning and what—what happened last night," she finished in a rush, eager to clear the air entirely, feeling the hot color flood into her cheeks yet again. Stricken, she looked up at him, then immediately looked away. She put her hands to her face and nervously smoothed back the damp tendrils of hair that had escaped her braid. "I—I don't know what happened. I guess I was tired or—"

"Never mind, Lucie. It was my fault," he interrupted gruffly. He reached out and turned her face up to his, finger and thumb under her chin, forcing her to look at him. "I shouldn't have done that—shouldn't have expected you to put in a full day right away like that. Forget it."

"I want you to know that I—I appreciate you taking care of me the way you did," she said, her voice almost a whisper. He took his hand from her face.

"I've had worse jobs, Miss Lucie." Boone grinned at her and she thought she just might faint again, this time with sheer, unexpected pleasure. "A whole lot worse."

I made a big mistake when I hired you.

What had Boone meant? Lucie had thought about what Boone might have meant ever since he'd asked her to stay on. If hiring her was such a big mistake, why didn't he want her to leave? Well, that's easy, she told herself for the umpteenth time. He's already lost three cooks in a month. Besides, she was getting along with Mattie. And Lucie was gradually realizing that most people wouldn't...and maybe that was why three cooks had left that month.

Mattie was bossy and cranky and nosy and demanding and crotchety as heck, and she didn't hesitate to use her age and poor health to get her own way. But, despite everything, Lucie was beginning to love her. Mattie loved to talk; Lucie loved to listen. Mattie loved to tell everyone what to do or the way she'd do it; Lucie loved to find out how to do things. For someone who would never dream of cooking for herself, Lucie was getting right into it. By week's end, under Mattie's watchful and demanding eye, Lucie had made a passable pot roast with roast potatoes and two veggies, had mastered biscuits—the color at least; they were still a little on the dense side, "bullets," Mattie called them—and had completed a series of disastrous pies. The ranch hands hadn't seen the pies. Even immune to Boone's cooking as they were, Lucie didn't think the pies would pass muster.

So she and Mattie ate them for lunch. Three pies that week: an apple, a cherry and a blueberry. They'd just picked off the burnt bits on top and the soggy underdone bits on the bottom and called it pudding. Mattie had laughed until the tears rolled down her cheeks. That was the day Lucie had realized, with a fierce surge of protective emotion, that she cared for this old woman, Boone's grandmother, she who had never known a grandmother's love…or a mother's, not that she could remember. Right then, in her heart, she claimed Mattie for her own.

She deserved a little happiness, transitory though she knew it was. She deserved the simple happiness of learning to care for this old woman, this stranger, someone else's grandmother. Somehow, Mattie, and Lucie's growing relationship with her, filled a part of the past Lucinda Crane Douglass had been denied.

Lucie's true past, what she could make of it, was a puzzle she'd been trying to piece together over the past couple of years. She'd learned that the people she'd called Mother and Father had been her real mother's distant cousins, who'd wanted her because she had Douglass blood in her veins. As far as she could figure out, the fact that she was a Douglass was the only thing that mattered to them. Why had they kept her adoption a secret? Lucie asked herself for the thousandth time. Why had they pretended that she belonged to them, was their daughter, their flesh and blood? What had happened to her own parents? What had happened to her sister?

Bonnie Snowden, once her college roommate and now a Boston private investigator, was slowly turning up pieces of the puzzle. She'd found that Lucie's father had been a drifter, a man named Raymond Crane, perhaps the man that her mother had run off with against dire threats of retaliation from her family. They'd never married. Bonnie had tracked down a former landlady, in a decaying part of Pittsburgh—perhaps the place Lucie remembered in her dreams—who'd told her as much. Had her mother been as afraid of her family's power to harm the man she loved as Lucie was today of being tracked down by her guardian?

Bonnie, on the other hand, she trusted. Bonnie was the only one in the entire world who knew where Lucie's despair had led her, the only one who knew how or why she'd finally escaped Concord in the dead of night two weeks before in a desperate bid for freedom. She didn't care what Uncle Charles and all the others thought. She'd return, but only on the day she turned twenty-five. Until then, her life was her own.

She couldn't have managed without Bonnie. Bonnie had arranged to forward bank drafts from time to time so that Lucie could get her hands on cash without carrying identification. Her escape from the Douglasses had been planned for too long and with too much care to have some bank teller or car-rental counter clerk recognize her. Credit cards were out of the question. And her uncle's influence was not to be underestimated. Even the slightest clue, a withdrawal from her bank account, a phone call to a friend, would give him the point he needed to start tracking her down. He'd forced her into line before; Lucie knew he'd do it again, if he could find her.

She'd outsmarted him this time…but good. He'd never find her here. She was traveling light and free and happy for the first time in her life. She'd never been anonymous; she'd never been plain Lucie Crane. She was plain Lucie Crane now.

Lucie had promised to contact Bonnie from pay phones from time to time, to keep in touch, to let her know that she was all right, and to find out if Bonnie had any news of her sister, if, in fact, a sister existed in more than Lucie's dreams. Bonnie seemed to think it was possible, from the kind of information she was beginning to uncover, but though she cautioned Lucie against getting her hopes up, Lucie couldn't help but believe in the miracle. *A sister!* She had to believe that it was true, to believe that somewhere there was someone who truly belonged to her. *Family. Flesh and blood.*

Lucie tried to think well of Jack and Myrta, knew that she ought to, that it was only charitable, now that they were dead. But she couldn't...she just couldn't forgive them for lying to her all those years, for letting her believe that they were her real parents, that she'd been born to a couple who seemed to despise their own child. The betrayal had eaten at her for twelve years, ever since she'd discovered her birth certificate. The betrayal had poisoned her life.

They were dead now, Jack and Myrta, and, still, she couldn't find it in her heart to forgive them. Dead but not gone, she thought, and shuddered. Their cold, grasping Douglass hands still reached out and clung to her, from the grave. *Flesh and blood, flesh and blood.*

They'd made sure, with the help of crafty family lawyers, that, until she was twenty-five—in two more months—her life was not really her own. Until she was twenty-five, Uncle Charles controlled her inheritance, Uncle Charles controlled every detail of her life. But he couldn't control her here. She'd found the perfect hideout. The Sawtooth Valley. Beaver Creek Ranch...the Double H. They'd never dream of looking for her here, not in a million years.

She just had to keep Boone from asking a lot of questions. She wasn't a very good liar. So far, since she'd fainted that night, he hadn't brought up the subject again. If he did, this time she was prepared. She planned to tell him she'd lost her ID, and then borrow Bonnie's Social Security number the first time she got to Ketchum and a phone. She'd straighten it out with Bonnie later. She'd make up a name and permanent address and use Bonnie for next of kin, if he asked, and then would cross her fingers in hope that he'd never check it out. Somehow she didn't think he would. Somehow she knew Boone Harlow had a lot more on his mind running the Double H than wondering about the background of some casual employee he'd picked up on the Star Route one summer day. In two months she'd be gone, in three months he'd have forgotten all about her.

And why did that thought hurt so much? Lucie frowned and carefully replaced the hodgepodge of trinkets and Harlow family treasures she'd just dusted on the mantel in the family room. Several were rodeo trophies dating from years back, bucking broncos and cutting horses with Boone's name, and Carson's, engraved in silver, but dark and tarnished with age. A woman came in every two weeks to wash floors and vacuum and dust, Boone had told her, but Lucie didn't mind helping out between times. She was tidying up, unable to sit still with her thoughts, keeping Mattie company while the old woman watched one of her morning television programs.

She looked over. Mattie was sound asleep, snoring gently, her glasses askew on her nose, wiry gray hair springing haphazardly out of the old-fashioned, almost invisible hair net that she wore. Lucie smiled. Why did the thought of leaving the Double H and this crotchety old woman—and her dark, brooding grandson, if the truth be known—hurt so much, when she was a stranger here, always would be, a stranger who'd only just arrived?

"Say, what d'you think, Boone? That new cook of yours going to last?"

Boone looked up from where he was wedged under the roller mechanism of the old baler, catching just a glimpse of his friend's blond head between the wheel and the blue sky. What he wouldn't give to buy some new equipment. Not much chance of that, not this year....

He grunted as he shifted out from under the baler, aware that Lyle's casual inquiry had irritated him. Was it the lazy male appreciation he heard in Lyle's voice? Couldn't be. He'd known Lyle Hendricks all his life; they'd shared everything since they were eight years old. Besides, Lyle was married. Happily married. Boone frowned as he finally eased himself from under the haying machine. He wiped dirt particles and debris off his face with a greasy sleeve. And if Lyle didn't happen to be married and had a passing romantic interest in Lucie Crane, what could it possibly matter to him?

"Well? Mattie gonna run her off, or ain't she?" Lyle persisted.

"Mattie likes her."

"Hot damn!" Lyle stood up and wiped the silver-smooth metal shaft he held in his hands with an oily cloth. "You're kiddin' me, Boone!"

"Nope." Boone was clear of the baler now and dug through the tool box standing open to one side of the machine shed. Lyle had offered to come over at noon to give him a hand. Between the two of them, they'd repaired the old John Deere often enough to know they could probably pull it off once more. This time, though, it looked as if the baler had them beat. The ratchet that controlled the size of the bales the machine made was broken, and Boone was pretty sure he couldn't get that part anymore.

"What about you, Boone? How'd you like having another woman in the house? Alice was askin'," Lyle added quickly as Boone glowered at him.

"You ask too many questions, Lyle," Boone said. "Always have." He bent again to paw through the box of greasy black used parts stored in a corner of the shed, frowning. He needed a spare hose, too. Maybe there was one in here...

"Ah, hell, Boone. You don't know when you got it good," the other man said, grinning as he threw down his rag and tossed the heavy metal shaft from one hand to the other. "Kinda looks to me like you got lucky and hit the jackpot all by yourself this time, with—"

"What are you trying to say, buddy?" Boone knew that everyone in the valley, everyone from the mailman to the artificial insemination technician, had been trying to hook him up with a woman ever since Carson had left, even since before Carson had left. But it wasn't going to work. Boone knew what he was doing. Even a valley girl such as Becky, Carson's girl, couldn't bear the thought of spending the rest of her life in the back of nowhere, out here in the Sawtooths. And the isolation and poverty of the place had killed his mother, a city girl from the East. You couldn't expect a modern woman to give everything to the land the way he did, the way the Harlows before him had. He was resigned to an affair from time to time, maybe, and a solitary life of ranching, doing what had to be done. He couldn't expect a woman to share it, and he didn't expect to find one who would. He wasn't looking, had no intentions of looking. Lyle's wife, Alice, was different. Sure. But there weren't too many like Alice. Or Mattie.

"It's true, man. Ever since Carson took off with Becky McNeill two years ago and left you high and dry, we been trying to fix you up with some nice woman. I have, Alice has—hell, everybody has. But where has it got us? Have you popped the question yet to any one of them nice valley girls we been setting you up with? Nope. 'Cept for you moseyin' down to Twin Falls from time to time—" Lyle gave his friend a sly, knowing look "—don't seem like you've got time for women anymore. Ain't natural, Boone."

Twin Falls! Boone thought about that for a moment.

Yeah, he had had an on-again, off-again affair with a teacher friend in Twin Falls for a while. Nothing to set the world on fire, though, and they'd both known it. But that was two years ago. It hadn't worked out and now she was marrying some accountant with a big insurance company. He wished her well; she knew he did. They were still friends. Nearly two years without a woman…when you got right down to it, that was the trouble now, this thing with Lucie. He could barely look at her without thinking about getting her into his bed. It was just hormones. That's all it was—pure and simple.

And he was no teenage boy, to be jerked around by his hormones. Boone set his jaw. Maybe he ought to take Lyle and Alice up, maybe he ought to meet a few of the women they'd been trying to set him up with lately. Just to get them off his back for a while. He thought of the teacher in Twin Falls again, all dark hair and eyes, all woman. Hell, Lucie Crane was all arms and legs…and big blue eyes. And that hair, red-gold and soft as silk. Boone strode back to the baler and threw himself down to ease himself under it again. Lucie Crane wasn't even his type…and he was her boss. *What the hell was he thinking about?*

"Ho tells me you've taken her on until fall roundup?"

"Ho talks too much." Boone turned his attention deliberately to the problem at hand, the broken machine. He knew Lyle had let the subject drop…for now. Trouble was, his friends were way too interested in his life, considered they were doing him a favor. They couldn't believe that living the way he did was what he wanted. He *was* settled down, damn it, he just wasn't married. They couldn't believe that a man could be happy by himself. It was just a question of attitude, he told them. Boone had made up his mind on that a long time ago.

Two months. He thought about how long Lucie'd promised to stay on as cook, if he could keep her. If he could keep his feelings to himself, keep from offending her and maybe having her hit the road again. Why was it that during roundup and branding and when you were trying to cover the range shorthanded during calving season two months went like a grass fire? And yet the thought of staying on his best behavior for the next two months under the same roof with Lucie Crane felt like a life sentence? Felt like forever.

Chapter Six

If she hurried, maybe Boone would take her along.

Lucie pulled on a clean T-shirt and quickly tucked it into her jeans. She opened her dresser drawer, located her wallet, quickly checked to see that it had money, then remembered the wad under her mattress and pulled it out. Seventy, eighty...a hundred dollars should be enough. She shoved the money into her wallet, tucked the wallet in her small nylon backpack, the one she used for a purse, and slung the pack over her shoulder. She needed some clothes, she needed an alarm clock, but mostly she needed to find a pay phone and call Bonnie.

Lucie froze for a moment. She heard a door slam in the hall and the quick thud of stocking feet down the stairs. Boone rarely wore his boots in the house, she'd discovered. That, at least, was not like the movies. Boone obviously respected the people who had to keep the place clean—probably because he'd most likely pitched in and done his share over the years. Lucie took a quick look at herself in the mirror, licked the palms of her hands and smoothed the flyaway hair at her brow and temples. Then she wrenched open the door and flew down the hall after Boone.

"Wait!" She raced for the stairs. He was just picking a hat off the rack by the front door, a slightly dressier version of the one he usually wore. He already had his boots on. His scowl, as he swung toward her, had her forgetting the lines she'd rehearsed so carefully.

"Problem?" He settled the Stetson on his head and put one hand on the door knob.

"Yes! I want to go with you. To Ketchum. I've—I've got a few things I'd like to do in town." Her words tumbled out and did nothing to erase his expression. If anything, he looked more annoyed. "I've already checked with Mattie. She's—"

"You're not responsible for Mattie."

"I know, but she says she'll be fine. She's going to read for a while and take a nap." Lucie didn't know why she felt she had to explain herself, and that she'd already checked about a trip to Ketchum with Mattie. As Boone said, Mattie was not her responsibility.

Boone looked at her for a moment without the slightest change in those unreadable dark eyes, then he nodded. "Okay," he said finally, grudgingly. "Get in the pickup. I'll be right there." He wheeled and went down the hall toward the room where Mattie slept.

Heart hammering, Lucie slipped out the front door and meekly walked around to the passenger side of the pickup truck. Whew!

These past couple of days had been murder with Boone. She hadn't seen him that much, and when she did, he rarely had anything to say. He'd eaten in silence the few times he took his meals with them instead of the men, content, apparently, to let Mattie and Lucie do the talking. After supper, he usually left the house until dark. She'd rarely see him before breakfast the next morning. Which suited her just fine, Lucie reminded herself. She still didn't trust the strange feelings she had when he was around; the less she saw of him, the better.

The trip to Ketchum wasn't much different. At first, Lucie tried to maintain at least a semblance of a conversation, but she soon ran out of things to say. Boone said as little as possible. Finally, annoyed that he wasn't even making an effort, she turned to look out the window, at the mountains that rimmed the valley, at the dusty hills and the verdant irrigated bottomlands. It was easier. She could think her own thoughts and try and forget the disconcerting presence of her employer, not two feet away from her on the torn bench seat of the old truck.

Only once, as they were nearing Ketchum, driving slowly through the condo development that had helped turn the old ranching town of Ketchum into a center for Sun Valley alpine skiers, had Boone turned and addressed her. "You need some money?"

It startled her, the bluntness of the question as well as the unexpectedness of it. "No. I've got some. Thanks anyway," she added.

He turned to the road, then back to her again, his eyes probing hers. "You need anything, just ask. Understand?"

"Yes." Blunt as it was, it warmed her. She felt that she could rely on this man; he'd just told her she could.

"The point is, Miss Lucie," he went on dryly, as though he didn't want to leave any room for possible misunderstanding, "I'm not Santa Claus, but I do owe you for wages." Shocked, she looked at him again. "I don't intend to ask again who you are and where you come from and all that other stuff I need for the government, not after what happened last time."

His look was sharp, and Lucie felt herself blush slightly.

"So I'll give you your wages when you leave the Double H. We'll straighten the paperwork then. But, if you need money before that, just ask. I'll take it off your pay."

Boone couldn't have been plainer. He obviously wanted to make it clear that he wasn't doing her any favors. But Lucie heaved a huge silent sigh of relief all the same. Thank goodness! And the money...why, it was laughable that this rancher felt he owed her money. He'd never know how much she owed him, just for the giving her the chance to spend the summer at his ranch.

Boone dropped her off on Ketchum's main street, pointing out a sort of dry goods general store on one side of the street when she told him she wanted to buy a few extra clothes. He gave her directions to the grocery store, where Beaver Creek Ranch had an account, and told her to charge whatever she needed in the way of supplies. Then he pointed out a café halfway down the street and told her he'd meet her there in an hour's time, at three o'clock.

As soon as she saw him disappear, taking a left turn at the end of the block, Lucie hurried across the street to where she'd spotted a pay phone in front of the post office. She fumbled through her pocket to find the number she'd written on a piece of paper.

Fingers shaking with both excitement that Bonnie might have news for her, and fear that Boone might see her in the phone booth—although why that should matter, really, she couldn't say—she dialed the series of numbers. He knew nothing about her; she might have friends in Ketchum, or relatives. Or in Sun Valley. Or Hailey or Boise, for that matter.

"Bonnie?"

"Lucie Douglass! For heaven's sake, where are you? I've been worried sick when I didn't hear—"

"I'm in Idaho. I'm calling from Ketchum—"

"Idaho! How'd you end up in Idaho?"

"Never mind. I'm working, I got a job, I need to borrow your Social Security number for a while, in case I get asked for it." There was no need to tell Bonnie, not now, about the complicated series of train rides and bus tickets and hitchhiking that had brought her to Ketchum in the first place. Before Boone had picked her up.

"Don't laugh—I'm fine. Really! I'm staying at a ranch near here. It's a real ranch, Bonnie. Cattle, horses, dogs, cowboys." She ignored her friend's hoot of laughter. "No kidding. I'm cooking for a bunch of ranch hands. It's the perfect place. I'm going to stay here until my birthday. Uncle Charles will never dream of looking for me here." She grinned as she listened to her ex-roommate's mile-a-minute opinion of Lucie's culinary skills.

"You laugh, Bonnie, but this is the new Lucie Crane you're talking to here. I've dropped the Douglass, for obvious reasons. Any news?" She bit her lip as she listened anxiously, oblivious to the sound of traffic outside the booth.

Bonnie's sources told her that Charles Douglass was playing down his niece's disappearance. Bonnie wasn't sure if that meant he'd given up trying to find her or whether he was going to try something new. She'd keep an eye on him. As for tracing Lucie's sister, Bonnie had received some promising leads in California and Oregon, which she intended to follow up as soon as possible.

"California?" Suddenly it all seemed so hopeless, so foolish of her to keep hoping, keep praying. California was so very far away, with so many millions of people.

"Yes. It seems that an Eva Grace Crane was adopted by a family out there eighteen years ago. Whether it's the Crane we're looking for or not, I don't know. It doesn't coincide with the date of your adoption, it's a few years later. But the fact that your mother's name was Eve is encouraging. Maybe your sister was named after her. It's starting to look pretty positive."

"Oh, Bonnie—"

"Don't give up, Lucie, but don't put all your eggs in this one basket, either. If she's alive, or if she ever was alive, I'll track her down. She might be your flesh-and-blood sister, but don't forget you're still strangers. I know you've got a lot tied up in this. Family counts, but it isn't everything. Just don't set yourself up for disappointment. Not again."

Lucie knew exactly what Bonnie was talking about. The only reason her mother's cousins had wanted to adopt her was because Douglass blood ran in her veins. But they were hard, grasping, unforgiving people. She wanted to find her flesh-and-blood sister for other reasons…reasons of the heart. She needed to know to whom she belonged, and who belonged to her.

Lucie hung up slowly, realizing that her heart was pounding. Each time she contacted Bonnie, it seemed that the trail was getting warmer. First it was discovering where her mother had died, then it was finding records of Lucie's adoption and the landlady who remembered her mother. Now Bonnie was gradually sifting fact from fiction about Lucie's natural father, and her sister. It made Lucie want to go back sometimes, back to the East Coast to see what she could do to help. But, of course, that was foolish. Uncle Charles would discover her whereabouts in no time. Any man who'd tracked his niece for the past two years with a paid detective, until she didn't have even one private moment, until she knew every time she looked over her shoulder she'd find someone, some stranger, watching her, would have no trouble finding her if she surfaced in Boston. Besides, she was known there; her face was known. Here she was just plain old Lucie Crane—nobody from nowheresville. And that's the way she wanted it to stay.

Lucie wandered into a couple of stores and made her purchases: two loose cotton dresses, a skirt and a pair of sandals. The skirt and sandals she decided to wear, and stuffed her jeans and sneakers into a shopping bag. She'd worn jeans when she was traveling incognito, hoping strangers would take her, perhaps, for a teenager. But jeans were too hot for the kind of weather they were having and the cotton dresses were going to be a lot more comfortable. Then there was the matter of an alarm clock, although she hadn't overslept since the morning after she'd fainted. She picked out a utilitarian model in a hardware store next to the grocery, and by ten minutes to three she was strolling to the restaurant where Boone had said he'd meet her, pausing occasionally to look in shop windows as she walked.

Ketchum was an odd mix of old-style ranching and modern ski-and-tourist town. Even she had heard that the great American novelist, Ernest Hemingway, had been buried here, that Ketchum was his town, that he'd grown up on some dusty ranch in these very hills. Perhaps in the Sawtooth Valley, somewhere like the Double H, she mused, sorry that she couldn't remember the details. The ski mecca, Sun Valley, was only a few short miles out of town. Upscale boutiques and juice bars jostled for space with old-fashioned hardware stores and saddleries on Ketchum's main street.

Hardy's Café, where Boone had said he'd meet her, seemed to straddle the two cultures. Biscuits and gravy, a rather revolting hit of carbohydrates she'd already discovered endemic to Western roadside eateries, was offered on the hand-printed menu, along with avocado-sprout-cream cheese combos on whole wheat. Lucie found a table by the window, beneath some hanging greenery, ordered mint tea and settled in happily to watch people go by on the sidewalk outside.

Lucie saw Boone before he saw her. She watched him wheel expertly into a recently vacated parking spot across the street, then get out of the truck and stand for a few moments on the sidewalk talking with a couple of women who'd hailed him. The women, Lucie was relieved to see and angry with herself for even noticing, were several years older than Boone; one even had a child in tow. She watched as Boone grinned at the boy and reached down to ruffle the child's spiky blond hair affectionately. She poured out the rest of her tea from the pot and slowly stirred in a spoonful of honey, determined not to watch him any longer, but, despite herself, her eyes were drawn to the other side of the street again.

He was saying goodbye to the women and, as she watched, he smiled and tipped his hat to them. The gesture caught her somewhere just below her heart, and she felt herself take in a quick, almost painful breath. She continued to watch as Boone, eyes narrowed, waited for a car to pass, then strode purposefully across the street. *Toward her.* Toward the restaurant, Lucie corrected herself.

She was glad she'd seen him first. She had a few extra seconds to quiet her beating heart, to get her features under control, to hope the surge of emotion she'd felt flood her cheeks had subsided. She felt both confused and angry at the reaction she'd had as she'd watched him on the other side of the street. Sure, Boone was a handsome man, but she'd known a lot of handsome men. It wasn't that.... What was it? Perhaps it was the air of control he had, the air of natural confidence that surrounded him, his easy, relaxed friendliness with the women, the sense she got that he cared for them, deeply, truly cared, as a fellow human being, that he cared for the child. He had a certain quality of quiet maturity, of character, that she'd never before felt in a man, an inner strength that drew her, that intrigued her, that...*fascinated* her.

She took a deep breath. *That's* what it was, this attraction she felt toward this man. After all, even the slightest, faintest, silliest dream on her part—and she hotly denied to herself that she'd had one—that the attraction could be rooted in something else was preposterous. She wasn't twenty-five yet, he was thirty-six. She was an East Coast heiress, whose life had never been her own, a poor little rich girl, with roots going back to colonial New Hampshire, he was a fourth-generation Idaho rancher, as free and independent as the Western wind. She had no one, no one of her own blood in all the world, he had his grandmother and brothers and sister and...even if he didn't have a wife—and Lucie still wasn't clear as to why he didn't, he was certainly attractive enough, and she knew the fact that he wouldn't take one was breaking Mattie's heart—why, half the valley considered themselves Harlow family, or near enough.

No, she was simply impressed by the way Boone uncomplainingly shouldered his responsibilities: Mattie, the ranch which clearly wasn't doing all that well, the livelihoods of the men who counted on him for seasonal work, his younger brother's college fees—whatever. She admired the way he operated—simply, directly, openly. With no hidden agenda. That's all. Just a little bit of hero worship on her part. She should have felt relief at finally getting to the bottom of her strange mixed-up feelings toward the rough-edged rancher who'd hired her. She should have...but she didn't.

"Been waiting long?"

Lucie looked up, startled. She'd been so distracted by what had been going through her mind, she'd almost forgotten that Boone was on his way to join her.

"N-no, just about fifteen minutes."

Boone frowned at his watch. She knew by the clock above the counter behind him that it was ten past. "Sorry." He eased himself onto the bench opposite her and nodded and smiled as the waitress held up the coffeepot from a distance. If he noticed that Lucie had changed and was wearing a new skirt, he didn't let on. Lucie felt peculiarly let down. "How about you...you want coffee? What's this?" He gestured to the pale liquid remaining in her cup.

"Mint tea."

"Ah…" He smiled at her, then, with such focus, such single-minded intensity that Lucie felt her heart begin to flutter all over again. "Mint tea."

"Yes." She found herself smiling back. Just then, happily, the waitress arrived.

"How about a slice of Mary's lemon meringue pie, Shirl? You, too, Lucie?" He smiled up at the waitress. "I can vouch for Mary Hardy's cooking. She makes the best lemon meringue pie this side of Missoula."

"This the new cook I hear you've hired on at the Double H?" the waitress asked, smiling at Lucie.

"Word sure gets around," Boone grumbled, giving Lucie a direct, apologetic look.

"News is news, Boone," the waitress said easily. "Shirley Diamond, honey." She put down the pot of coffee and extended a plump hand to Lucie.

"Lucie Crane." Lucie shook the woman's hand, amazed. Even the waitresses were friendlier in Idaho!

"Now—how about a piece of that pie." Shirley eyed Lucie skeptically. "You look like you could use a little fattening up, darlin'. No offense."

Somewhat overwhelmed, Lucie decided to have the pie. Boone was right. It was absolutely delicious, and as she ate it, Lucie carefully noted its taste, its texture, the consistency of the mile-high meringue and the flakiness of the crust.

"Taking notes?"

"Mmm," Lucie replied, licking the last bit of meringue from her upper lip, noticing with dismay that Boone was watching the gesture with unreserved male interest. "Does Mary give lessons? I'd like to take some."

Boone laughed. "That's not a bad idea. If you were sticking around, I might be able to arrange something."

A sudden awkward silence fell between them. Maybe it was just her own nerves, her heightened awareness of him, and everything he said. Maybe it wasn't his reference to her term at the Double H that had caused them both to study their empty plates with such interest.

"Ah, Lucie, Lucie," Boone finally said softly, stretching out his long legs under the table and slowly stirring his coffee. He sounded vaguely regretful. "I don't know where you're coming from and I don't know where you're headed, but I've got one piece of real good advice to give you on your way through. Don't ever get mixed up with a hard-rock rancher. It's a hell of a life."

"Problems?" Lucie knew he was speaking metaphorically. She knew, so why did she feel the faint blush crawl up her throat at his words?

"Problems!" He pushed his hands through his hair in a frustrated gesture and slumped wearily against the bench seat, one arm stretched along the back. He looked out the window for a few seconds then back at her. "Every time I have to fix that—that— Well, I could say one or two things that shouldn't really be said in front of a lady and I know it wouldn't do a damn bit of good anyway.

"But every time I'm faced with jury-rigging another part for that damn baler, which I have to do three or four times a season, I think of how my father ran the Double H into the ground and it makes my blood boil."

Lucie had heard plenty of mutterings from Mattie about her irresponsible son, but, until now, hadn't realized just where that irresponsibility lay.

"Your dad wasn't much of a rancher, I take it?" she offered.

"Rancher! He wasn't much of anything." Boone looked at her, his eyes very hard all of a sudden. "He was a hell of a poor provider, couldn't handle money when he did have it. All he lived for was his dreams. And maybe my mother...in the beginning at least."

Boone got a faraway look in his eyes, a gentler look, that

made Lucie want to reach over and cover his hand with both of hers, to ease the pain she felt in his voice. But she didn't.

Boone sighed, then smiled. "He was a pretty good dad, I'll give him that. When he was around, which wasn't much of the time. But we had a lot of fun with him. He knew how to laugh."

Boone seemed to catch himself, as though he'd said more than he'd intended, and when he went on, his tone was grim. "The point is, he ran the ranch into the ground and I've been trying for the past eight years, ever since he died, to get it back on its feet again. It's working, I'm getting there." He laughed, a short self-deprecating sound, and drew his hand over his face again. "But it's a slow process, building an operation practically from the ground again. It's a twenty-four-hour-a-day job. I don't recommend it as a way of life," he finished with an ironic grin. That, Lucie knew, is what he'd meant by his advice never to get mixed up with a hard-rock rancher.

"One thing that would help," he muttered almost to himself, and frowned out the window again, "is if that damn baler didn't keep breaking down." He narrowed his eyes for a moment, as though considering a new idea that had just occurred to him, then looked at her suddenly. "You ready? Let's go."

He grabbed the check and stood up. "These packages yours?" He reached over and took a couple of the bags she was trying hurriedly to gather together. When she looked up, flustered, she saw his eyes on her skirt, on her bare legs. Then he turned, with a frown, and strode ahead of her toward the cash register. Lucie had to trot to keep up.

Boone nodded at a couple of regulars who waved him over, but he didn't stop to talk or to introduce her. She was just as glad, really, considering the way everyone seemed to stare. Either she was a bit of a novelty, coming into town with Boone as she had, or she'd grown a horn in the middle of her forehead since she left Beaver Creek a couple of hours ago!

"What's the rush?" she said as she stowed the packages on the seat in front of her feet. She slammed the door of the truck.

"Just thought of something," Boone said, looking through the rear window as he maneuvered, his arm stretched along the back of the seat. She was acutely aware of his hand, only inches from her bare shoulder. Hot! That wasn't the word for it in this country. Lucie rolled down her window to take advantage of the breeze.

At the grocery store, she got out to help him load the boxes he'd ordered earlier into the pickup, over his protests. A few moments later they were headed east, rattling along some graveled road Boone seemed to be very familiar with. At least he drove over to his side of the road at mysterious intervals that turned out to be the approach to a blind hill or a curve or a hidden intersection. Lucie shrugged to herself and turned gratefully to the breeze, eyes closed. This country driving wasn't for the fainthearted.

It turned out that Boone was headed to a run-down spread a few miles outside town. He spoke to a woman at the door to the ramshackle house with its paint peeling and flower beds long grown over with weeds. She nodded slackly as he talked, and shifted a naked toddler from one hip to the other. Her apron was torn and greasy, her hair was dull. But she smiled when Boone reached into his pocket and handed her some bills that he counted out into her hand.

Lucie sat up on the edge of the seat, trying to see better. What in the world was Boone doing?

Then Boone was in the truck, grinning like a boy who'd taken first prize at the country fair. He jammed the truck into reverse and stepped on the accelerator.

"Hang on to your hat, Miss Lucie."

"Oh!" The truck bounced and growled over the rutted yard and into the side field where Lucie could just make out rotting mechanical hulks of various shapes and sizes, almost lost in the long grass. She scrabbled and grabbed and slid around on the truck seat, bouncing once clear over to Boone's side as the truck lurched over a hummock of grass. That sensation, of hard warmth, of the scent of his skin and hair, of the deep rumble of his laughter as he caught her with his free arm for a moment to steady her, had her redoubling her efforts to hang on.

Finally the truck jerked to a stop and Boone opened his door. He reached behind the seat and pulled out a couple of greasy-looking tools. It seemed so silent suddenly, with the truck's engine turned off, a silence broken only by the lazy saw of unseen grasshoppers and the distant bawl of a calf. Lucie still hadn't seen anything that warranted Boone's air of supreme satisfaction.

"What's going on, Boone? Why are we stopping here?"

Boone came around to her side and opened the passenger door with a bow and a flourish. He grinned at her and tipped his hat rakishly. "You are looking at the proud new owner of a 1957 John Deere haymaker, Model 604, as is, ma'am." He bowed again and Lucie giggled. Then he reached his hand to her, as though to help her from the truck and she, delighted with the game they were playing, with the unexpected whimsy of the whole situation, put her nose in the air in her best imitation of a princess, held out her hand to him in a graceful, airy gesture and lightly stepped forward.

And missed the running board of the truck. And fell straight into Boone's arms. And had a brief sensation of a dark head looming between her and the bright sky, and tawny eyes shot with gold looking deep, deep into hers, and hard arms pulling her closer, tighter, into his embrace.

And then Boone's head bent toward hers and and she forgot everything else.

Chapter Seven

Lucie heard a soft grunt as Boone took her full weight and she felt a quick swirling sensation, as though the bottom of her stomach had dropped away. Then she realized that when he'd caught her, he'd swung her around and around, his action absorbing the unexpected effects of what amounted to her launching herself bodily into his arms.

Lucie felt her heart hammering a mile a minute...and something else. Boone's heart. Hammering against hers. His arms were still around her, hard and tight, and she could feel his breath hot on her cheek. Then he made a queer choked sound and buried his face in her neck, holding her even tighter. It felt so unexpectedly good to be held by him like this, to be held as though he'd never let her go, that Lucie wanted to stay right where she was, to stay in Boone's arms forever.

But that wasn't possible. She tried to concentrate on reality, to quiet her fluttering pulse. She told herself to open her eyes, to stop being such a ninny. Nothing was happening, nothing was *going* to happen, so why did she continue to embarrass herself and him by offering her face like she was, eyes closed, as though waiting for the kiss that would awaken her, that would open her eyes to a new, vivid world, a world of love and life, a world that included him? She opened her eyes, slowly, cautiously.

The blue sky looked much the same, the slight breeze ruffling the top of the long dry grass felt much the same....

"Oh...Lucie," Boone muttered hoarsely against her forehead, against her hair. "Lucie, Lucie."

Then, almost roughly, he thrust her from him, his eyes fierce and dark, his face stern. Only the harsh sound of his breathing gave him away.

"Sorry, I—I..." Lucie didn't really know where to begin and she stopped, her eyes searching his.

Boone shook her slightly, his hands iron clamps on the soft flesh of her upper arms. "Lucky I caught you," he said finally, his voice gruff, his smile seeming very forced.

"But—"

"Don't say anything else, Lucie," he breathed raggedly, looking at her. "Just don't." He loosened his hands on her arms, and she felt his thumbs slowly circle, gently stroking the rounded flesh of her shoulders. She shuddered, her eyes wide on his. Every nerve in her body was vibrating and she felt gooseflesh on her bare arms, despite the heat. Her entire body was on full alert...in response to this man. Her boss.

Boone turned from her and stooped to pick up the tools he'd dropped beside the passenger door. He said nothing more to her, just strode over to the rusting baler and eased himself under it, cursing softly as flakes of blistered paint drifted into his face and hair.

Half an hour later they were in the truck, heading for Beaver Creek Ranch. Boone had removed several wicked-looking pieces of machined steel from the innards of the old baler and had tossed them on a burlap sack in the back of the pickup. Lucie had waited for him as he worked, sitting silently in the grass, plaiting strands of brome and couch grass and meadow daisies, trying not to think of what had just happened between them, yet thinking of nothing else.

Had anything happened? *Really* happened? Hadn't he simply managed to save her from falling, when she'd made a fool of herself by pitching out of the truck the way she had? He must think her a complete idiot, holding out her hand to him like that, like some fairy princess! *She* was the one who had obviously gone too far. Whatever had happened back there—indeed, if anything had—hadn't seemed to affect him. He was ignoring her again, just as he had on the trip to town. Still, they were two adults, two independent people who could be expected to govern their actions by reason, not by wild emotion—or hormones.

Lucie stole a sideways look at Boone. He was frowning at the pavement in front of the truck, one hand on the wheel, the other gripping the door frame above the open window. Whatever his thoughts were, he wasn't sharing them with her. She shivered, as she'd done before, and took a deep, unsteady breath as she turned back to staring unseeingly out her own window. *This wasn't hero worship, what she felt. Not a bit of it.* For once in her life, Lucie decided silence really was golden, and kept her thoughts to herself the rest of the trip.

Boone slammed on the brakes in a cloud of dust in front of the ranch house, something he wasn't in the habit of doing. Mattie usually raised hell with him about the dust. He glanced irritably at his watch as he got out of the pickup. They'd left her alone for nearly four hours. Correction— *he'd* left Mattie alone for nearly four hours. As he'd told Lucie, Mattie was not her responsibility.

It was getting bad, though, Boone admitted to himself,

bad enough that he'd have to do something about it. Soon. Mattie couldn't really be left alone anymore, and he couldn't keep an eye on her and run the Double H, too. Somewhere, somehow, he'd have to scrape up the money to hire someone to look after her.

"I'll just check on Mattie and be right back to unload this stuff," he called to Lucie as he stepped onto the veranda. Lucie had climbed out of the truck and was standing there, unabashedly yawning and stretching her arms over her head. Balzac, hypocrite that he was, was barking and leaping at her feet, yowling and whimpering with delight to see her. Boone felt an uncomfortable pang and turned to open the front door, aware that he knew exactly what that mangy mutt was feeling.

Lucie. Another problem, a big problem, he thought as he walked through the house. But he'd known that the day he'd hired her. He'd known the day he'd picked her up at the side of the road that she was trouble, that the wild thrum of his blood he'd felt the first time he'd looked into those big, serious blue eyes had been rooted deep inside himself, so deep and so strong, a need he'd forgotten existed anymore. And he'd known somehow that she felt it, too. He'd known that and he'd still hired her. Boone cursed himself soundly for the fool that he was.

And then this afternoon... This afternoon didn't bear thinking about! He'd nearly lost it, lost it for good with her. Her launching herself at him the way she had... He knew it was accidental, but that sweet solid feel of her in his arms again, the softness of her body clinging to his, the smell of her hair in his nostrils, the surge of instant, blazing passion that he'd felt for her—

Boone paused at the door to Mattie's room and removed his hat. He slapped it softly against one thigh while he dragged his other hand shakily through his hair. Yeah, he'd nearly lost it. And where would that have left him? Left her? What he'd felt out there in the middle of Nellie Babbs's overgrown south field had been so hot and so pure…the kind of glorious white-hot energy that happens sometimes—rarely—between a man and a woman. Pure, strong, simple.

And dangerous as hell.

He took a deep breath and stepped into Mattie's room. She was asleep in her chair, her feet up on an ottoman, her knitting slipped to one side. Boone stepped up beside her and touched her cheek gently with the back of his hand. It felt cool and soft. She looked awkward, sitting slumped the way she was, but he wouldn't disturb her; he'd let her sleep. For a moment he stared down at his grandmother, feeling that comfortable, familiar surge of love he always felt when he was with her, letting it wash free and easy over him. They were soul mates, he and Mattie; they were kindred spirits. She was a true Harlow, as he was, although she'd been born a Rogers and married into the name. She loved this high country, as he did…and she was nearly worn-out.

Boone took a deep breath and quietly left the room. Mattie was getting frailer all the time. The doctor said her heart was feeble, enlarged, that one of these days it was going to give out. She was almost ninety, after all. He'd be awful lonely when Mattie went, as he knew she would soon. He wished he could have given her more, could have made her life easier these past few years. How he could have done that, he wasn't sure, nor was he sure she'd have taken anything from him anyway.

Boone squinted as he stepped into the sunshine again. The tailgate of the pickup was down, but there was no sign of Lucie. She must be unloading the groceries, he thought, noting the rock wedged against the doorjamb to keep the kitchen screen door open. He strode to the back of the truck and carefully lifted out the baler parts on the burlap sack. He'd throw these in some solvent now, then he'd clean them up and try to get that machine working again after supper.

Besides, Boone thought, absently reaching down to scratch the ears of the dog nuzzling his knee as he walked toward the machine shed, just now he'd had about as much of Lucie Crane as a man could be expected to handle.

He deliberately put her from his mind. What a stroke of luck it had been recalling Hank Babbs's collection of derelict vehicles. Why, for years Hank had been collecting machines of one kind or another that nobody else wanted. Boone remembered Hank telling his father, years back, "Why, the day'll come when that stuff you fellers call junk'll be *worth* something!" Ho Pickens bought most of his parts off of Hank. Boone should have thought of that earlier. What luck that Hank had had the old baler Boone needed.

He frowned. Poor Nellie. Hank's wife had been only too glad to take two hundred dollars for the baler. She probably hadn't seen that much money in a while, by the look of things around the place. That broken-down hulk was worth its weight in gold to him. He'd been right; there were no more parts available for the ancient baler he'd inherited with the ranch. Now he'd have spare parts for years; he'd keep that old John Deere jury-rigged forever! Boone grinned. Wait'll he told Mattie; she'd have a good laugh.

He got back to the pickup and frowned when he noted that the kitchen door was still open and a few cartons of groceries still sat in the hot sun in the back. He picked up a heavy box of canned goods and carried it into the kitchen. No Lucie. Figured, he thought, spotting the open door to the pantry, the light on. She should have left the groceries for him to unload in the first place. Most of the boxes were too heavy for her to carry anyway. Not that that would stop Lucie Crane. He had the feeling she was about as determined as Mattie when she got her mind made up....

He shifted sideways to carry the cardboard box through the pantry door, with a grimace throwing it down on a

wooden table in the corner. Then he turned, away from the
door, and automatically reached out to grab the cord that
turned off the overhead light. At the exact same instant, he
heard a loud "Hey!" from the corner, from behind the door.
And as he wheeled, startled, Lucie stood up from where
she'd knelt to stow supplies into a cupboard. She bumped
the door with her hip as she scrambled to her feet, and it
silently swung closed on its well-oiled spring mechanism.

It wasn't pitch-dark—there was a small window high up
in the south wall, with a faded chintz curtain across it. But
after the brilliance of the sun outside and after the brilliance
of the 150-watt light bulb overhead, the room seemed very
dark. Boone automatically reached for the wildly swinging
cord with his left hand; at the same time Lucie grabbed for
the cord with her right. They were inches away from each
other, and when their hands touched, connected, they automatically joined them, without thought, without intent.

It had happened in the space of a breath. They were,
Boone realized, like two dancers, two shadows, two strangers in a dream, engaged in a wary pas de deux, a courtship,
in the semidarkness, and he could no more stop himself
from reaching out and pulling her against him, his left hand
releasing hers and traveling up her arm, her bare skin,
slightly damp and sticky in the heat, to her shoulder, the
roundness, the mystery, to end tangled in her thick disheveled braid, at her nape, he could no more stop himself from
touching her the way he did than stop breathing. He held
her tightly with his right arm, held her head stone steady in
his left hand, and, as he felt her arms reach up to encircle
his neck, to wrap around him freely, strongly, the stretching
action pressing every part of her against him, he bent his
head and claimed her mouth.

Claimed her fiercely and strongly, unerringly, claimed her
with the abandon he'd felt in her presence all afternoon, the
abandon he hadn't dared let loose, claimed her hotness, her

sweetness, her softness for his own. Their mouths clung, tasting, absorbing, moving this way and that, teeth against teeth, tongue twining with tongue, as though they could never get enough of each other. *Never.*

As he knew he could not. He groaned as he felt her response, timid, surprised initially, tentative, then as fierce and passionate as his. And finally, after what seemed like forever, after what seemed like the longest kiss it was possible to share with a woman, after he felt his breathing change to match hers, his heart speed to pound as one with hers—he felt its matching rhythm under her ribs and in the pulse beneath his thumb—after he felt his knees weaken, and knew if she let him he'd take her right here, among the canned goods and boxes of potato chips and the sacks of flour and sugar, he felt fear, real fear. The knowledge that he'd nearly lost complete control of the situation, that her passion was feeding his, her sweet womanly response sending his desire blazing higher, nearly out of control, that he was only moments from doing something that he knew he would regret—that she would regret... He knew it and he knew it was up to him to do something about it. *Now.*

Only that absolute knowledge made him raise his head, aware that he could taste the sweet salt tang of blood, not sure if it was his, or hers, or when it had happened, or how.

"Boone...oh, Boone," she whispered against his throat. He could hear in her voice that she was close to tears and he held her tightly, both arms hard around her, his breath ruffling her hair. He swallowed, tested his bottom lip with his tongue. His lip was bleeding slightly. She'd—he'd— who knows? The thought made him smile. And that saved him. He wanted to laugh. He didn't.

"Boone?" She sounded so bewildered, that he wanted to shake himself. Now look what he'd done! He looked down at her in the half-light, saw the moisture trembling in the corners of her eyes, saw the fullness of her lips, swollen and tender...from kissing him. Knowing that it would never happen again, *could* never happen again, he kissed her again, this time beginning, at least, with tenderness. But it was hopeless; it was as though, once lit, the fire between them would never die, *could* never die, and this time when he raised his head it was to hear her strangled whisper, "Don't! Please don't—" and to hate himself.

"I won't, Lucie," he got out hoarsely, thrusting her away from him roughly, wincing as he saw the confusion in her eyes. "I'm sorry—I'm sorry I hurt you. It won't happen again. I promise."

And he turned from her, pushed open the swinging door, and walked out.

Lucie stood there for a moment, listening to the sound of her own heartbeat in the small room, to the echo of his heels down the hall. She shivered and ran the tip of her tongue over her lips, felt the fullness, felt the taste of him still in her mouth, felt tiny, unstoppable bubbles of joy rise in her and burst, in her center, again and again. She couldn't let the joy expand in her the way it wanted to, couldn't let it spill over, didn't dare. It was too frightening...just now. She needed to think about what had happened. For, this time, something *had* happened, and there was no going back. Only forward.

Lucie smiled to herself in the semidarkness, feeling her mouth tremble with emotion. He'd misunderstood her. But thank goodness he had! What she'd been trying to tell him was that she'd wanted him to go on kissing her, to go on holding her. *"Don't stop, Boone. Please don't stop,"* is what she had meant to say.

The next couple of days were such a jumble of unexpected upset and nerve-fraying suspense that Lucie wasn't able to take the time she needed to explore her feelings about what had happened between her and Boone. She wasn't able to establish, quietly, irrevocably, within herself, a new way of being with him, a new rapport. She was too worried about Mattie.

That night, after tossing and turning for what seemed like hours, Lucie had finally fallen into a restless, dream-filled sleep, only to be awakened abruptly in the darkest hours after midnight by Boone. He was standing at the end of her bed, fully dressed. He hadn't touched her, but she'd awoken instantly, fully, and sat up to look at him as he stood there burnished by moonlight, his face in shadow.

"Mattie's sick," he said.

"How—?"

"I don't know. This isn't the first time this has happened. I'm taking her to Ketchum, to the hospital."

"But, Boone—" Lucie leapt out of bed, unthinking, and stepped toward him. She'd automatically reached out to touch his arm, but he moved away stiffly, before she could touch him. "Maybe I can help." She shook her head wildly. What could she do? "Can I help her get dressed? Or—"

"She's dressed. Go back to bed, get some sleep." His eyes were in shadow. "I'll be back in a couple of hours, in the morning—unless she's worse than she usually is. I—" He paused for a few seconds, and looked at her. She couldn't see him, but she could feel his gaze on her. "I just wanted to let you know."

Then he was gone.

Lucie ran to the window and watched as Boone carried Mattie out of the house and carefully put her into the front seat of the ancient Buick that Boone referred to as "Mattie's car," a vehicle that saw no use unless Mattie was going somewhere, he'd told Lucie with a smile. Mattie liked her own things, and her independence, he'd told her, with the same small indulgent smile. Now Mattie was going to the hospital, and true to type, she wouldn't ride in Boone's pickup, even if she was ill. Lucie felt her eyes fill with tears.

If anything happened to Mattie…! She let the tears roll down her cheeks and felt a few drops hot on her knuckles that were clenched white and tight on the sill. If anything happened to Mattie…!

With a strangled cry, Lucie put her head down on her clenched fists and sobbed. It felt good to weep at last, to let the broken, ragged sounds of grief flow freely. It felt good to let the roller coaster of emotion she'd been on for the past six months, ever since she'd made her decision to run away, finally find release. And the mixed-up emotions of the past twenty-four hours with Boone…and the tender feelings she had for Boone's cranky old grandmother. The anguish she felt at the sight of Boone taking Mattie away was greater than anything she'd felt when the people, whom she'd believed most of her life to be her parents, had died. It was even greater than the grief she'd felt when she'd begun to piece together the sad short life of her natural mother. She hadn't known Eve Douglass; she knew Mattie. She supposed she'd loved her own mother; she couldn't remember, she'd been too young when she'd lost her. But she knew she loved Mattie Harlow. God couldn't take Mattie away from her, not when she'd just found her, not when she'd just claimed her for the family she'd never had. He couldn't! It wasn't fair; life wasn't fair. Life never had been fair for her.

Lucie wept as though her heart would break, thankful that she was alone in the house with no one to hear her. She wept until she finally realized how cold and stiff she was, and crept back to bed to await the morning.

Chapter Eight

Three days later, Mattie was home again.

Lucie had just pulled a pan of cookies out of the oven—anything more complicated for dessert still eluded her, but the ranch hands didn't seem to care—when she heard the unmistakable *thump, thump, thump,* of Mattie's walker in the hallway.

"Mattie!" She flew to the open door and stood there, her eyes wide with apprehension, her hand, still in an oven mitt, held to her mouth.... Was she all right—? Still, if Mattie was walking on her own...

"Oh, for heaven's sake, girl, I ain't dead yet," Mattie snapped, then stopped and looked at Lucie directly. "Got some new red pills this time. Don't s'pose they'll do much good, either. Nothing wrong with me that bein' twenty years younger wouldn't cure." Boone was standing silently behind his grandmother, watching them. Lucie looked from her to him, then back again.

"Oh, Mattie!" Lucie stepped forward and wrapped her arms around the old woman, bending her head to hide the tears that swam in her eyes. She didn't want Boone to see. Mattie felt like a little bird, all sharp, brittle bones and the softnesses of skin and hair. Lucie pressed a kiss onto the wiry gray crown. "Oh, Mattie, I was so worried about you," she whispered, then stepped back, blinking fiercely. She sniffed loudly and managed a smile. She was well aware that Mattie might not exactly welcome such an emotional homecoming.

"Hmph." Mattie worked at a frown, then her lined face broke into a flicker of a smile and Lucie saw her faded blue eyes begin to twinkle behind the smudged lenses of her glasses. "Hmph. Well. I see you got yourself a new dress while I was gone. That's something. Hmm. Do I smell fresh gingersnaps?"

The moment of homecoming was over. And Lucie laughed with real pleasure at the way Mattie stumped her way over to the counter to inspect the fresh cookies, finally choosing one and then another and stumping her way back to the kitchen table.

Still smiling, Lucie turned to Boone, to find him looking at her, an unfathomable look in his dark gaze. He reached up with one hand and settled his Stetson firmly. "Well, I'll be getting back to work." Without another word, or even a nod of farewell, he stepped out the door and Lucie heard the screen door slam behind him.

If she hadn't been so thrilled to have Mattie back, she would have wondered a little at his attitude. Boone was on her mind constantly these days, but that was about all. Since the day they'd gone to Ketchum together, she'd barely seen him. He finished breakfast by himself before she got to the kitchen in the morning and had his evening meal with the haying crew. She hadn't had five minutes alone with him since the episode in the pantry and, really, now that she had

had the time to consider the situation, what would she have said to him if she had had the chance? It seemed that he was giving her the opportunity to handle the situation as he seemed determined to do—by ignoring it.

And maybe that was the wisest course to take. After all, romance was not on her agenda, not her current agenda anyway. Perhaps after she returned to New Hampshire, after she turned twenty-five in six weeks, after her life was her own again and Uncle Charles would no longer have any say in how she lived—yes, perhaps then she would be open to romance. Finding a man who would love her as she loved him and marrying that man and having the family she so desperately wanted, the family that had been so cruelly denied her, was very much on Lucie's agenda. But a short-term romance in the Sawtooth Valley? It was completely out of the question.

And then there were the many subtle and not-so-subtle references to Boone's bachelor state. It was an unending source of irritation to Mattie, she knew, and Ho Pickens had referred to it. Obviously there was a great deal more to her employer than she knew, or could possibly know. Perhaps he'd been married before, unhappily, and wasn't keen to repeat the experiment? That was a common enough scenario today, and who could blame him?

But no, she didn't believe that, not really, and surely someone would have mentioned it if he had been. There'd been a few occasions when she had caught Boone looking at her with such directness, such puzzled yearning almost, such curiosity, that had made her quite sure that a man who had been married before would not look at a woman that way. Then there were the sly references to the teacher in Twin Falls.... Perhaps he was in love with a woman who'd left the valley, who'd moved to Twin Falls to take up a career, leaving him behind.... If that were the case, he'd feel guilty about what had happened in the pantry, and that might explain the way he'd avoided her since.

Lucie squelched her runaway imagination firmly, aware that the thought of the teacher in Twin Falls always hurt, had hurt ever since Mattie had suspected Lucie of being that very person the first day she'd arrived. Lucky woman, to be loved by Boone Harlow, she thought sadly. The wayward thought had slipped out before she could stop it.

"Mmm?"

"I *said*, I was wondering when you'd get around to wearing a dress. Looks awful nice on ya, too." Mattie inspected Lucie's creased summer sundress closely, her face tilted up, the better to peer through her bifocals.

The dress was one of the ones Lucie had bought in Ketchum. It was pale green, very plain, with a row of gathers round the hem. Impulsively Lucie pirouetted, the full skirt swirling around her.

"I always said a dress suits a woman more 'n' slacks. Mind you, slacks is easier, 'specially for riding and gardening. Boone notice?" Mattie added slyly, her eyes bright with interest. "Eh?"

"'Course not," Lucie said airily, pirouetting again and again, across the length of the kitchen, pleasing herself. "Why would he?"

Mattie just sighed.

"Boone? What *is* wrong with Mattie? Really wrong?"

Lucie was perched nervously on the top rail of the corral. The rail wasn't that high, really, and it was rock solid. No, what unnerved her was definitely Boone's presence beside her, leaning against the topmost weathered pole so that his shoulder and crossed arms were only inches from her knees. She'd been surprised when he'd gruffly suggested at noon that she might like to watch the new wrangler working with a couple of two-year-olds later that afternoon. She'd been surprised at the invitation, but she hadn't hesitated for a second to say that, yes, she'd be there. Mattie was napping in her room.

Boone glanced at her quickly. She just caught a glimpse of those dark eyes, flecked with gold in the sunshine, before he turned his attention back to the young wrangler with the filly in the corral. The filly was balking, standing stiff-legged in the dust while the wrangler urged her on.

Boone sighed. "Mostly old age, Lucie. And an enlarged heart. Doc says her blood pressure is sky-high, probably what contributed to her stroke last year."

"Is that why she had to go to the hospital this time?"

"Yeah." Boone hesitated, seemed to tense, and suddenly called out to the wrangler. "Keep her head up, Gene! Reins high. When she ducks it like that, she'll feel it and she'll soon learn. Higher!" Boone watched for a moment, intent on the horse and rider in front of him, and Lucie watched him. His face was half hidden in shadow from the brim of his hat, but she could see the lines around his eyes from years of squinting into the sun, his skin permanently tanned from an outdoor life. He looked his age. A man in his prime. Mature, capable, shoulders broad enough to carry any load, his body taut and relaxed at the same time in his work-worn jeans and faded chambray shirt...a man ready for anything. Lucie looked quickly away, holding up one hand to shade her eyes.

"That's it—you've got it!" Boone called to the rider, and she saw his body visibly relax. She realized that he was as much in the saddle, at least mentally, as the wrangler. "Yeah. This happens, every couple of months." It took a few seconds for Lucie to realize that he was still talking about Mattie. "The doc gets her blood pressure down, adjusts her medication and sends her home again. That's all they can do." Boone straightened and looked at Lucie, a piercing, level look that held her still. "Mattie hates the hospital. She hates doctors. She's always scared she's going to die there, away from home."

Lucie saw the shadow of pain behind his words. She didn't know what to say, so she said nothing. Silence, she was beginning to understand, carried a lot of meaning in this country. Boone loved his grandmother. He wanted to carry out her wishes. But he couldn't. The doctors and the medication and the resources of the hospital were necessary; he had to rely on them from time to time, as her condition worsened.

"Mattie's just crabby, you should know that," Lucie said, needing to reassure him. "She knows you're doing the best you can for her." She wanted to reach out and pat his shoulder, but, of course, she didn't. Partly she knew it was an idiotic thing to do, and Boone surely wouldn't appreciate it with the wrangler looking on, and partly she knew that if he rejected the gesture, if he stiffened, she'd...she'd not be able to bear it.

"Does she?" Boone murmured, looking up at her with an ironic smile. His gaze held hers, just a second or two too long, his smile warmed, and then he held his hand out to her. "Come on. I'll show you the new foal."

"A new foal!" Lucie's momentary awkwardness was forgotten. "You didn't tell us about a new foal!" She automatically reached for his shoulders when he put his hands on her waist to lift her down lightly, and when she was standing on the ground again, she looked up, meeting his smiling eyes, terribly aware of the few inches that separated them. She'd let go of his shoulders immediately, as soon as he'd put her down, but it seemed to her that he'd kept his hands on her waist just a little too long. She hoped he guessed that the flush of excitement and the pulse that she knew betrayed her, were in anticipation of seeing the new foal.

"Happened night before last," Boone said, conversation-ally, strolling beside her in the direction of the barn.

"Colt?"

"Filly."

"Quarter horse, I suppose."

"Is there any other kind of horse worth buying feed for?" Boone grinned at her as he pushed back the heavy sliding door to the barn, and Lucie grinned back. She ducked inside the cool, hay-smelling, horse-smelling darkness, suddenly so glad to be alive that she didn't know how she'd be able to stand it.

The filly was a palomino, red-gold and cream, although with her bristly little knob of a tail and crimped-up baby mane, she didn't show much beauty yet. But she had plenty of promise.

"Oh, Boone, look at her funny little blaze! Come here, little darling," Lucie crooned to the foal, stretching out her hand. Amazingly, the foal stepped up to the stall door and nuzzled Lucie's fingers for a few seconds before snorting in surprise and bolting back to the safety of her mother's flank.

"May I go in to see her? Will her mother mind?" Lucie glanced from Boone over to the far corner where the foal's dam calmly pulled hay from a rack and munched it, swing-ing her head to gaze at the visitors as she chewed, ears flicking with interest. She was sorrel, a lovely cinnamon red from nose to tail.

"Don't see why not," Boone said, stepping closer and unfastening the bolt that secured the door. "Willow's an old hand at this. This is her fifth foal. I don't think she'll mind, will you, old girl?"

Boone walked up to the mare and rubbed her behind the ears as she bobbed her head at him and nickered a soft welcome. Lucie saw that he was distracting the mare, so that she could approach the foal. She sank to her knees in the deep straw that littered the big box stall, and held out her arms. The little foal obligingly trotted right up to her and began nibbling at her sleeve. Lucie laughed and the foal threw its head up, and grabbed at her collar. Lucie laughed again. Boone watched them both from a distance.

"Oh, isn't she delightful?" Lucie said, looking over to the corner where Boone stood. "What's her name? Hey, you—leave that alone!" The foal had nibbled at her hair. Lucie tossed her braid back over her shoulder and wrapped her arms around the foal.

"She hasn't got a name yet," Boone said, walking over to the two of them. He squatted down beside them, reaching out with one hand to scratch the foal's crooked blaze. He smiled at Lucie, and she felt her heart wobble. "Want to name her?"

"Me?"

"Why not?" Boone drawled. "Hey!" He cupped the foal's jaw in his hand and gently pulled her away as she grabbed at Lucie's hair again. Then he reached for Lucie's braid and put it behind her shoulder, out of reach of the curious foal. His eyes, as he touched her shoulder, so fleetingly, were on her braid, not her face.

"Why—why I'd love to. When I was home, I always—" Lucie caught back her rush of words. She'd been about to say that the stable manager had let her name the foals that had been born in the Douglass stables. They'd all had proper, unpronounceable registered names, but Lucie had given them their everyday names.

"You always—what?" Boone's casual enquiry sounded a little too casual to her ears. Was she simply being paranoid? Should she simply confess everything and ask for his understanding, his cooperation, until she turned twenty-five in a few more weeks? No, it was too much to ask a stranger. She could involve no one in her scheme; she could trust no one to keep her secret. And Boone had enough to worry about with Mattie and the Double H without taking on her burden, as well. As she knew, instinctively, he would.

"Nothing. I—" She looked guiltily at him. "It's not important." She buried her face in the foal's neck. It smelled delicious: like hay and milk and warm, clean horse and with that indescribable, irresistible baby scent that new puppies and kittens—that all new creatures—had.

"I want to name her 'Happy,'" she said, raising her head and looking solemnly at Boone. A faint change of expression flickered across his eyes as he looked at her, only inches away, but Lucie couldn't judge for certain what it was.

"Happy?" There was a faint smile in Boone's lazy drawl.

"Yes. She looks happy and she seems to be a happy little thing and—and that's how I feel ever since I got here." It came out in a tumble of words, unexpected and unplanned and absolutely true, Lucie realized, the instant it spilled out. She'd never been so happy in her life as she was in this wild, remote Idaho valley.

"'Happy' it is, then," Boone said and stood, holding his hand out to help her up. She stood and looked up at him, and he reached out and tipped her chin up with his other hand. "You're a funny little thing, you know that, Lucie Crane?" he said, smiling.

He studied her face for a moment, and Lucie felt her breath catch in the back of her throat. His hand was warm on her chin, his fingers rough and hard. "You say you're happy, Lucie. I'm glad to hear it." His voice was very quiet and deep. "But I can't say that's a word I'd have picked to describe you. *Spunky,* maybe, or *stubborn* or how about plain *mysterious?* Or—" Boone took a sudden deep breath and turned away, releasing her and taking a step toward the door of the stall.

When he faced her again, holding the gate open, she knew he'd just been teasing her. The intensity that had crept into his eyes a moment ago had vanished. Perhaps she only imagined it. "Or, how about *late for dinner?* Let's go, sunshine."

The day after she named the foal, Boone seemed less edgy, less tense, less wary of her. Or maybe she'd imagined that, too, because she liked having him around so much and she didn't dare ask herself why, afraid, she knew, of what she might discover.

Even the weather changed, and maybe that was the real reason why he spent more time at the ranch house. A few days of rain meant the haying had to be interrupted for a while, and after a boisterous last supper, most of the crew headed off for a few days in town. That meant less work for Lucie, but she realized that she was getting used to the routine, and had begun to look forward to the banter and teasing from the ranch hands. She knew she missed it.

Lucie spent more time with Mattie, and she'd taken on the project of taping some of Mattie's stories.

"It'll be something for your great-grandchildren to remember you by someday," Lucie had said when Mattie'd protested. "Who'd ever believe you'd learned to ride before you were five and didn't have indoor plumbing before you were grown-up? And what about that story you told me about the time your dad led a pack train through a hornet's nest on the Redfish Lake trail?"

Mattie had laughed then, and said that, yes, some things were *worth* remembering, and she'd settled happily to the task. They usually spent an hour or so at it, in the afternoon, before Mattie's nap. Mattie would knit and ramble, and Lucie would listen. Sometimes Mattie would want to talk after supper, with Boone listening in and reminding her of stories she'd told him when he was a boy, and Lucie would quietly turn on the tape recorder.

Soon she'd be gone—too soon, Lucie thought with a

pang—back to New Hampshire. And Mattie would be gone someday. These stories, though, would live. Stories of hardship and courage and sharing, of young brides making do with what they had, raising children and chickens, and never giving up. They were living stories of a pioneer America, an America younger than the place she'd come from, an older place set in its ways and in the ways of what had gone before. The West was new and young and exciting. It had been then, in Mattie's day, and it still was to Lucie. These stories, which she hoped one day to transcribe and compile somehow, were her contribution to the Sawtooth Valley, to the Harlow family. The valley that she'd always remember; the valley that had once felt like home to her.

It was an evening just like that, an evening about a week after she'd named Willow's foal, when an unexpected knock on the front door brought a flush to Mattie's cheeks and a sparkle to her eye.

"Company! Put on the kettle, dear. Boone'll get the door."

Lucie got up to put on the kettle. Unexpected company was always welcome in the country, she knew that. Still, she'd felt the briefest twinge of disappointment when she'd heard the doorbell. She loved these quiet evenings, just her and Mattie and Boone, Boone usually reading or sitting in an easy chair with his feet up, in the cluttered family room, staring out the window…thinking, perhaps. It lulled Lucie into believing they were a family, a real family, and foolish as she knew she was, she still craved the illusion.

"Alice! For heaven's sake—" Mattie's last words were muffled as a young woman with short black curls swept into the room and bent down to envelop the elderly woman in a big hug. When she straightened, her merry blue eyes immediately sought Lucie's, and she smiled.

"You must be Lucie," she said, her bright eyes darting quickly from Lucie's sandal-clad bare feet to the halo of flyaway hair that Lucie knew looked as untidy, no doubt, as it felt. The young woman took a step forward, extending her hand. "I'm Alice Hendricks. Welcome to the Sawtooth Valley, Lucie. I've heard plenty about you and I must say I've been dying to meet you."

Lucie shook her hand and smiled, a little self-conscious under the other woman's unabashed inspection. She wished she'd known someone was coming; she would have changed, done something with her hair. She hadn't wanted to fuss too much about her appearance before, even though she'd had the thoroughly feminine urge to do so when Boone had started spending more time around the ranch house in the evenings. But she hadn't; she would have died of embarrassment if she'd thought he'd even suspected that she wanted to look nice for him. As, of course, she didn't—

"Ah, Lucie Crane..." Lucie's attention was taken by the entrance into the kitchen of Boone and another man, nearly as tall as Boone, blond and good-looking with a windblown, outdoors look and a wide grin. Should she know him...? She looked uncertainly at Boone. He was frowning, but immediately stepped forward to make the introductions.

"Lucie...I'd like you to meet Lyle Hendricks, a friend of mine. Alice's husband." Had he emphasized the 'husband,' with a dark look at his friend? "They've got a spread on the other side of the valley, the Crazy J, a couple of miles from here."

Alice stepped up and wrapped her arm around her handsome husband's waist. He looked down and they grinned at each other for a long, conspiratorial moment. Boone, Lucie noticed, was looking extremely uncomfortable.

"Land sakes, boy, where's your manners?" Mattie gestured toward the other chairs at the table. "Sit down, sit down, Alice. Lucie here's making a cup of tea. Or would you prefer whiskey? Boone? Bring out some of that cake

Lucie made yesterday." Mattie was in her element. Her eyes sparkled, her cheeks glowed.

Lucie realized just how quiet the old woman's life was, how welcome this diversion was. She herself had been thankful for the peace and quiet, for the silence she'd found in this valley. It had nourished her soul. But Mattie had never known anything different. Seeing people—other people beside her grandson and the ranch hands who came and went from year to year, and now Lucie—this was as good as a party to her.

Within half an hour, the reason the Hendricks had dropped in—one of the reasons—became clear. They were inviting the Harlows to a party. Of course they didn't mean to include her, she assumed, she was just the hired help....

It didn't work out like that in the Sawtooths. "Don't be silly. Of course you're invited—Boone don't you dare come if you don't bring Lucie," Alice ordered, when Lucie demurred. When Boone said fine, that he'd stay home since he wouldn't dream of talking Lucie into something she didn't want to do and he didn't feel like going anyway, Alice changed tacks. Then it was Mattie who allowed there was nothing she'd like better than to go to a party at the Hendricks' and she wasn't going to go unless both Boone *and* Lucie went. And she couldn't imagine her grandson— or Lucie, come to think of it—denying an old lady something like that, something she'd set her heart on, not at her age....

That settled it. Alice made them both promise to come, and Lucie laughed at the way it had been handled, uncomfortably aware of Boone's continued reluctance. What was behind it? He seemed to be privy to something she wasn't and kept staring daggers at his friend. Lyle just grinned back.

Mattie was up long past her usual bedtime, and when Lucie finally helped her to her room, at Mattie's insistence over Boone's protests that he'd help her, everyone said good night and she did, too. After she'd helped Mattie, she'd slip up to her own room. Lucie's head was awhirl with thoughts of going to the Hendricks' party. With Boone. And with Mattie, of course.

Later, perhaps an hour later, Lucie heard the sounds of Alice and Lyle leaving. She lay staring at the slatted shadows of the moonlight on the white-painted tongue-and-groove ceiling. She didn't feel the slightest bit sleepy. She glanced at her clock alarm…half past eleven. If she wasn't asleep in an hour, she'd slip downstairs and get the P. D. James paperback mystery she'd started reading that afternoon. It was in the kitchen. By then Boone would have gone to bed. Somehow, she didn't want to face him. Certainly not by herself.

That was odd. Why not by herself? It occurred to her, then, just how much she had unconsciously come to rely on Mattie. She even relied upon her, idiotic as it seemed, to protect her from her grandson! Lucie was nearly twenty-five, she didn't need protection. And protection from what? Beyond that episode in the pantry—Lucie still felt her knees melt when she thought of it—Boone had been the perfect gentleman. Completely indifferent to her, as far as she could see. Disinterested. And that's the way she wanted it. Didn't she?

Lucie looked at the clock again with a sigh and threw back the covers. She went to the window and looked out. It was past midnight, but she could still see the outline of the White Cloud range on the other side of the valley, etched black against the sky. Dark, solid, comforting in its unmoving, immovable bulk. Permanent, unchanging…safe. Frowning, Lucie turned to go downstairs. The last thing she needed was to start getting maudlin…. Of course she was safe here, felt safe. And once she was home again, she'd be free of her uncle's machinations and she'd be free there, too, for the first time in her life.

Lucie tiptoed down the stairs. By now she knew each creaky riser, each squeal of protest in the wooden floor. She retrieved her book, from the kitchen counter where she'd put it that afternoon when Boone had joined her and Mattie for tea. Was she mistaken, or was he even more solicitous than usual about his grandmother these days? That episode in the hospital had put a scare into everyone....

Lucie paused at the bottom of the stairs. A flickering bluish light at the door to the family room told her that someone was still up. Lucie silently pushed open the door, which had been left ajar.

Boone was stretched out on the sofa, one leg slung off the cushions and propped at an angle on the floor, the other foot resting on the arm of the sofa. One hand was behind his head, the other flopped loosely over his chest. He was asleep.

Lucie tiptoed closer. Should she wake him? So that he could go upstairs to bed? Indecisively she bent for the remote control that was on the floor beside him, and turned off the set. The sound had been turned off already, but the sudden absence of the flickering light made her feel that now she really was alone in the room with him. As though the stark tumbling shadows of an old Chaplin movie had constituted another presence in the room.

She looked down at Boone, noting the tired lines in his handsome face, the way his lashes shadowed his cheek as he slept. His breathing, measured by the slow rise and fall of his chest, was deep and easy. She wouldn't disturb him; she'd just—Lucie looked around the room and stepped over to grab an afghan from Mattie's chair—she'd just cover him. It was cool already in the house and would be cooler by morning.

Lucie held her breath as she draped the afghan lightly

over his long body. It didn't begin to cover him properly, but it was better than nothing. Then, although she knew she shouldn't, she couldn't resist standing there for a few seconds longer, letting her thoughts and feelings about this rough-hewn man, the dark stranger who'd already affected her in some way, had already left an indelible mark on her heart—by his example, by his loyalty, by his quiet courage and humor in the face of whatever life handed him, by the regard he had for his grandmother. That's all it was, really, Lucie thought, taking a deep shaky breath. He was just an honorable man. And she hadn't known very many.

She turned to go.

"Wait!"

Boone's hand shot out to grab her wrist and she turned back, startled. He pulled on her arm and she bent. His eyes looked clear and dark in the half-light from the moon outside. She felt her heart surge in her breast.

"I—I thought you were asleep. I'm sorry if I—"

"You didn't wake me," he said, his grip still hard on her wrist. "I wasn't asleep. I was thinking."

He could have fooled her. He swung his other leg to the floor and sat up, letting go of her wrist to run his fingers through his disheveled hair. He yawned, then looked at her, his gaze, she thought, lingering on her crazy nightshirt, the one that, along with the teddy bear on the front, had the words Hug Me. How childish it suddenly seemed!

"Sit down, Lucie." He patted the seat beside him, and, awkwardly, Lucie sat, perching stiffly on the edge of the cushion, thinking how much wiser she would have been to sit in Mattie's chair, well away from him. She clutched her paperback novel to her midriff, as though it could protect her. From what? From him? From herself?

"I know it's late, but I've got something to tell you, Lucie, something I should have told you a long time ago."

Chapter Nine

"Yes?" Her voice sounded thin and tentative and, irritated, she frowned and cleared her throat.

"First of all—" he studied her for a few brief seconds, then went on "—I want to let you know that I'm going to be hiring someone to help take care of Mattie." He ran his fingers through his hair again wearily, his frown deepening. "She's too frail to be left on her own and I can't handle it myself anymore. I've put in a request with an agency that deals with that sort of thing."

Lucie put her hand on his arm. "Let me. I can do it, Boone! I'd like to—"

"No!" Boone stood up suddenly, and Lucie's hand dropped to the sofa cushion. "That's not what I had in mind—"

"But she *likes* me, Boone. She doesn't like everybody. You know that. She'd be no trouble, honest—" Lucie broke off, biting her lip as she saw his black look. Hire someone else to take care of Mattie? It was unthinkable!

"No." Boone paced to the window, stared out for a few seconds, then paced back again, hands in his pockets. Irritably he stopped in front of a floor lamp and flicked it on. Lucie was blinded for a moment by the glare. She put her hands to her eyes.

"Why not?" His refusal even to consider her offer had angered her. "You wouldn't have to pay me anything." *That* was a mistake. He looked at her grimly, and rocked back on his heels.

"*If* I said you could do the job—and I won't—I would naturally pay you. But the question doesn't arise, because I'm not hiring you," he said flatly.

"Why not?"

"Because—because you've got your hands full with cooking and other things. You've got enough to do."

"I don't. I've got plenty of spare time in the afternoons."

"You don't want to be tied down to an old woman twenty-four hours of the day—"

"What's the difference? What would I do with my time?" Lucie waved her hand. "I like it here. I don't want to be anywhere else."

"It's not much of a life for someone like you, a young woman, single, burying herself away—"

"Who says?" she said defiantly. "I *like* it here, Boone Harlow. Can't you get that through your thick cowboy skull?"

"No," he said softly, and Lucie felt the sudden heat of his gaze on her hair, then her lips, then her eyes. She willed herself to remain calm, to ignore what his gaze was doing to her nerves. "No, I can't. I'm afraid I can't, Lucie Crane," he said very softly. For a couple of seconds he stared at her, and if he hadn't finally turned with a grimace and a soft curse, she would have fled from the room herself.

"Go back to bed, Lucie," he said, and tossed the afghan back on the chair. "We'll discuss it in the morning." He held the door for her and she walked toward him. Then, when she was just a pace away—

"By the way, I thought you'd appreciate me letting you in on Lyle and Alice's little scheme."

Scheme? She looked up at him, puzzled.

"Yeah. It's a setup. That's what I should have told you before. I've been through this plenty of times with them. It's pretty clear to me what they're up to with this party business next weekend—"

"Which is?" she said, irritated by his roundabout explanation. Everything about him irritated her just now, and she was tired, too. Bone tired. She wanted to get to bed. Why wouldn't he let her look after Mattie? As long as she was here, anyway?

"They're matchmakers, Lucie."

"Y-you mean, you and me?" she stammered, feeling the heat rise from her throat to scorch her cheeks.

"Yeah." He looked down at her and grinned and she felt her heart do a double flip in tantalizing slow motion. "To put it bluntly—yeah, you and me. They've been trying to get me married off for years and they're always organizing little get-togethers of one kind or another to introduce me to eligible women. And they think that now, now that a good-looking woman has shown up all on her own at the Double H—"

"That's—that's *terrible!*" Lucie said, staring up at him, aghast. She deliberately ignored what his casual description of her had done to her pulse.

"Isn't it?" Boone kept smiling at her. "But I figure, if you know what's going on and I know what's going on, nobody's going to get taken in. Right?"

She shook her head, not exactly sure what she was agreeing to with him.

"Except maybe Lyle and Alice, which is fine by me. And Mattie. And probably Ho Pickens. He's in on this, too, if I know him." He grinned again. "And I owe them all a couple anyway," Boone finished softly. "I thought I'd better warn you, Lucie, because I wouldn't want you to get any, well, wrong ideas at this party of Saturday. You know...about what they're up to. It wouldn't be fair to you."

Fair to her? On that note, Boone waved her up the stairs, and she went, not entirely sure whether what she was feeling was flattered or furious.

"So what's the big problem, Boone Harlow? Any particular reason why can't you find a wife on your own?" Lucie looked up, a teasing glint in her eyes, then gasped a little when he suddenly guided her through an intricate turn on the dance floor. He smiled. He'd watched her pick up a country-style two-step with Lyle's brother, Tom. Her first ever, he'd guessed, from the way she'd stumbled and laughed. That was earlier, when they'd first arrived. The "little get-together" suggested by the Hendricks turned out to be an all-out country dance at the Beaver Creek Grange Hall. Everyone from the north end of the valley was there.

Boone tightened his arm around her waist, ostensibly to steady her, but really, he knew, because he liked the feel of her in his arms. She was a good dancer, real good, and he liked that because he liked dancing, too. It was different, a different sort of physical activity from what he was used to, although he'd noted that cowboys generally were good dancers. Had to do with rhythm, he supposed—riding, dancing....

He looked down at her again, thinking about the way the top of her head would just tuck nicely under his chin if he pulled her close enough to find out. Then, looking over her head to where they'd left Mattie sitting at a table with a couple of other women, he deliberately forced that thought from his mind. It was dangerous to let his mind drift in that direction.... Everything about Lucie Crane was dangerous, he was discovering.

"Well?" she repeated. "What's the problem?"

"No problem," he said, smiling down at her. "And I'd be happy to find myself a wife—if I wanted one. Trouble is," he said softly, and wondered if his voice held any of the regret he sometimes felt lately, "I don't want a wife. That's the simple truth of the matter. Alice and Lyle have a hard time believing me, that's all. Not to mention Mattie, and Ho and just about everybody else in the valley."

"Oh."

He looked down at her quickly, a little surprised at her brief, noncommittal response, but she was looking over his shoulder. He turned to follow her gaze. Mattie was looking toward them. She had apparently just said something to one of the other women that had made them both nod and smile. He glowered at his grandmother, but she wouldn't have seen him clearly anyway across the room, even if her eyesight had been better.

Then he frowned at the band...was it his imagination, or had they played this last song twice already and were starting it a third time around? Ho Pickens was in the band....

He never should have given in to Lucie over Mattie. Lucie had begged him, and then the agency had phoned to say they had a person lined up but she was on another job and wouldn't be free for two weeks. So he'd relented. Why, Boone thought to himself angrily, was he so convinced it was a mistake? She and Mattie got along like a house on fire, Lucie seemed perfectly capable of taking care of her—and that was more than could be said for her cooking. Damn it, it just made him edgy, that's all. After all, what if Mattie got attached to her? She was leaving soon, it wasn't much more than a month now to fall roundup. Boone was startled at the sudden pain he felt as he thought of Lucie leaving, then looked cautiously down at her. She'd brought sunshine to the Double H, she'd brought sunshine into Mattie's life and...

"Why is that?" she asked, looking up at him unexpectedly. He could tell by the change in her breathing that she was nervous, that she'd surprised herself at her own question.

"Why is what?" He frowned. He wasn't entirely sure what she was talking about. He'd been caught up in his own thoughts, to take his mind off the way she felt in his arms, the way he felt, the way he wanted to hold her that way forever.

"Why don't you want to get married? Don't you believe in love?" He saw her bite her lip quickly, as though she could catch back her words. "No—don't answer that. It's none of my business." She smiled up at him, a brilliant smile that seemed fragile around the edges. "Just making conversation." She glanced, desperately it seemed to him, toward the band. "Do they always play this long?"

"Lucie. Look at me." He waited a few seconds, until she looked up at him again. "Sure I believe in love. Some people find it, some don't. I'm not looking for it. Marriage isn't for me and the reason for that is that it'd take a very special woman to put up with what I have to offer, which isn't much. The fact is, I don't believe that kind of woman exists anymore, the kind that could make the sacrifices that have to be made living this kind of a life." He held her closer and maneuvered her expertly away from a boisterous couple that had already bumped into him once. "Not even here in the Sawtooth Valley. And if there was such a woman, well, it doesn't seem too likely I'd be in love with her, too, does it?" He scowled at the other couple, but they paid no attention to him.

Lucie was silent. Boone looked down at her, at the top of her head, glinting red-gold in the subdued light of the hall. Her hair wasn't in her usual braid; she'd brushed it out and had done something with it, something that left most of it pinned high on her head in some mysterious way that women had, soft tendrils spilling here and there, curling against her neck. She stumbled a little, and he caught her against him tightly.

"Boone. I—I..."

"Tired?"

"A little."

"Want to sit down?" He knew that she wasn't really tired, that it had been something he'd said that had made her want to be alone, made her want to be away from him. That angered him, and he fought the sudden need he had to stop right there on the dance floor and haul her against him, hold her tight, just him and her, in full sight of every busybody in the entire valley.

"Maybe after this dance," she said, smiling faintly.

"Sure." He knew his voice was gruffer than he'd intended. The new skirt she was wearing swished and snapped as she whirled, a flash of vivid color, brushing against him, making him wonder what she wore under it. Forbidden thoughts. She felt light in his arms, feminine, warm and...and incredibly desirable. He knew she'd bought the outfit especially for the occasion; he'd been surprised because she'd asked him for money, the first time she'd done so since she arrived, and she'd been nervous asking him. He could tell it had been something she wasn't comfortable doing. It had raised questions in his mind again, about who she was and where she'd come from, questions he tried hard not to think about.

The shirt she'd bought to go with the skirt, some cream-colored silky material, allowed him to feel the warm satin of her back beneath his hand, as though it was really her bare skin he felt, under his bare hand.

"Excuse me..."

Boone turned his head abruptly. It was Tom Hendricks.

Lucie'd danced with him earlier, twice, while Boone had danced with someone else. He couldn't even remember his partner's face now, he'd been so aware of Tom with Lucie, so aware of every smile she'd given him.

"My turn, buddy." Tom grinned at him. "Looks like a fella's forced to cut in." He nodded toward the quartet of banjo, fiddle, accordion and guitar. "They don't show no signs of slowing down."

To his own surprise, Boone shook his head and frowned at the younger man. "Sorry, Tom," he said curtly, not sorry at all. "The lady's dancing with me."

"Fine...fine!" Tom held up his hands in a gesture of amiable acceptance. "Whatever you say, man." He ambled off and asked someone else to dance.

"Hey!"

Lucie sounded indignant. He agreed; maybe he should have consulted her, maybe she'd prefer to dance with Tom. But just then, the thought of Tom with his hand in hers, with his hand on the silk of her waist...he—he couldn't stand the thought of it. She stumbled a little again as Boone changed direction and edged her toward the end of the hall, toward the big doors that opened onto the velvety summer darkness.

"Boone—what was that all about?"

"Just what I said," Boone growled. "The lady's dancing with me." He tightened his grip on her hand suddenly. "Let's get out of here."

He pulled Lucie behind him, through the doorway into the cooler darkness. Several young men lingered at the door, smoking, a few with cans of beer in their hands. One of them started to say something, but at one look at Boone's fierce expression, he seemed to think better of it.

"Boone!" Lucie pulled her hand from his as he walked with her around a corner of the building, into the darkness there, away from the lighted squares of the windows in front or the larger one of the door at the side. The sky was brilliant with stars. She bumped into him as he stopped, and he turned and took her by the shoulders. Now that his eyes had adjusted, he could see her easily in the starlight.

"I want to talk to you, Lucie."

"So...talk." He searched her eyes in the half darkness, but he couldn't read her expression. She sounded annoyed. How was she going to take it? What he was going to say to her? What would she say? More to the point...what did he want her to say?

"I suppose you've noticed the way people are staring at us in there."

"I noticed."

"I, uh, well, I wondered if you want to do anything about it. One way or another. You know why they're doing it...?"

"Yes." He had to bend his head to hear her whispered reply. "Yes, you told me."

"I'm sorry about this, Lucie. I really am." He let go of her arms and turned angrily to lean against the railing that ringed the building. "It's a hell of a thing to put anyone through, especially a stranger like you."

A stranger. That's what he wanted to believe she was. But she wasn't a stranger anymore, not to him, although he knew nothing about her. Nothing at all.

Lucie made a small, choked sound, a sound that might have been assent, or encouragement for him to continue.

"Look, I don't know the first thing about you. For instance—" He hesitated, then steeled himself for the question. "Are you married, Lucie?"

"No." Her soft reply nearly washed away the defences he'd built so carefully against her. Lord, he hadn't known until now just how much he'd wanted to know, needed to know....

"Got a boyfriend back where you come from?" Why

didn't she tell him to go to hell, that it was none of his business?

"Not really. No one important."

"Because, damn it, I can put a stop to this—this harassment, if I have to. I don't want you hurt, Lucie, or embarrassed over this foolishness or—"

"Why are you asking me all this, Boone?" Her voice sounded soft and anguished in the darkness. He ached to touch her, to offer her comfort.

"Because the way I figure it, Lucie, either we pretend we're—well, we pretend we like each other and hope that Lyle and Alice and all the rest will back off, give us a little room. Or we make it clear we don't, in which case they'll be working on you as well as me, trying to get us both matched up. I'm used to it, but I don't think you should have to put up with—"

"I do like you, Boone."

It took every ounce of willpower he'd ever drawn on to stay exactly where he was, his elbows on the wooden railing, staring off into the darkness. Her soft reply, so innocent, so...so wistful, had hit him like a ton of bricks. He cleared his throat, with difficulty. "And I—I like you, Lucie. That's why I don't want to see you hurt over this. You're a very, uh, a very nice young woman and you don't deserve this kind of a hassle—"

"Never mind, Boone." She put her hand on his arm and he tensed. "Let's do it—let's pretend we like each other and...well, you know. I know it's just a game. You've explained it all, so you don't have to worry about me."

"Don't I?" he asked her softly, turning his head to face her in the dim light. Her face looked white in the starlight, her eyes pools of darkness. He wasn't worried about her...he was worried about himself. He had to tell her, he had to tell her just what she was getting into...she seemed so innocent. Didn't she know what it was like, what it *could* be like between him and her?

"What about me, Lucie?" he asked her softly. "Have you thought what it might be like for me? I said I liked you—well, it's more than that, a lot more." He saw, felt, her quickly indrawn breath, the way she held it. She took her hand from his arm. "It's not a game...but I have to pretend that it is. The truth is, I want you, Lucie. I've wanted you, the way a man wants a woman, ever since the day I met you. I've controlled myself, because that's the way it has to be. Except for that time in the pantry—" He bit his lip. Lord, this was hard! He took a deep, shaky breath and began again.

"Look—this valley killed my mother. She was young, she was beautiful, she was used to a city life, used to soft, city things. My father brought her here and she had four kids, no help, more work than she could handle, no support from my father and...and she died, Lucie." He turned to look at her. "She died. She tried her damnedest, she had a lot of spirit, old Philadelphia spirit, but after J.J. was born, she just seemed to give up. She died when J.J. was three months old. That's when Mattie and my grandfather moved in with us. I remember it. I was about fourteen." Boone stared out over the sagebrush again. He was conscious that she'd put her hand on his arm again and he wanted to push her away, but he knew that would hurt her, hurt her badly. He willed himself not to move, to continue.

"I hated my father for a long time after that. I thought he'd been to blame for what happened to her. But it wasn't his fault. I don't blame him now. He ran the ranch into the ground, he wasn't much of a father, but, hell, he lived for other things—dreams, stuff I couldn't understand then." Boone took a deep breath. He'd never known telling the truth could hurt so much. "Now I know there're the kind of things that are the most important part of a man."

He'd never told anyone what he was telling Lucie now. But she deserved to know his reasons, deserved to know why he did what he did, what he had to do.

"Is—is that why you're so sure you'll never marry?" Her voice was soft and hesitant in the darkness. He smiled, knowing she couldn't see him. Nothing ever was the whole truth....

"Yes. That's part of the reason. I see no point in history repeating itself, do you?" He turned to look at her. "My brother left a couple of years ago because the woman he was involved with couldn't face spending the rest of her life on the Double H. And she was born and raised in the valley! No—" Boone straightened and ran his fingers through his hair, before turning to face Lucie "—it's pretty clear to me that, even though I love what I do and couldn't live any other way, it's a poor life, a hard life. There's no money in it and not much satisfaction. No modern woman's going to put up with it past the honeymoon stage. Women like Mattie did it, but they didn't know any better. If they had—" he smiled ruefully at Lucie "—they probably would have headed for the bright lights, too."

"Alice?"

"Yeah. Lyle got lucky there. There probably are one or two left, Lucie, if a man had the interest to really hunt around. I'll admit it. The point is—I don't," he said flatly.

"So? Where does that leave us? I mean," she went on quickly, "where does that leave your plan for tonight?"

"Are you game to go ahead, knowing what you know about me now?"

"I am."

Boone wanted to bend down and kiss her face, turned up so solemnly to him in the moonlight. "Knowing that there's nothing I'd rather do than hold you in my arms and kiss you and make love to you...but that, if I did, that's as far as it'd get between us? Ever?"

"Y-yes."

"That the only reason I'm even suggesting this crazy plan is because you'll be gone in a month and, knowing that bunch in there, it's the only way we'll get any peace between now and then?"

"I understand." He saw her smile and her eyes met his gamely.

Boone grinned and reached for her hand. "Okay, partner. Let's go in there and give them something they can *really* talk about."

They'd done that all right. Lucie still blushed a week later to recall how he'd kept her by his side, arm around her waist, most of the evening, how he'd turned back any claims to dance by any other men, how he'd smiled at her, how he'd kissed her once or twice briefly, how he'd grinned even more when he'd seen her blush. How he'd winked when he thought no one was looking.

It was that, that wink, that reminded her of the game they were playing. It had been only too easy for her to forget. For this, Boone's undivided, male attention, the way he looked at her as though she were the only woman on earth, this was exactly what she'd wanted all along, she was beginning to realize. It frightened her to ask herself why. It frightened her to think what this man was beginning to mean to her....

They were playing with fire. He knew—he'd told her so—and she knew.

She tried to keep her mind on Mattie, and her job. She tried to concentrate on the stories she was taping—Mattie had told her dozens already and was beginning to complain that she didn't know any more. She was grateful that Boone had absented himself from the ranch house since the dance. Of course, she knew that he was very busy, that there were a million and one things to take care of on a big, working ranch like the Double H, but she knew, too, that his absence made it easier for her.

He didn't know—couldn't know—her real feelings toward him. She knew he believed he was doing her a favor: he'd told her how he felt, what he wanted; now he was keeping clear of her. Even on the one trip to Ketchum she'd made with him, a trip during which they'd barely exchanged a word, she'd been shocked at how little interest she felt in making the weekly call she'd promised Bonnie. Bonnie's news that she'd tracked her sister down to the Sacramento area, her news that she'd definitely lived there as recently as six years ago, didn't have the result it would have had two weeks before. She was happy—of course, she was!— but two weeks ago she'd have wanted to jump on the nearest plane and fly to California to help track down the sister she'd dreamed of finding, the family she'd prayed she'd one day find. Now…now it was different. Her sister was something to look forward to in the future, her life in New England seemed lost in the distant past. The silent man who'd driven her to town and the grumbling old woman they'd left at the ranch, with Alice keeping her company—they were her family now. At least that's how it felt. Beaver Creek Ranch was where she wanted to be.

Mattie was confused by the turn of events. Lucie thought Mattie seemed more confused than usual the past day or two, but Mattie's confusion was nothing new. Mattie had complained about Boone's absence in the evenings several times and told Lucie she wasn't doing a very good job of looking after her man, and when Lucie tried to soothe her, to calm her, Mattie accused Lucie of trying to put something over on her.

"You're just like that grandson of mine, afraid to settle down, scared you might get hurt," she grumbled. "'Course you're gonna get hurt—life hurts! Young people! Haven't got the brains God gave 'em when it comes to looking out for themselves.''

"Would you like me to bring you a cup of tea?"

"Hmph! Tea might be nice," she allowed. "What I'd really like is a couple of great-grandchildren. Why don't you marry that grandson of mine and be done with it?" She peered up at Lucie. "Eh?" she said, hopefully.

"Now, Mattie, don't get yourself worked up." Lucie spread a blanket over the old woman's knees and went over to the television. "I know you'd like to see Boone married, but I think you'd better leave that up to him, don't you?" *Worked up!* It was her heart—Lucie's!—that was hammering like a schoolgirl's as she adjusted the set. She couldn't blame Mattie; from what Mattie'd seen the night of the party, it would have appeared that she and Boone were... well, fond of each other.

Lucie blushed as she walked down the hall to the kitchen to put on the kettle. She hadn't considered what Mattie's reaction would be when she'd agreed to Boone's suggestion. It had just seemed at the time like the best short-term solution, she hadn't dreamed of the follow-up, of the consequences back at the Double H, of how their scheme might aggravate Mattie's burning desire to see Boone married.

She walked back to the family room, carefully balancing a tray with tea and milk and Mattie's favorite gingersnaps. She'd made another big batch the day before....

"Mattie!"

Lucie put down the tray hurriedly, slopping the milk over the side of the pitcher. She bent over the old woman, who'd slumped to one side in her chair. Mattie's color was poor, bluish gray, and Lucie had to bend to see that she was still breathing, shallow and raspy.

"Mattie, Mattie, darling...*what's wrong?*" In her panic she shook Mattie slightly, then fumbled for her bony wrist.

She could barely feel the old woman's pulse for the pounding of her own heart. Mattie's pulse was there, barely there.

My God! Lucie stood up, her hands to her head. What should she do? Should she call for an ambulance? But it was forty miles to Ketchum. Mattie might be dead by then. Dead! Boone had said he'd be working in the machine shed most of the afternoon. Or had that been yesterday? Lucie took a deep breath and told herself that she had to calm down, to get hold of herself. She loosened the old woman's clothing, praying under her breath that everything would be all right.

Then she raced down the hall, out of the kitchen door, into the brilliant sunshine. She was halfway to the machine shed before she heard the screen door slam shut behind her.

"Boone! Boone!" She was screaming and crying at the same time and nothing mattered anymore, nothing at all. Nothing mattered except finding Boone. "Boone!"

Chapter Ten

"Lucie! *What the hell's the matter?*"

Boone stepped out of the shadows of the open machine shed door and grabbed her by the shoulders as she ran up to him. He held her, hard. "What's happened? Are you hurt?" His face was as grim as she'd ever seen it, his eyes, shards of ice stabbing into hers.

"N-no." He let go of her. "It's Mattie, Boone. She's sick, really sick. You've got to come and see her." But she hadn't finished before Boone took off at a run toward the ranch house. Lucie stumbled behind him, her vision blurred with tears.

Later, Lucie didn't know how she'd done it. Somehow she managed to drive Mattie's lumbering Buick all the way to Ketchum, not stopping until she'd pulled right up to the emergency doors of the hospital. Boone had ridden in the back seat with his grandmother, cradling her small body in his arms, talking to her softly in his deep voice, soothing her. Lucie'd had to take one hand off the wheel more than once during the trip to wipe her eyes.

All at once, there had been a bustle of activity as a pair of orderlies transferred Mattie to a hospital gurney and whisked her off down the hall. Boone stood for a moment, looking at her. Lucie stood behind him. Then, feeling his pain as hers, she moved up beside him and touched his arm.

"She'll be all right, Boone. I know she will. The doctors will take care of her," she whispered. Boone looked down at her with a strange look on his face, a half smile—for her, she knew—and yet with a trace of bewilderment in his eyes, as though he'd just remembered her presence and wondered who this stranger was and how she'd got there, beside him. Lucie burst into tears.

"Hey...Lucie," he said softly, and hauled her into his arms. She felt him rest his chin on the top of her head and she tried hard to stem the flow of tears, drawing courage from the iron strength of his arms around her...but she couldn't stop. Here she was, weeping like a ninny, and it was *his* grandmother who was sick!

"Hush," he said, drawing back and looking down at her. "Don't cry, sunshine." He traced the path of tears on her cheek with one thumb. "You're right. She'll probably pull through. I've been through this with her before, a dozen times. But if she doesn't—" he paused, and Lucie looked up, his features swimming before her "—hell, she's an old woman, Lucie. She's not afraid to die."

They went to Admissions and Lucie waited while Boone filled out forms and answered questions. Then they went down the hall to the acute care ward where Mattie had been taken. She still hadn't regained consciousness, and Lucie was almost sorry she'd come when she saw how tiny and gray and weak Mattie looked, in that high white hospital bed, in a wrinkled hospital-issue nightie and surrounded by bottles and tubes and monitors. Boone stepped forward and took his grandmother's hand in his. It looked so small and wrinkled, the blue veins standing out in the white, puffy flesh against Boone's much larger, tanned, work-hardened hand. Lucie fished an already much-used tissue out of her pocket and blew her nose again.

Boone turned, his face grim. "Let's get out of here."

He didn't say anything on the long trip back to the Double H. Lucie felt exhausted. She was glad that he was silent. She didn't want to talk; she had nothing to say. Besides, she was getting used to Boone's long silences. He left her at the garage where he parked Mattie's car, and went back toward the machine shop. Halfway there, he stopped. He turned toward her and pulled his hat down low, against the sun, and said, "I'm going in to see her again after supper. You can come with me if you want."

The next day, Mattie was conscious, and feeling much better, Lucie thought: she was complaining. And that meant she was on the mend. She was still in acute care, though, and the doctor told Boone he was quite concerned: her heart was still beating erratically and it wasn't responding this time to the medication they were trying. She'd be in hospital awhile if they couldn't get her condition stabilized soon.

But Lucie was just happy to see her awake and complaining. That was the Mattie she knew best.

"Pull that shade, will you?" Mattie gestured weakly to the window when Lucie and Boone arrived. "Enough to blind a body," she grumbled. "Even if I was feeling fine, which I ain't." Lucie had laughed and gone to adjust the curtains. Mattie started on Boone.

"Lucie taking good care of you, Boone?" she'd inquired slyly, her voice not much more than a whisper, but a gleam of the old devilment in her eyes. Lucie plucked Mattie's glasses off her nose and polished them with the tail of her shirt, giving Mattie a stern look of warning as she did so. As usual, the old woman's glasses were covered with smudges and fingerprints.

"Everything's fine, Mattie." Boone patted her hand. He evidently didn't know what Mattie was referring to, Lucie realized with a flood of color. If the old girl was going to start on *that* again, she must be feeling better.

Lucie tried to change the subject. "Would you like us to bring you anything when we come again, Mattie? How about your knitting?" Mattie'd finished the afghan for Ho Pickens, although she hadn't given it to him yet, and had started on a pair of mittens that she'd said were for Lucie.

"No. No knitting for me, dear. Not yet. I haven't got the strength for it."

Lucie'd known that; she just wanted to remind Mattie of home, of what she had to look forward to when she came back.

"How about some gingersnaps?" Lucie whispered, conspiratorially.

Mattie managed a weak grin. "Wouldn't say no to that, but they probably wouldn't let me have 'em. Nurses might eat 'em before I get better."

Lucie was relieved that Mattie had been diverted from her favorite topic these days: Lucie and Boone. But it didn't last. The next day, Mattie had been moved to a regular ward, much to Lucie's relief. Boone, she noted, was happier, too, although he didn't say much. He challenged his grandmother to a game of checkers, a game she usually loved, but this time Mattie said, no, she still didn't feel up to it. Boone sat in an armchair beside her bed and picked up a magazine that was lying on a table. Boone's idea of a visit seemed to be mainly sitting with his grandmother in companionable silence, pretty much the same as he did at home.

Mattie sighed. "Tell you what, Boone. There *is* something you can do for me. If you really want to make an old woman happy.''

"Mmm. What's that, Mattie?" He smiled, looking up from the magazine. "You know I'd do anything I could to make you happy. All you have to do is ask, darlin'.''

"Hmph. So you say."

Alerted by something in her tone, Lucie straightened from where she'd been unpacking a few of Mattie's personal things and putting them into drawers in the hospital room.

"Boone...marry Lucie. She's a good girl and she'd make a good wife for you. I know you both and I know what'd suit you and you know I don't care for too many of the younger generation these days, especially them flibbertigibbit city girls. You'd be making an old woman real happy, Boone, before she dies. If I could just—"

"Hold it. Hold it right there, Mattie," Boone interrupted flatly. He hadn't looked Lucie's way, beyond that first lightning look of shared surprise, and Lucie was glad he hadn't. She knew her face must be brick red with shock and embarrassment. "Nobody's dying. And nobody's getting married just to make you happy, Mattie. You can forget that nonsense. I know what you're up to, and you're not going to get away with it, sick or not sick. I said, *I'd* do anything I could—"

"But you *could*, Boone, you could marry her. She's a dear little thing, and she fits right in— Oh!" Mattie winced and put her hand on her chest, under the blanket, and Lucie stepped forward.

"Mattie, dear. Don't talk," she said quietly, soothingly, tucking the sheets around the old woman. "You need to rest. Don't get yourself all agitated about—about foolish things." Her cheeks burned. But she couldn't reproach Mattie now; it was too important that the old woman rest.

The nurse shooed them out, and they left, Lucie embarrassed and Boone angry. He told her brusquely not to pay any attention to his grandmother. She'd been nagging him for years to find a wife. It was just the sort of thing he'd warned her about, he said.

Why did that hurt? Lucie asked herself that night, lying awake in her bed under the eaves, watching the shadows shift across the ceiling as the moon rose. Why did it hurt so much that Boone didn't even think it was worth discussing? After all, it was partly his fault, ever since the dance at the grange hall, that Mattie'd believed there was something between them. The fact that Boone could brush the whole thing off so lightly, as though a marriage between them was so plainly preposterous…well, it hurt. But, of course, it *was* preposterous, Lucie reminded herself. She knew that as well as he did. And why did *that* thought hurt so much? She didn't dare look into her own heart to find out why. She didn't dare think of it at all. She didn't dare allow herself to think of him lying just down the hall from her, alone in his big bed. Was he lying awake, too? Was he staring out the window, watching the same moon rise? She shivered and turned on her side and pulled the covers up around her chin and silently recited *Hiawatha* to herself until she fell asleep. It had never failed her.

Next day, when they went to the hospital in the afternoon, Mattie brought up the subject again. This time, Lucie was even more concerned about Mattie getting herself worked up, because the doctor had told them that her condition wasn't getting any better. If anything, it was marginally worse. Bed rest might help. The new drugs he was trying might have an effect. They'd just have to wait and see.

Boone put up with Mattie's querulous demands with a good humor that Lucie could see was somewhat forced. He was getting very irritated with his grandmother. But when Mattie finally turned to her and asked her why she wouldn't marry her grandson, why she was just as stubborn as he was, and if anyone cared about making an old woman's last days happy ones, Lucie made a desperate plea across the bed to Boone.

They could figure out what to do about it later; they could get out of it somehow, once Mattie was home and safe, but now it was absolutely crucial that Mattie quit worrying, that she calm down and get the rest she so desperately needed.

"I'd be pleased to marry your grandson, Mattie," Lucie said, as lightly as she could manage. "There's just one problem—he hasn't asked me." She felt her hands tremble but her voice, thank goodness, was steady.

Boone stared at her across the white expanse of Mattie's bed. If ever a man looked thunderstruck, Boone Harlow was that man. Lucie watched him, holding her breath, crossing her fingers behind her back so he couldn't see. He swallowed, slowly, his eyes fathomless as midnight.

"Well," he began slowly, his eyes never leaving hers, "if that's the only problem, I guess I can do something about that." He paused, then went on, "Lucie Crane...will you marry me?"

"Yes," she whispered, feeling something, something close to joy, rise within her and nearly smother her. "I will." And she knew, deep in her heart, that despite the very practical reason behind his offer, despite the fact that they were only going through a charade for the sake of Mattie's health, she meant what she said. She'd marry this man in a heartbeat; she hadn't realize the power of what she felt until now, until this very moment.

Their eyes held for a few more seconds across the hospital bed, and then they both looked down. Boone smiled. Mattie was cackling with delight. She grabbed their hands and joined them across the blanket, over her midriff, her tiny gnarled hands joining Lucie's slender white one with Boone's large tanned one.

"Now," Mattie said, beaming with complete satisfaction, "that wasn't so hard, was it?"

The next day, Mattie seemed marginally stronger, strong enough to ask where Lucie's ring was; what kind of an engagement was it if she didn't have an engagement ring. She insisted Boone take the ring that had belonged to his mother from the jewelry box on her dresser at home, which he did, and put it on Lucie's finger. He didn't go so far as to do that; he just left it on the table after breakfast the next morning for her to put on herself. Then he took his hat from the rack by the door and went out. Lucie put on the ring— two diamonds and an emerald in an old-fashioned gold filigree setting—acutely aware of the oddity of sliding his mother's ring onto the third finger of her left hand, as a mark to the world of Boone Harlow's intentions, sliding it on alone, sitting by herself in front of the window of a house that would never be her home. The pain of that knowledge, the truth of it, shook her, but still she put the ring on and knew herself for the fool that she was.

She'd fallen in love with Boone Harlow after all, a man she'd practically had to beg to ask her to marry him, for farcical reasons, a man who'd never marry her for good, strong, simple reasons that he'd had the honor to tell her about. He'd been honest with her, honest all the way, even when he'd told her how he wanted her, how he wanted her in his bed, warning her of how he felt, but telling her at the same time that he'd never want her for more than that.

She was the charlatan. She was the one who'd betrayed these people, who'd betrayed Mattie terribly, first by hiding the truth of who she was, now with this—this pretend engagement. Mattie believed in her, Mattie trusted her. What would she say when Lucie said goodbye? What would they both say when they found out that she was not what she'd seemed to be, when they found out that she'd only been using them for her own selfish purposes? As a place of refuge until her own tangled affairs could be sorted out, until she could claim her inheritance and be her own woman, free to make her own choices, free to live her own life.

Lucie put her head down on her arms quietly and wept. What a mess she'd made of her life! What a mess she'd made of everything!

How the news got around so fast, Lucie never quite figured out. But then she'd never lived in a community like the Sawtooths before, had never heard of the speed or reliability of the so-called moccasin telegraph. Next morning, before breakfast was cleared out of the way, Ho Pickens was at the door.

"Well, well, well," he said, shifting his weight from one foot to the other, his greasy Stetson in his hand, his bright eyes fixed on first her, on the surprise that Lucie knew was on her face, then without missing a beat, to the black look of disgust on Boone's. "Ain't that wonderful news. Just wonderful!"

"What's that, Ho?" Boone drawled, suspiciously cool.

"Why that you two's figurin' to get married!" His smile didn't waver. "Heard it from Alice, don't know who she got it from."

Lucie made a vague gesture to the half-cleared breakfast table and Ho didn't need any more encouragement. He hung his hat on the rack by the door and pulled up a chair, practically rubbing his hands with delight. Heavens, Lucie thought, she'd certainly underestimated the determination of the valley folk to see Boone married off!

"So! When's the big day?" He took one look at Boone's frown, then quickly added, "Or would that be pryin'?"

"It'd be prying, Ho," Boone said dryly. He reached for his own hat from the rack and jammed it on. "Now...if you'll excuse me," he said with heavy irony, his hand on the door, "I've got work to do around here."

And he left her to fend for herself with his nosy neighbor!

Lucie didn't know if she was quite up to handling Holcomb Pickens.

"I see true love don't seem to have changed him none—don't mind if I do," Ho said, reaching for a biscuit on a plate on the table and nodding at Lucie's offer of tea. "That's a Harlow for ya—they runs dark, but they runs awful deep. Ha! I knew he'd crack, I jest knew it!" Ho slapped his knee and Lucie winced. "Jest took the right woman, that's all. Alex Myers owes me fifty bucks over this one," he added mildly. Lucie looked at him in shock and amazement.

"Yessirree." He regarded her with supreme satisfaction and respect, as though she'd just performed some world-record-setting feat, against impossible odds, some feat that he'd had the foresight to lay his bets on early. He chewed and mumbled through the biscuit crumbs, then washed the lot down with a swig of tea. "Ooohee! Didn't I figure the day we picked ya up comin' back from Ketchum that somethin' might spark between you two? Didn't I—"

"Care for some more tea, Ho?" Lucie said, interrupting him. She didn't want to hear any more about it. It was wretched the way the people in the valley had interfered in Boone's life. Sure, they were only trying to be helpful, but no one knew better than she did what it felt like to be manipulated and hounded and harassed to satisfy someone else's agenda. She'd left, but Boone couldn't leave—he belonged here. The more she heard about it, the madder she got—

"From what I've seen, Boone's quite capable of handling his own affairs. What about the girlfriend I heard he had in Twin Falls?" Lucie said, defending Boone, not thinking for a second that it might be an odd defense to make from someone so newly affianced.

"Oh, he—, er, heck, Miss Lucie, you don't have to worry about her none," Ho confided, wiping the crumbs from his chin with the back of his hand. "I heard she married some bean counter from south of Twin Falls a coupla weeks back. More her style. Boone warn't real sweet on her anyway. He just tried to let on he was." He winked at her. "Wanted to kinda keep us off his back, if ya know what I mean."

He was an exasperating old fellow, but Lucie couldn't help but like him. She smiled and poured them both another cup and settled back to listen to a few more stories. Ho Pickens had no shortage of stories to tell.

The next day, Boone asked Lucie if she wanted to go out riding with him. He said he had to check on the condition of some pasture a couple of miles from the ranch house, and thought she might like the chance to get away from any more drop-in company the likes of his garrulous neighbor.

"You ride, don't you?" Boone asked her, casually enough she thought.

"Of course I do!" she replied. She loved riding and had been good at it, too. As a teenager she'd even convinced the dour people she'd called Mother and Father to let her show some of the Douglass Arabs. She'd taken her share of prizes in the ring.

But when Boone had given her a leg up atop a monstrous bay gelding, in full Western regalia, she'd quickly had second thoughts.

"Just a minute, sir," she'd muttered under her breath as the horse danced sideways. Boone had pushed back his hat and was watching her with interest. "Just let me get these— oh!" The reins seemed awfully thick, and the saddle—! It was hard and broad and she couldn't feel the slightest movement of the horse beneath it. No matter, Lucie thought grimly to herself. She took a rein in each hand, in the approved manner, the way she'd been taught by the best riding masters New England had to offer, and she kicked the horse smartly in the ribs.

He took off like a shot, into a full fast gallop. Lucie hauled back on the reins, startled at the instant reaction she'd gotten from the gelding, and he slowed to a trot. She'd heard these quarter horses couldn't be beaten in the short run, over the quarter mile, but she hadn't actually wanted to find out for herself! She began to post, trying to regain her poise. It wasn't easy in this rig. The stirrups seemed overly long; maybe she'd get Boone to adjust them....

Boone caught the gelding's bridle as she came to a stop beside him. "What the devil are you doing, Miss Lucie?" he asked softly.

"What does it look like?" She wiped her upper lip with the back of her hand. She was beginning to perspire in the heat already. "Riding."

"Ah." Boone regarded her very intently. She thought she saw a gleam of amusement in his tawny eyes. "And what was that all about—that bobbing around?"

"Bobbing around?" She looked down at him in amazement. "Why I was—I was just posting!"

"Posting?" Boone began to grin. Lucie felt that she ought to be indignant—he clearly was laughing at her—but she didn't feel indignant. She felt like laughing, too. She couldn't believe that he'd actually asked her to go with him today. She'd hoped for weeks to get out riding. After all, she was living on a real, honest-to-goodness working Idaho ranch—she might as well get some fun out of it.

"Posting. You know, when the horse trots. A posting trot," she explained clearly and carefully, as though she were informing a child. "*T-r-o-t*, the gait between a walk and a canter." She was teasing him, and she knew he knew it. His smile turned her inside out.

"A canter, hmm?" Boone reached up and she took her foot out of the far stirrup, lifted it over the high, bothersome horn these saddles had, and slid into his arms. For a few seconds he held her immobile, in the shadow between his body and the horse. Her pulse shifted into double time. Then he grinned and let her go.

"I think we've got our wires a little crossed, Miss Lucie," he said, taking the horse by one rein. The animal obediently fell in behind him as he strode back toward the barn. "Wait here."

Lucie waited expectantly by the corral, sitting in a patch of dusty grass and leisurely scratching one of the half-dozen ranch dogs behind the ears. What was Boone up to? She'd rarely seen him in such a lighthearted mood, especially these days, and she wanted nothing to jeopardize it. She'd wait, although her curiosity was killing her.

Ten minutes later he emerged, leading behind him a black gelding Lucie hadn't seen before. The horse carried full English tack, the tack she was familiar with. Then Lucie blushed, blushed hot and red. Of course! Boone had known in a flash that she'd never ridden Western in her life.

"Meet Henry," Boone said, with a smile. He patted the gelding's neck affectionately. "He's a horse my sister bought before she left home. He's getting on, but he's a good old boy. Rides both English and Western." He grinned down at her.

"You knew?" Lucie said, guiltily, feeling her cheeks still burning.

Boone looked at her cheeks, her chin, her mouth, her eyes. It didn't help her embarrassment any. "It was pretty hard to miss, Miss Lucie," he said softly, and handed her the reins.

He gave her a leg up, and she was back on familiar ground. Everything felt exactly as it should. All she needed was her hard hat and boots. Henry responded beautifully, and the saddle, although obviously very old and a little neglected, was of the very best quality. *Hermés, Paris* she read on the four small silver plugs set into the saddle's seat. The very best, indeed.

She watched Boone swing into his own saddle, with the ease and economy of movement that marked a natural rider and an athlete. He sat on the horse as if it were part of himself. She almost felt ridiculously stiff and unnatural, posting along as she rode next to him. "Bobbing," as he'd put it. But the prospect of the next couple of hours riding with him filled her with absolute delight. Nothing could dim that.

"The tack belong to your sister, too?" She was looking forward to meeting this mysterious sister of Boone's someday. His brothers, too. Would she be here long enough to meet them? She looked at him finally, when he didn't answer.

Boone shot her a quick sideways look and frowned. "The saddle belonged to my mother," was all he said, then he spurred his horse into the lead, and any chance for conversation disappeared.

Later, when they'd climbed into some of the benchland at the foot of the Sawtooths, Boone had become quite talkative—for him—and pointed out some of the sights of the valley below. He'd shown her where Redfish Lake could just be seen, glittering in the distance, and told her how it was the origin of the Salmon River, the mighty river that Lewis and Clark had called The River of No Return, the river that fed into the Columbia and then the Pacific, many hundreds of twisted miles to the west. In Lewis and Clark's day, almost two hundred years ago, it had been red with salmon returning to spawn in its waters, hence the name. Now, with pollution and dams to contend with, fewer and fewer fish returned. Fisheries monitors had been lucky the past year, he said, to spot only a handful. Another example, he said, in what to Lucie was one of the few displays of controlled passion Boone had ever shown her, of what man's greed was doing to the planet.

"Up here," he said, waving to the wide-open grassy areas

around them, parched and brown in the summer heat, "huge sheep flocks at the beginning of the century had pretty well destroyed the grassland up here, and the delicate balance of everything in this ecosystem that depended on it.

"Now," he continued, with an ironic glance at her, "it's the cattleman who're doing it. Some of them, anyway. The National Forest Service, which is in charge of what happens here in the valley, has been trying to protect the land from overgrazing but they've had to put up with harassment and lawbreaking from the very people they're trying to help—the ranchers."

"Harassment?"

"Guns, threats...some people still think this is the wild West, Lucie, and that they can take the law into their own hands," he said with a cynical smile. "You ought to know that."

Boone didn't elaborate, and Lucie followed him slowly down a sidehill, gripping Henry's broad back with her knees and realizing just how handy a horn on a saddle might be in this rugged Western terrain. Luckily the horse was experienced and they reached the bottom without mishap. Lucie breathed a sigh of relief. Somehow it was essential that she not embarrass herself any further: she wanted Boone to think well of her, to think that she was competent at riding, if not at cooking. He'd teased her more than once about her shortcomings in the kitchen.

For an hour or two, she even forgot about Mattie, and she felt guilty about that when Boone came into the kitchen just as she was putting supper on the table that evening and told her that he'd received a phone call from the hospital. Mattie wanted to see him, and the doctor felt that it was important that he come.

"Give her my best," Lucie said, trying to keep the worry from her voice. If the hospital had called, it must be urgent.... "Tell her I'll be in to see her tomorrow."

In a way she was relieved that Boone was going to the hospital by himself. After an entire afternoon spent with him, she felt exhausted, both physically from the unaccustomed rigors of riding, and emotionally, from the incredible strain of being alone with him, knowing how she felt about him, unable to express herself or let him know by even an unwary look what was in her heart. Boone had enough on his plate, with his grandmother ill, his ranch problems, this idiotic public engagement he'd got tangled up in—thanks to her—without finding out that she'd fallen in love with him. That's all he needed, a lovesick cook on his hands, when what he really needed from her was support, and help to weather this crisis with Mattie.

The strain she'd felt that afternoon was on top of the strain she felt every day that they were alone together in the ranch house, every night that they spent there, each alone in a big bed, every time she caught him looking at her, when he thought she wasn't watching. The simmering undercurrent of awareness between them, even knowing that Boone was well in control of himself—and that thought irritating her—had brought many sleepless nights so far. And would bring many more, she knew.

This afternoon had brought the situation into sharp, painful focus for her. Instead of dreading her birthday, because it would mean leaving the ranch and going back to Concord, she ought to be praying for the day to come. There was nothing for her here—Boone had made that crystal clear—and the sooner she left, the better. The sooner she left, the sooner she could take up the search for her sister, her *real* family, the sooner she could start living her own life and start forgetting about the Harlows—about Mattie, who'd become like a grandmother to her in the past month, a grandmother she'd often wished for and had never had, and—and about Boone. Somehow, she knew deep in her heart, that forgetting about Boone might be a long time coming. If, indeed, it was possible at all.

When was he coming back? Lucie finished up the dishes after the men had left for their various evening pursuits in the bunkhouse, aware of the deep silence in the old house. She watched television for a while until finally she switched it off in disgust—she couldn't concentrate on the programs, and each time she thought she heard something, such as the growl of the pickup's engine, she'd race to the window. Only to see nothing but the blackness of the night beyond the yard lights.

Finally she put on a new nightgown she'd bought and went to bed. There was no point in waiting up for him. It was not her place, and, besides, perhaps he'd gone to visit someone. Friends…a woman. Boone obviously had a life— and deserved one—that she knew nothing about.

But she slept fitfully, and more than once, crept to the window to look down the long, dark valley. Stars and moonlight, and the far-off cry of a coyote, a mournful wild sound that sent shivers down her spine. Finally, not even sure she'd dropped off, in that state of alert confusion that occurs when the dreamer isn't sure she's been dreaming, Lucie sat bolt upright in bed.

It was silent outside. But hadn't she heard the slam of a truck door? Hadn't she heard the noisy yawning and whining of Balzac as he roused himself from his position on the back step? And wasn't that the sound of someone walking around downstairs? Boone must be back!

Without thinking, Lucie threw back the blankets and went down the hall.

"Boone?"

No answer. She paused, then quickly padded down the rest of the stairs in her bare feet. He was in the old-fashioned formal living room, the room that had once been a parlor, a room lined with the dour faces of the men and women who'd gone before him. He hadn't turned on a light, but was standing in front of a window, fully dressed, still wearing his jacket, staring out into the blackness outside. He was leaning, stiff-armed, on the windowsill. Lucie felt, more than saw, the stiffness in his body, the tension, the way he gripped the wooden sill. He didn't turn when she entered the room.

"Boone?" Her voice sounded soft and thin in the thick darkness of the room. "What's wrong? How's Mattie...is she all right?"

It seemed an eternity before he indicated that he had even heard her, another eternity until he turned, shifting toward her, his body outlined by starlight. His face was deeply shadowed, turned as he was, away from what light there was, outside. She couldn't see his expression; could only hear his voice, thick and strained.

"She's dead, Lucie. Mattie's dead."

Chapter Eleven

"Dead!"

Lucie wrapped her arms around herself, suddenly shaking uncontrollably. *Mattie dead? What was he saying?*

"She's dead, Lucie. Just before midnight. Her heart finally gave out, the doctor said, and she'd had another stroke before I got there." Boone's voice sounded flat and oddly detached.

"But—but I never said goodbye to her," Lucie began, her voice a whisper. She felt her eyes fill with silent tears that spilled over and ran down her cheeks. *Mattie dead!* It wasn't fair! She'd just begun to know her, to love her—

"Neither did I." Boone turned back to the window and stared out again. "She was unconscious when I got there. She never regained consciousness. And—and—" Boone faltered and caught back his words. With an oath, he slammed his fist into the wall beside the window.

"Oh, Boone...oh, Boone," Lucie said softly. "I'm so

sorry." She went to him and reached out to touch his arm. He winced, and she saw the flash of pain on his dark features. Then he turned to her and grabbed her by the shoulders so hard, it hurt.

"I let her down, Lucie. I can't forgive myself for that. She hated hospitals, she hated doctors. She wanted to die at home. And—and—"

"You can't blame yourself, Boone—"

"Why not?" he interrupted with another oath. "She was my responsibility. She depended on me to do the right thing. I failed her, Lucie. I let her down."

"But you had no idea she was dying. You thought she was getting better—we both did. So did Mattie. She—she was always so...so..." Lucie couldn't speak anymore, and lowered her head, so that Boone wouldn't see her tears.

"Ah, Lucie, sweetheart—" Boone pulled her into his arms and held her. She put her arms around him and sobbed against his shirtfront. She felt the pressure of his chin against the top of her head, and she gave herself over to the grief she felt, the overwhelming sense of loss....

Finally, sniffling, she pulled away. "I'm sorry, Boone. I'm—" She managed to smile weakly. After all, it was *his* grandmother who'd just died, not hers. She should be the one offering comfort, not him.

"Hush," he murmured and pulled her close again. "Don't talk." Lucie stood in the shelter of his arms, her own arms tight around him, for a very long time. She had no idea how long; in some ways it felt like forever. His body warmed hers through the thin fabric of her nightgown, his arms were hard bands of strength, strength, she knew, deep in her soul, she could always count on. She heard the thudding of his heart under her cheek, heard and felt it so deeply that it seemed to become one with her in the darkness, as though they were one grieving entity, not two, together in body, together in soul.

Finally, Boone took a long breath and drew back, raising his hands to her face, cupping her face with his palms, wiping the tears from her cheeks with his thumbs, hard and rough and infinitely tender.

"She was an old woman," he said, his voice quiet in the absolute silence of the room. "She wasn't afraid to die. She'd told me many times that she expected to meet Edward again—that was my grandfather—once the Lord managed to round up a replacement for her. That's how she put it." Lucie saw his faint smile in the darkness and it nearly broke her heart all over again. "She was a believer, you know. Behind that gruff, ornery manner was a simple woman who lived a simple faith." He hesitated, and Lucie felt her tears run afresh. He traced their course with his thumbs. "She didn't suffer, sweetheart. I held her hand when she died. She might have died in the hospital, but she didn't die alone."

"I know. I—I'm sorry, Boone, for carrying on like this—"

"Don't be sorry, Lucie," he interrupted sternly, almost angrily. "Don't ever be sorry for what you feel. Feeling's what—" he cleared his throat, and when he spoke again, his voice sounded even gruffer "—feeling's what makes life worth living. Now—" He took his hands from her face and quickly slipped out of his jacket, draping it around her shoulders. "You're cold. Why don't you go back up to bed?"

"What about you, Boone? You must be exhausted. Can I make you a cup of tea or anything?" She sniffed, hunching up one shoulder to wipe her eyes on the smooth leather of Boone's jacket.

"No. I'm going to go to bed soon. I just want to stay down here for a while. I've got some thinking to do."

His voice was quiet but firm. Lucie could take a hint—he wanted to be alone. Without another word she went up-

stairs, pulling the jacket close around her. He was right—
she was cold, with a cold that went clear through to her
bones. She didn't think she'd ever be warm again.

It was nearly two in the morning. Lucie lay for a while,
frozen, feeling the endless hot flow of tears that slipped
down her cheeks to stain her pillow. *Don't ever apologize
for feeling.* Finally, fitfully, she slept, but she awoke again
just as the first thin streaks of gray touched the early morning sky. She knew what she had to do, what she must do.

Quietly she slipped out from under the quilt and padded
down the hall on bare feet. At the entrance to Boone's room
she paused, her heart hammering in her ears. *Don't ever be
sorry for what you feel.* She loved him. He needed her.

With a deep breath for courage, Lucie went into his room,
stopping at the foot of his bed. When had he finally gone
to bed? He was fully clothed, just bootless and hatless. His
arms were folded across his chest as he lay on his back,
atop his blanket. Perhaps he was cold, too. Outside the curtainless windows the first shard of light was brushing the
top of the highest Sawtooth peak. It was still hours before
morning.

Quietly, carefully, Lucie sat down on the far side of the
bed. Boone didn't move. His breathing was deep and easy
and for a long time Lucie sat there motionless, studying him,
feeling within herself the ever-widening circles of the love
she felt for him, the feeling for him that had enriched and
nourished her life already, far beyond anything she'd ever
dreamed.

She turned, onto her knees, and bent toward him.
"Boone?" She stroked his cheek lightly with one hand and
his eyes opened instantly, although she'd only whispered
his name. He didn't move, but the look in his eyes said
everything. *What are you doing here? Am I dreaming? Yes,
Lucie, I want you. More than anything, more than every-*

thing. I want the comfort of your body, of your smile, of your arms.

"Do you mean this?" he whispered finally, his voice rough, his gaze not leaving hers for a second. His eyes were calm and clear and warm, filled with growing wonder, filled with gathering desire. She knew he must see her intentions in her eyes, her feeling for him, because she knew she need not answer him. He reached up to cup her face in his hands as he'd done before. She nodded. He drew her down toward him. She shut her eyes, just as their mouths met.

Yes, yes…more than anything!

Boone's mouth touched hers tenderly, lightly. He barely moved, as though not trusting himself to move, to reach out to her, as though they were both caught in a rare and precious dream. But she felt a tremor run through his body beneath her hands, her palms on his chest, her fingers digging into the hard muscles beneath the cloth. A wave of knowledge swept through her, that she held the key to their coming together, that she held the power....

She broke away from him, even though her soul cried out, even though her body protested that she must press closer, must never be separated from him ever again. She straightened, until she was kneeling on the bed beside him, sitting back on her heels. She saw his eyes glittering in the half-light, watching her. Neither had spoken; Lucie knew that neither would.

Slowly, carefully, her fingers trembling, she unbuttoned the row of pearl buttons that fastened her nightgown. Thirteen, no, fourteen…had she ever counted them before? Then the thin cotton garment lay open over her left breast, and she felt the tension tight as coiled steel in the man before her as he wrenched his eyes from hers, finally, and looked at her naked breast. She looked where he looked, to see what she had offered, and saw the white globe of her own breast, outlined by moonlight, glowing palely in the dimness, the dark center hardening, burning, swelling proudly, under the gaze of the man who would be her lover, the man she had said she'd marry, the man she loved with all her heart.

Boone stared at her for a long, trembling moment, a moment in which she took no breath, nor did he. And then, letting out his breath in a tortured, ragged sound, he reached out and gently pushed aside the right strap of her nightgown, so that it slipped off her shoulder, too, and the whole garment spilled down to settle at her waist.

She could hear the silence of forever in the room. Then Boone made a sound, deep in his throat, a strangled sound, a moan of pure need, a sound she'd never heard before. And before she knew what he was doing, he'd pulled her down, and with one rough movement, had rolled over so that he was above her, his hands on either side of her face, holding her, and he was plunging his tongue into her mouth, possessing her and groaning, growling his fierce need into her mouth. Teeth met teeth. Tongue mated with tongue.

Lucie gasped at the heat that rolled through her, gasped at the suddenness, at the urgency. She felt every atom of his passion as it met hers, as it joined with hers, loosed, finally, as it fed her own, as it swept over her so fiercely and so strongly, that she had to twist her head to one side and cry out or she knew she would burst.

At her cry, a cry she didn't even recognize as coming from her own throat, Boone levered himself up, and stood beside the bed for a moment, ripping off his own clothes, his glittering gaze never leaving hers.

Then he was with her again, heated flesh meeting heated flesh, hard meeting soft, the rough hair of his chest against the smoothness, the tenderness of her bare breasts. Her nightgown was still gathered around her waist, forgotten. She cried out, once, before his mouth sought hers again, then again, her voice oddly muffled, as his body possessed hers in one powerful movement. There was no tenderness, there was no courting, there was no shape or pattern to their lovemaking, this was mating—pure and hot and glorious.

Lucie clung to him as he moved fiercely within her, she moaned into his mouth as he kissed her, wholly, deeply, as she felt the shudders of tension ripple again and again through the rock-hard muscles of his back as she held him tight, as tightly as she could. She heard him cry out, a choked and tangled cry, and felt him make a sudden, unexpected movement. Then she held him as he cried out again and bent his head over hers so that his hair blinded her and she felt the heat of his seed spill into her. And she didn't know whether the salt she tasted was from her tears or from his.

Saturday, the day they buried Mattie Harlow, dawned bright and windy.

Boone stood at the graveside and listened to the wind-blown words of the preacher, half hearing, half thinking, half remembering. The whole valley had turned out to see one of their own returned to the soil, the dust from whence she'd come. From whence they'd all come. To his right stood his sister, Jane, tall and handsome, beside her J.J., the youngest Harlow, dark and brooding and ever quiet. He hadn't been able to track down Carson. To his left stood Lucie, her bright head just reaching his shoulder. At the church she'd held back, saying the front pew was reserved for family. But Boone had taken her arm and escorted her to their place at the front. She belonged there beside him. Their bogus engagement had nothing to do with it: Lucie's bond with his grandmother had run deeper than blood.

He reached for her hand now and squeezed it. She returned the pressure, yet didn't look up at him. Black, he thought, looking down at her briefly, had never suited a woman as well. The valley normally didn't go in for mourn-

ing clothes, not like city folk still did. There was no fashion
here to the rituals of death; men put on their best suit, the
one they wore to church, if they were churchgoing men, the
one they'd worn to their wedding if they weren't. But Lucie
had worn black, a new dress with her red-gold hair done up
in some complicated fashion—he still couldn't look at her
without thinking of it wild and loose, spread out on the
pillow beneath him, her arms reaching up to him, holding
him tightly, her eyes alive, eager with passion....

Boone deliberately tried to blank out the thought, to turn
his mind from the vision of her as she'd come to him that
night, the night Mattie'd died, the vision of an angel in the
shape of a woman, the source of life itself. But every time
he looked at her in her plain black dress, it was impossible
not to think of the way it contrasted with the milk-white
skin beneath it, not to think of the way the warm silk of her
skin had felt beneath his hands, the way it had fitted against
him, so soft and yielding and close...and then he was lost
again.

It scared him, what Lucie Crane had done to him. He'd
thought what he felt for her was a simple case of lust—
burning, driving lust. And there'd been that, too. But that
wasn't all; it wasn't that simple. He was beginning to realize
that with Lucie Crane nothing was simple.

That morning, after she'd come to his bed, he'd arisen
early, sleepless. They'd made love with a fierceness, an
abandon, a perfect melding of soul and spirit that he'd
never, ever felt with another woman. He'd been ashamed at
how he'd lost control that first time. It shook him badly; it
had never happened to him before. But then he'd promised
to make it up to her. And he had. To see the sheer passion
on her face, the beauty, as he took her to the heights, again
and again, before they cried out together, each consuming
the other in the white-hot crucible of spirit-made-flesh. He'd

known the instant it had happened that he'd never be the same.

And that wasn't what he'd wanted to feel. And that's why, after she fell asleep, innocently, wholly, warmly, in his arms, he'd lain there sleepless, waiting for the dawn. Who was she? Who was this woman he held? He'd seen her head for a pay phone time after time when he'd taken her to Ketchum. Who was she calling? Why didn't she tell him, even casually? Why did she guard herself so closely, so secretly, so carefully, when in his arms she could give him everything?

He thought of that first day, the first time he'd seen her after they'd made love. He'd given the men breakfast—cold cereal—and told them about Mattie. He'd given them time off until after the funeral. Then he'd written a note to Lucie and left it on the kitchen table.

By the time he got back from Ketchum, after picking up J.J. at the Hailey airport and making arrangements with the funeral home, it was nearly three o'clock. Jane, he knew, had planned to arrive before noon. He'd never forget the first glimpse he'd had of Lucie, the instant he'd walked in the door.

She was laughing with Jane; her face was flushed and glowing, her hair awry, her arms floury to the elbows with something she and his sister were making. She'd turned, and their eyes had met, and the soft glow he'd seen in her blue eyes had made him set his jaw grimly just to keep control. He felt the fever she'd freed in him burn again and nearly consume him and he wanted nothing more than to toss J.J. the truck keys, tell him and Jane to beat it and go find a bed and breakfast to stay at and then sweep Lucie into his arms and carry her upstairs to his bed. It was all there, all there in his eyes, and he knew she knew by the way she blushed and looked down and hurriedly turned back to Jane again.

He'd taken a deep breath. *Get a hold of yourself, Harlow.*

It hadn't been easier, either, that evening, when Jane laughingly said that she assumed he and Lucie were sharing a bedroom, after all they were engaged now and both grown-ups.

"There's no need to pretend on my account, big brother. Or J.J.'s," she'd teased him, her eyes dancing. Boone knew she was pleased as punch that he was engaged. Or, at least, they all thought he was engaged. Time enough later to straighten out *that* whole business. Boone had given his sister a level look that told her quite clearly it was none of her business and she'd laughed and let it go at that. Lucie, he'd noted, had blushed a dozen shades of red and had said nothing.

It had been hard, real hard, to say good-night to everyone and go to bed alone these past two nights. To watch Lucie go up to her own bed. Lucie, beyond a very self-conscious expression that he took to be embarrassment, had avoided the subject. It was as though the night they'd spent together—the few short, glorious hours they'd spent together—had not happened. But, of course, it had, and nothing could possibly be the same between them again.

"J.J. tells me you're one of Boone's strays?"

"Strays?" Lucie looked up from where she was sitting on the floor of the attic. She and Jane were sorting through Mattie's old trunks to see what could be given away and what could be thrown out. Lucie had been touched to hear Boone say that Mattie had made him promise to give Lucie her knitting supplies and her extensive collection of tattered cookbooks. Now she'd learn to knit, if it killed her; it was a sacred trust.

"No offense, of course." Jane smiled. She was tall and had the Harlow eyes, their tawny gold a striking contrast to her jet-black hair. Boone had told Lucie she ran her own catering company, or something like that, in Twin Falls.

"Boone's always been a softie—he and J.J. If ever there was a wounded rabbit or a nest of partridges that the tractor'd run over, Boone or J.J. would be the one to bring the little chickies home for Mattie to nurse back to health in a little box behind the kitchen stove. That brother of mine hides a very tender heart behind all that gruff, tough exterior. A lot like Mattie, come to think of it," she added, her brow wrinkling. Then she laughed and looked up at Lucie. "Except Mattie was a lot noisier!"

Lucie smiled, but she didn't really know what to do. Should she tell Jane the truth? That her engagement to her brother was just a fiction they hadn't gotten around to revealing yet? Boone hadn't said anything to her, she hadn't been alone with him since the morning she'd gone to his bed.

Lucie still blushed when she thought of that. Boone's storm of passion, his abandon, had swept away any reservations that she might have had. *Don't ever be sorry for what you feel*, he'd said. She loved him; and no man could be as tender as he'd been, as intense, as passionate, without feeling something in return. Perhaps not love, but surely consideration, respect, friendship.... Friendship! What a laugh, she reminded herself. Friendship is *not* what you feel for Boone Harlow. But there'd been no repeat of the fierce lovemaking of that morning and Lucie had the feeling there wouldn't be. It had happened, it had changed their relationship irrevocably, but it had been an aberration. It wasn't going to happen again.

"Jane...I think there's something I'd like to tell you."

"Yes?" Jane had gone to the side of the attic to the knee wall that made the ceiling so low, she had to stoop. She was looking through some large flat objects that looked like canvases, stacked against the wall.

Lucie *had* to tell Jane, to tell someone, she couldn't go on letting people—the whole valley—think she and Boone were really going to get married. She'd seen the way Boone had looked grimmer and grimmer with each congratulation on his engagement he'd received the day of the funeral. She'd seen the way he'd looked at her over the heads of the crowd: annoyed, apologetic.

"Boone and I aren't really engaged."

"What!" Jane looked over at her in apparent dismay. "What do you mean you're not really engaged? What's going on?"

"Well..." Lucie began, twisting the diamond-and-emerald ring she wore. "We just—we just decided to pretend we were going to get married because Mattie'd set her heart on it. She was so insistent at the hospital that I—" Lucie's cheeks flamed as she thought of her part in the farce. "I told Boone I'd marry him if he'd ask me. So he asked me. But it was just to get Mattie to settle down—we both had no intention of following through."

To her surprise, Jane was grinning. "Maybe you didn't, Lucie. But I wouldn't be surprised if Boone did. He never would have asked you if he hadn't meant it."

"No! I tell you, it was just because Mattie was so agitated," Lucie began. It astonished her that Jane seemed to take the news so lightly.

"Look—" Jane held up both hands, palms toward Lucie "—I don't know a thing about you—J.J. says Boone doesn't, either—but I do know my brother. Trust me—he wouldn't have asked you if he didn't intend to stand by his offer. Now," she continued, eyes twinkling, "if you've got other ideas, I think you ought to let him know. Here, could you give me a hand with this? I think these are the ones J.J. is supposed to get."

"What are they?" Lucie looked down at the objects Jane was sorting through. They *were* canvases, covered with cobwebs, but she could see the vivid colors, the sweep of composition through the layer of dust on each one. Jane's dismissal of her confession seemed final. No point in going on about it. And she felt slightly irritated that Boone had obviously told J.J. quite a few details about her, details he'd been only too happy to pass along to Jane. Well, she decided grudgingly, they *were* family.

"These look like paintings," she said, suddenly interested in the work at hand.

"They are." Jane dusted her hands on the knees of her jeans and stood up. "Whew! What a mess. I'll tell J.J. that his pictures are here and he can cart them back to Seattle with them if he wants them."

"But—" Lucie was completely bewildered. "What are these? Who painted them? Whose are they?"

"Boone's never told you about these old pictures?" Jane looked amazed. "Our father left them to us. The Harlow legacy, you might say." She smiled ironically. "Drove Boone crazy. He always hated Dad for abandoning the ranch and spending all his time painting and off on trips up the canyons by himself. He blamed Dad for what happened to Mother." Jane thought for a moment. "I don't suppose he holds it against him any longer. Boone's got his own dreams now. Amazing what growing up can do to a person's perspective, isn't it?" She looked to Lucie for agreement.

Lucie swallowed, then nodded. Did it? Did it change a person's idea of what really mattered? In a way she felt that coming to Idaho as she had, had been a symbol of her own coming of age. Certainly she'd been an adult at twenty-four, but she'd never wrenched control of her own life from the well-meaning but misguided, overbearing people who'd always managed to make her life miserable. Her adopted parents, her Uncle Charles....

And as for priorities, even her search for her sister had gradually faded into the background in the last while, onto a mental list of "must do someday." Her revenge against Jack and Myrta and all the Douglasses who'd made her own and her natural mother's lives wretched, the desire to outsmart her uncle, the man who symbolized all that pain for her now, the fierce desire for revenge that had given her the courage to leave her home in the middle of the night, to hop a westbound freight train for an unknown destination, even that seemed not much more than foolish now. Perhaps what Jane said was true...people changed.

"Anyway, Dad left us each a dozen or so of these. That's Boone's lot over there," Jane said, pointing to the far wall. "Mattie's left J.J. her lot—probably because she was so mad about all his talk about writing poetry that she figured he's the one who deserved them." Jane laughed. "She always said she wouldn't have those paintings around, never forgave her own son for neglecting what she thought his duty was."

Lucie stood back and looked at a couple of the paintings. They weren't bad. They were mainly landscapes, with scattered herds of cattle tucked in the folds of hills, some of horses and riders, others of the Sawtooth range that loomed behind the ranch. "They're really rather good, Jane. Don't you think so? Western art's all the rage these days, you know."

"Is it?" Jane put her hands in her pockets and shrugged. "Maybe J.J. can sell a couple and raise part of his college fee this year instead of depending on Boone for money like he usually does. I hung a couple in my apartment because they reminded me a little of home—" she skewed up her eyes and looked critically at one of the canvases "—once I got over not wanting to be reminded of home, that is!"

Lucie helped Jane cart the paintings to the kitchen. They dusted them off, amid sneezing fits and much laughter— Lucie had discovered a broad streak of the Harlow whimsy in Jane, a trait she'd only glimpsed from time to time in

Boone...the day he'd bought the old baler, for instance—
and Jane helped Lucie organize supper for the ranch hands.
Cold baked ham, potato salad, bean salad, lemon squares
for dessert. Jane was a thousand times more adept in the
kitchen than Lucie was, than Lucie knew she would ever
be. Still, she didn't mind. It was a joy to watch an expert,
to lend a hand when she could. And her own cooking was
improving—several of the ranch hands had mentioned it,
shyly, politely, and Lucie had blushed with pleasure.

But there was a serious side to Jane, too, and before
they'd finished up in the kitchen, she turned to Lucie and
said bluntly, "Look—about what you said up there earlier,
up in the attic...this business of being engaged to Boone, if
it means anything or not. If you decide you want my brother,
stand up and fight for him, Lucie." A grimace crossed her
face, a grimace she quickly caught and masked. "He's a
typical Harlow, I'm afraid. Hardheaded as hell, but he's
worth fighting for. He's a good man. I think you know
that," Jane finished softly. But her smile was tremulous
around the edges, and her eyes were shadowed with pain.
Lucie knew that what she was saying meant a great deal
more than Jane let on.

"I know what it's like, Lucie," Jane said after a few
seconds. She put her hand on Lucie's arm, and continued,
"It's old news now, nothing I want to talk about, really—
but I had to learn my lesson the hard way. It's not too late
for you."

J.J. left that afternoon, and while Boone was gone to drive
him to the airport at Hailey, Jane decided to go across the
valley to visit a friend she'd known since grade school. She
invited Lucie to come with her, but Lucie declined the invitation. She wanted to be alone. So much had happened in
the past couple of days, so much that she needed to think
about.

She wandered down to the slow-moving creek that meandered through the fields along the flank of the mountain before turning down the valley to flow near the ranch house. Balzac walked sedately at her side, seeming to sense her melancholy, her need for dignity, for healing silence.

The sun was hot on her shoulders as she walked, hot through the thin cotton of her dress. The valley was quiet, not a man-made sound to be heard, but the grass was alive with crickets and grasshoppers and the darting brilliant shapes of butterflies. The air was alive with the scent of hay drying, and dust and sage and clover, all the rich mixed scents of summer.

Lucie stopped at one cattle guard to wait for a couple of curious white-faced calves to approach her and the dog. She smiled. She now knew what a cattle guard was—her expensive Swiss education hadn't taught her that! Cattle guards, Boone had told her, were at the entrances to field for an extremely useful purpose: to let vehicles through without the necessity of getting out to open and close a gate, but to keep cattle back. No cow of any brain, he'd told her, would trust herself to maneuver across the wide-spaced steel rails without putting a leg through and perhaps suffering serious injury.

"*You're* not going to grow up to be a cow of very little brain, are you?" she murmured to the bravest calf. He allowed himself to be scratched on his bullet-hard white-whorled head before trying to capture Lucie's hand with his sinuous milky tongue. She laughed and pulled her hand back and the calf galloped stiffly back to its mother, tail high in the air.

She continued on, humming quietly to herself. She loved this country, she truly did. She could see why Boone was so bound to it, why Mattie had been. In fact—she looked at the snow-capped mountains before her, aware that Boone's father had painted that very scene in one of the canvases she'd helped to carry down earlier—so had Boone's father. He'd let the ranch run down, to pursue his dream of painting, but what had he chosen as his subject? The country around him, the country he'd loved...as his son did. It all amounted to much the same thing.

Lucie found a shady spot under a huge cottonwood and leaned against its gnarled trunk to watch the smooth dark flow of the water before her. Beaver Creek. The ranch was its namesake. She twisted a rope of grass between her fingers and took a deep, shaky breath.

What was she going to do...fight for him? Jane had said he was worth fighting for. She didn't need Jane to tell her that. Life, suddenly, was way too complicated. If they hadn't made love...if they hadn't made love, they could have continued to drift along, much as they had done since she'd arrived, until she left in a couple of weeks.

But that hadn't happened. They hadn't drifted along. They had made love. There was no going back. Lucie closed her eyes and shivered in the green shade and wrapped her arms around herself, remembering. Yes, they'd made love...but would they go on as they'd begun? Could they?

Chapter Twelve

What was a man to do?

Just tell her straight out, plain and simple, that it wouldn't work between them and that there was no point continuing on with an affair? Much as every fiber of him, body and soul, regretted it? That taking up where they'd left off before his sister and brother arrived at the Double H was only asking for trouble? Big trouble. Boone groaned inwardly as he signaled for the turn to the ranch road off the pavement of the Star Route. How to explain *that*, without causing more damage. How to explain that he didn't want to make love with her, that they oughtn't to, when that's all he *did* want, all he'd thought about since the morning she'd come to his bed.

And then there was the small matter of one bogus engagement. Especially now that the whole damn valley was in on the act. Even at the funeral he'd had to listen to more congratulations than condolences. Mattie would have approved. Boone had to smile when he thought of how the news had spread around the valley like wildfire. Hell's bells, he had to hand it to his grandmother. It was Mattie's parting shot, her best one, her last attempt to control him from the grave, to hope that social pressure might make a difference where her nagging hadn't.

How wrong she was. It didn't make a bit of difference, not to him; it just made it a little trickier figuring out how to call the whole thing off. How to handle it. Someone else was involved, someone who didn't need her feelings hurt any more than he probably already had done. Sweet Lucie Crane. Damn! Boone slammed the steering wheel with his right hand. Every time he looked into those big blue trusting eyes…those eyes that still hurt somewhere, somewhere deep, he felt guilty as hell.

And that was another thing—why hadn't she ever come clean about where she'd come from, where she was going? He took a deep breath and frowned as he mulled over the complex reasons that might lie behind her silence. Even thinking about Lucie's life before she'd come into his, where she'd called home before she'd come to Beaver Creek, who she called from the pay phone every trip they made to Ketchum—even thinking about it scared him deep inside, scared him in a way he didn't want to think about. On the other hand, maybe her continued silence was good news; maybe it meant she didn't care to go on with an affair with him any more than he did. It was just…hell, just something that had happened. Once. Yeah, maybe that was it. And, he thought, shifting down as he approached the ranch yard, they were in one hell of a mess if she was as good at lying to herself as he was.

His sister's car was gone. Boone felt a twinge of disappointment. He knew Jane didn't plan to go back to Twin Falls until tomorrow; that meant she'd probably gone somewhere and taken Lucie with her. He had to talk to Lucie—

they had to get a few things straightened out between them, but…maybe it was just as well she wasn't here. It wouldn't hurt to think things over a little longer, to run over what he planned to say to her.

There was a note on the kitchen table. From Jane, it looked like. He picked it up and read it aloud. "'B—I'm off to see Connie P. for the afternoon. Lucie's gone for a walk. Tell her Bonnie called. Says it's urgent. See you later—J.'"

Bonnie? Who the hell was Bonnie? And Lucie had never—to his knowledge—ever received a phone call here at the Double H. Fear touched Boone somewhere deep, scraped a bone somewhere under his ribs. It was weird, it was an ominous feeling, as though he and Mattie had had Lucie to themselves for a long time, too long, and now Mattie was gone and the world Lucie had come from was calling her back. Calling her away from them, away from the Sawtooth Valley, away from…away from him.

Boone stepped outside into the sunshine. Where had she gone? He put two fingers to his mouth and whistled. He waited, listening. As he'd expected, he heard a couple of excited yelps in the distance and in another couple of minutes, Balzac streaked into the yard, whining and jumping.

"Down, boy," Boone said to the excited dog. "Okay, let's go find Lucie. C'mon, fella." And he followed the dog back along the road that led up the creek.

She must have fallen asleep. She'd slid down to lie at the base of the big cottonwood, her dress hiked up around her knees, her nimbus of red-gold hair spread on the grass. That's why he hadn't seen her, not at first. That's why he'd frowned and stopped fifty feet away, at Balzac's sudden soft whine. The dog froze, one foot in the air, tail straight and stiff, in a pointer's stance inherited from one or another of his many mysterious, no-name ancestors. Then he nosedived to flop down beside his mistress, big brown eyes looking up from between grizzled forepaws, tail lazily circling, thumping the ground, daring his master to object.

Boone stood there a moment, hands in his pockets, amazed to discover that he felt jealous...jealous of a dog! Balzac didn't hesitate; Balzac knew exactly what he wanted and went for it. Too bad people couldn't be as straightforward, Boone thought, walking forward, careful not to put his boots down too heavily on the soft turf. Should he wake her? He stood for a moment, hands in his pockets, looking at Lucie, looking at how the afternoon sun danced and dappled her from head to toe in the shade of the gently waving cottonwood. Her dress was pale green, the grass was a rich green, here so close to the life-giving waters of the creek, the shade she slept in was thick and green from the leaves above. Only her hair struck the odd note, shining burnished and bright against the grass, against the pale curve of her cheek.

Boone crouched and maneuvered himself so that he faced slightly away from her, so that he couldn't look at her without turning his head. It was a test, he knew, a subtle test of his own will, and he cursed himself softly for his foolishness. He reached irritably for a stalk of long couch grass and leaned against the tree trunk, staring at the familiar peaks through narrowed eyes. From long habit, he put the stem in his mouth and bit off the soft sweet end, the half inch or so that held the plant's sun-warmed sap. Damnation! Hell and damnation.

He glanced at Lucie, then away, then back again. He couldn't stop looking at her, at the way she breathed so slowly and evenly, at the way she wrinkled her nose as the passing breeze ruffled loose tendrils of her hair against her cheek, at the sloping curve of her hip, of her woman's belly, of—Boone cursed again softly to himself and looked away.

He closed his eyes, feeling the ache of desire well deep within him, all over again.

She warmed him. She warmed him from the inside out. She seemed so innocent—and she was, but yet she wasn't, at the same time. No innocent could have made love with him as she had, with such fire, with such focus, with such fierce passion. It was her response to him, her abandon, that had driven him wild. That, and the fact that he'd wanted her in his bed from the first moment he met her.

He'd often thought that, yet could it be true? Really true? He'd never felt that way about a woman before, never so fast, never so sure. He and Jill had dated off and on for nearly four months before they'd made the move from the living room to the bedroom. And even then it had been a conscious move. Sure, their lovemaking had been enjoyable—sex usually was—but it was totally different from what he'd felt with Lucie. In fact, it was difficult to call what had happened by the same name. Sex. Sure, it was basically the same thing—about as much as driving a tractor was like winning the Indy 500.

Boone pulled at another stalk of grass. Could he be wrong? Could there be a chance of it working between them, him and Lucie? A real, honest-to-goodness relationship? Craziness! Should he *try* to make it work—

"Boone." Her voice was soft as the breeze. He turned, wondering if the pleasure he felt showed in his eyes. He tried to keep his face indifferent, his expression closed. He had to. It was going to hurt, but it had to be done.

He cleared his throat. "Lucie. I, uh—"

"You came to meet me." It was a statement, but a statement that held a question in it, a soft wonder that he'd do such a thing. She reached out languidly, lazily, and touched his arm. He should have moved away from her, so that she couldn't touch him. But he didn't…he couldn't. "That was a nice thing to do," she continued softly, sleepily. "Thanks."

"I followed the dog." Boone bit at the stem of grass in his mouth then pulled it out and threw it down irritably. *Followed the dog?* What kind of a stupid thing was that to say?

"Good old Balzac." Lucie's eyes widened as she turned her head to look for the dog. He was thumping the ground with his tail, tongue lolling happily at her mention of his name.

Stupid damn dog! Boone felt himself getting more and more irritated. He put his arms around his knees and clasped his hands. She had hiked herself up to a half-sitting position. Her face was sleep-warmed and soft and he could see the wrinkles in her skin, on her arms, that the grass had made as she'd lain there. He wanted to roll over and pull her into his arms and kiss her, under the old cottonwood. He wanted her to keep still, not to say anything, he wanted them both to just feel…he wanted them both to think of nothing else, certainly not of tomorrow or next week or next month.

Boone made a sound of exasperation deep in his throat and stood suddenly. He walked to the creek's edge. Sure, walk away, Harlow. Okay, now he'd seen how *he'd* handled things…what would the dog have done?

"Boone?" Her voice sounded puzzled behind him. He wheeled and walked back to where she half sat, supported by her elbows. He threw himself down again, this time a little farther from her, hoping the desire to take her in his arms would be correspondingly less. It wasn't.

"J.J. get off all right?"

"Fine."

"His—his plane on time?"

Boone gave her a direct, piercing look. "Yeah." She looked confused. He swore silently to himself. *Obstreperous bastard. All she's doing is trying to make conversation with you.*

"Look, Lucie—" He hesitated, then plunged on. "I've been thinking. About the last couple of days and…well, since Mattie died." He stole a look at her then wished he hadn't. Those big blue eyes of hers were regarding him so seriously, so soberly. She was listening to every word he said, waiting, he knew with a flash of insight, waiting for the ax to fall.

"Yes?" He barely heard her whispered encouragement. His eyes were drawn to the twisting motion she was making with the ring on her third finger. His mother's ring.

"It's a hell of a note that the whole valley found out about this, but—" He shrugged. Then he forced himself to look at her, not to look away. "I want you to know that we don't owe anything to a promise made to a dead woman. She's dead, Lucie. Dead and buried. We both know why we did what we did." He hesitated, and the awful silence drove him on. "I—I guess that's all I wanted to say."

She looked down at her lap and twisted the ring off her finger. She handed it back to him. "Here," she said, simply, and he thought he saw the sheen of tears in her eyes. It could have been the sun through the leaves.

He took the ring and his hand touched hers briefly. It hurt, it hurt like crazy, seeing her take that ring off, seeing her reach out to give it to him, taking it in his own hand. It was almost physical, as though something that was his, something that was rightly his, had been torn away from him, ripped away from him forever.

Lucie had looked away, was plucking absently at the grass beside her. Finally she looked up. "Didn't work," she said and gave him a tremulous smile. "Mattie died anyway."

"Yeah." He felt himself smile faintly. "But she died happy." Lucie caught his eye as they shared a lightning-quick memory of the old woman they'd both loved. Then she looked away again.

Boone felt himself clear his throat. He took Lucie's hand. He couldn't remember planning to do that, but he did it anyway. Without thinking, without planning, just…just feeling.

"Lucie…" He stopped, then took a deep breath and went on. "I've always been a lone wolf, ever since I was a boy. I've always believed I was happiest that way. And I was— I am. I guess I had a certain picture in the back of my mind of what kind of a wife I might hook up with someday—if I ever did. I didn't figure it was any too likely. I sure never had any intention of looking around for one. Now, I've— uh, I figure I may have changed my mind on that."

Boone paused. Part of him was shocked at what he was saying to her; part of him wanted to go on. "The fact is, Lucie, I've gotten kind of used to you. I've gotten used to your ways, how you do things. I can't really imagine the place without you, after you're gone. And you've had a chance to get to know me over the summer, more than any other woman's ever done. I—hell, Lucie! What do you want to do? Do you think it could—" He froze, then got out what he had to say all in a rush. "Do you think it could work between us?"

She was looking at him. He'd felt her fingers tighten in his as he'd talked. Her hand felt small and strong in his. It felt good, it felt right. "What do you mean?" It was the barest of whispers.

"Do you think we'd be good together? Do you think we should go through with it?" Boone felt his heart pounding like a hammer mill. His throat had tightened, and he'd never felt so scared about anything in his whole life as he did right now.

"You mean…*get married?*"

"Yeah."

"Are you—are you asking me to marry you?"

"Yeah."

"For real this time?"

He felt a smile begin to tug at his mouth, as he watched her expression change. He shrugged. "Yeah. For real this time."

"Oh, Boone!" She smiled at him so happily, so brilliantly, so radiantly, that it was like the sun coming out again for him. He reached for her hand and slid the ring back onto her third finger, then curved her fingers around it and closed his hand over hers.

"I take it you'll marry me, Miss Lucie," he said gruffly. He smiled down at her, wondering where that pain in his chest had gone, where that weight that had held him down for weeks now had gone. He felt light and young and...and happy.

"Oh, yes! I'll marry you." She threw her arms around his neck and he pulled her close against his chest. "Oh, Boone!" he heard her murmur into his shirt at his neck. He barely heard what she said. "I promise I'll make you a good wife, Boone. I promise you won't be sorry." She rubbed her face against the fabric of his shirt, hard, then pushed away from him and looked up.

"You're not asking me to marry you because you feel sorry for me, are you?"

"No," he said slowly, realizing it for the truth, looking deep into those eyes, those blue, blue eyes a man could lose himself in—if he didn't watch it. "I'm not asking you because I feel sorry for you."

She buried her red-gold head against his chest again and he held her tightly, feeling her shoulders tremble. He knew nothing about this bit of a woman in his arms, this woman who had the power to exasperate him endlessly, who had the power to make him laugh. He knew nothing about her, but he knew what he felt: she was his, she belonged to him, he'd never let her go.

Then he pulled her onto the grass with him, and rolled over so that he was under her. She was laughing. He loved the sound of her laughter. Her hair fell forward to brush his face, her eyes looked deep and clear as the mountain stream that ran beside them. Her hair smelled like grass and sunshine.

"Lucie Crane." He whispered the mystery of her name, then pulled her down to him and kissed her.

When they walked back to the ranch house a couple of hours later, walking slowly, both of them, and scuffing at the dust as they went, Lucie knew she'd never been happier in her entire life. She'd never dreamed such happiness existed. The man she loved, the man whose arm was even now draped loosely over her shoulder in a subtle gesture of possession, the man who'd just made love to her in a grassy bed at the side of a mountain stream—this man had asked her to marry him! And this time he meant it. She'd never felt as she felt right now, as though her skin and bones were too small to contain the immensity of her happiness, the luster of her joy.

She didn't say much as they walked back; he didn't have to. The faint smile on his mouth, the softness in his eyes— they said it all. He might not love her—not yet—but, by damn, if Lucie Crane Douglass had anything to do with it, he was going to in the end. She intended to make him so happy, that someday he'd wonder how he'd ever thought he'd be better off staying single. She would make such a difference in his life, that he was going to wonder what he'd done before, without her. Nothing—not even the prospect of coming into her full inheritance in a couple of weeks, of finally avenging herself and her mother, the woman her own family had scorned and cast out for falling in love with the wrong man, of finally beating all the Douglasses at their own game—nothing filled her with so much pleasure as the simple prospect of staying here at the Double H, fixing up the house a little, paint here, paper there, and, maybe, one day, filling the big old house with the sound of children's laughter again.

Boone's babies. Her babies. Little Harlows. All kinds and sizes of them. Lucie smiled to herself and glanced up at the man she'd promised to marry. Family. Her own, finally...and Boone's. Wait a minute, she told herself firmly, slow down. He's just asked you to marry him. You'd better wait a while to count your chickens.

"What's so funny?" Boone held her shoulders a little tighter as they walked.

"Nothing." She smiled up at him. "Just a personal reminder not to get ahead of myself."

"As you tend to do, Lucie Crane," he said dryly, but with a gleam of humor in his eyes.

"I'll admit it," she agreed.

Suddenly Boone stopped and pulled her into his arms. "Listen, Lucie—" She looked up at the sudden gruff note of urgency she heard in his voice. "Let's get married right away. Let's not bother with any of the usual nonsense— let's just go to Ketchum tomorrow and do it."

"Boone!" She felt a flush rising to her cheeks. It was so unlike Boone to embrace her like that, right where any passing ranch hand could see them. It was so unlike him to sound so urgent, so eager to marry her. Did it mean more than she thought it did? Could it mean what she hoped it did? "What's the hurry?" she asked him softly. "It's not as if it matters all that much." She blushed again, then added, "I feel as though I'm already—well, your wife."

She saw him hesitate, his eyes searching hers intently, then, with a sigh and a quick smile, he relaxed and released her. "Yeah. I guess you're right." He fell into step beside her again. "I just—I don't know, I guess I'd feel better if we were married."

"Worried what people might say?" she teased.

"What they might say about you," he admitted, with a wry smile.

"Don't worry about me, Boone. I've been looking out for myself for a long time," she said lightly. *All her life.* She had to tell him—soon. "What people might say doesn't concern me a whole lot. Never has. Besides—" She gave him an impish grin. "The whole valley's tickled pink at the prospect of marrying you off, and you know it."

"Yeah," Boone said. But he was frowning slightly. "I suppose you're right. Oh!" He stopped her at the gate to the ranch house. "I forgot to tell you—Jane left a note on the table with a message for you. Said someone named Bonnie called, said it was urgent—"

"Bonnie!" Lucie felt the color drain from her face. Why was Bonnie calling here? She'd given her the ranch number to be used only as a last resort, in a genuine emergency.

"Hey! Lucie?"

She looked at him, aware that her expression must have revealed her shock. "Yes?"

"You all right?"

Boone's tone was grim, his eyes narrowed. But she was in no position to think about that now. *Bonnie!* She must—she must have definite word on her sister. Or she must have information about Uncle Charles. Perhaps he'd found out where she was hiding, had sent one of his goons after her....

"Lucie?" She realized that Boone had grabbed her arm to get her attention.

She tried to smile...succeeded. "I—I'm fine, Boone. I'll just call her right back. I—I'll get the charges from the operator." There'd be long distance charges. Of course she'd pay them. But she was engaged to Boone now; she belonged here—

"Never mind that."

Boone hesitated, as though waiting for her to tell him what it was all about. And she would, too, later.... Now she had to find out Bonnie's news, why she'd called—

"Thanks," she said automatically. Boone let her go. He was still frowning. She bit her lip, her mind already elsewhere.

"Don't mention it," he said, but she didn't feel the sting of the sarcasm in his voice, either. Boone tugged at his hat, adjusting it. "I'll be working behind the barn if you need me."

If she needed him. Lucie hurried into the ranch house and quickly dialed. *Lord, how she needed him, how she'd always need him.*

"Bonnie?"

"Oh, thank heavens you called, Lucie! I could hardly wait to tell you. I've found her—I've found your sister!"

"Eva?" The name sounded unfamiliar, thick, on Lucie's tongue. Her knees felt shaky all of a sudden, and she groped behind her for a kitchen stool. She closed her hand over the wooden stool, worn, satin smooth, and drew it toward her. *Her sister...she really had a sister!*

"Yes! Eva Baldwin, now. She's alive and well and living in San Francisco—Sausalito, actually. Turns out she'd lived with your father for a few years after your mother died, then when he got killed in some rail yard accident or something, she was adopted by this California couple. She's married now, Lucie, and she's got two children and—and—Lucie? You there?"

"I'm here." It was barely a whisper. The tears rolled down her cheeks. "Oh, Bonnie...thank you, thank you. Thank you so much. You can't—you can't believe what this means to me." She sniffed loudly and wiped ineffectually at her wet cheeks. "Just now when everything's turning out so... And, Bonnie—I'm getting married, too. Can you believe it? He's asked me to marry him—again—and I've said I would and he wants to get married right away, but he doesn't know anything about this and—''

"*What? You're what?* What do you mean—'again'?''

Lucie could hear Bonnie's utter shock and amazement clearly through the phone lines, bounced off a satellite or two, all the way from Boston. And that made her laugh. She began to giggle. It was just nerves, she knew, but...it was just so funny, how other people thought she was so completely incapable of managing her own life. As a matter of fact, considering all that had happened this afternoon, she thought she was doing a very good job of it.

"Eva.... My sister! I just can't believe it, Bonnie. I—I don't know what to say. After all these years of wondering, in a way I feel kind of scared—''

"Getting married? Lucie, are you out of your cotton-picking mind? You can't get married! You know what your parents' will said—you're jeopardizing everything. No man's worth that—''

"This one is.''

"If your uncle finds out, you're finished—''

"That's just it, Bonnie. I'm not supposed to get married until I'm twenty-five, not without my uncle's approval. But—'' she giggled again. "It doesn't say anything about falling in love, does it? And my birthday's coming up in two and a half weeks. Then I'm a free woman—can you believe it? A free woman!'' Lucie's tears started afresh. "Just like I am out here, where nobody knows me.''

"Lucie, girl. Get a hold of yourself. Maybe I should catch a flight out there, see what's going on.''

"No! Don't do that, I couldn't risk it. What if—what if Uncle Charles has someone watching you?'' She was terrified, suddenly. She shouldn't even be talking to Bonnie on Boone's telephone. She wouldn't put anything past her uncle's goons. They dressed Ivy League, but they were goons, just the same. "Look—I'll call you later, from a pay phone. In a day or two. Promise! I'll tell you everything then. Oh, Bonnie— I'm so happy! You just can't imagine how happy I am."

Then, when Bonnie had reluctantly hung up, Lucie put her head down on her arms and sobbed. A sound behind her, the scrape of a boot heel on the linoleum, a cleared throat, made her sit bolt upright, fear hammering at her heart. She turned, hastily wiping her eyes.

"Oh!" It was Boone. How long had he been standing there?

"Happy, huh? To tell you the truth, sunshine, you don't look so happy to me."

Chapter Thirteen

His voice was quiet but intense. "Want to tell me about it?"

"Oh, Boone...I—I don't know where to begin." She blew her nose with a tissue she'd found in her pocket, then wiped again at her puffy eyes. She must look a mess!

Boone walked toward her slowly, until he stood just in front of her. She heard each step he took. Separately, clearly, distinctly. She looked up, her eyes swimming with tears, and he reached forward and pulled her into his arms. His arms were a shelter, warm and protective, from the storm of emotion she'd been feeling. "How about at the beginning, Lucie? Hmm? That's always a good place."

She looked up, saw his faint smile and serious eyes, and blew her nose again. "Okay...okay." But she couldn't start at the beginning, could she? She couldn't just burst out with everything now, just when he'd asked her to marry him, *really* marry him this time. He'd wonder why she hadn't told him before. And she should have. No, she couldn't tell him the whole story now. This wasn't the right moment. She needed time, more time, time to organize in her own mind what she wanted to say. But the discovery of her sister, of how Bonnie had finally tracked down Eva...that was different.

"Who's Bonnie?" He was helping her, giving her a place to begin.

"Okay. Bonnie's a friend of mine. We've, uh, we've known each other since we were kids. She's my best friend, and she's, well, she's a private investigator now and—" She saw Boone's eyes narrow. "Bonnie's been doing something for me, kind of a job. She's been trying to track down my sister and my father and find out if I have one and—"

"Hold on! One thing at a time. Have one what? Where's your sister? Why did she have to track her down?"

Boone smiled, and the patience she saw in his eyes, the warmth, the interest, gave her the courage to go on. *Relax, Lucie, there's no need to tell him everything—not yet.*

"Okay." She took a deep breath. "My real mother died a long time ago, Boone, and I was adopted—by some cousins of my mother's." She looked at him, he was following what she said intently. "I had a sister, at least I *thought* I had a sister, an older sister. I used to dream about her sometimes. But the people who adopted me never told me anything about her, or even if I had one—"

"Why not?"

"I don't know. They never told me I was adopted, either. I just found out once when I was about twelve, by accident. I found a copy of my birth certificate in my father's—er, an old book, and it had my real mother's name on it, which wasn't the name of the person I'd always thought was my mother. That's when I realized that they weren't really my parents. I wasn't their real daughter."

She looked up at Boone again. It seemed very confusing,

even to her, but he was nodding, showing her that he followed what she was saying.

"What about your real father?"

Her father? Lucie swallowed, feeling again the pain of abandonment, of betrayal, of rejection, of scars that had never really healed, perhaps never would. She looked up at Boone, praying that he'd understand, that he wouldn't judge her. "He—" Her voice was just a whisper. "He was a drifter, Boone. Bonnie managed to trace him somehow...I'm not sure how. I don't think he ever married my mother."

If Boone was shocked or surprised, he didn't betray it. "'Drifter,' huh?" Boone smiled again and she felt his arms tighten around her. Then he bent to kiss her lightly. "He must have been quite a guy, drifter or no drifter, to have a daughter like you. Hmm? Should have stuck around."

"Oh, Boone!" Lucie tried to smile, then bent her head weakly against his chest and sobbed again, tears flooding afresh. Her throat ached. She felt his arms tighten around her again.

"Hey, there, sweetheart...slow down. There's plenty of time." He held her, rocked her slightly as she balanced on the kitchen stool, soothed her with his low words of comfort, of encouragement. Lucie wept for a while, then she raised her head again. She was beginning to feel better. She'd never told her story to anyone but Bonnie. It felt good, so good, to tell Boone, to let some of the ache in her heart trickle away, to ease the pain she'd carried there for so long.

"So when my parents—the people who'd adopted me— died, I decided to try and find my sister, if I really had one. Now I've found out that my sister does exist. She wasn't just a shadow in one of my dreams—" She looked up at Boone, smiling through her tears. "Her name's Eva, Boone, Eva Baldwin and she lives in California. And she has two children. I thought I was—I thought I was all alone in the world. And now I find that I'm not. I have a sister and I'm an aunt to two little children. My own flesh and blood! You don't know what this means to me, Boone.''

''No.'' His voice was quiet, a little restrained, she thought, but then she was so overwhelmed with her own happiness that she wasn't really a very good judge. ''I guess I don't know what it means, Lucie. I've always had plenty of people around that cared about me. Neighbors, family, my sister, brothers...Mattie.''

''Oh, Boone, I'm so sorry! I forgot—I didn't mean to remind you of Mattie and how you have no one now—''

''You're wrong.'' He put his finger on the tip of her nose and smiled. ''I have you, sunshine. Did you forget about that?''

''And I—I have you, Boone,'' she said shyly. He looked at her for a couple of very long seconds and then bent down and covered her mouth with his. She reached up to touch his face, to pull him down to her, to bring him closer. She was hungry for his warmth, for his taste, for his strong, sheltering arms. *What if she'd never—if she'd never met this man!* She couldn't think about that; it was an eventuality too horrible to contemplate, especially now when the feel of him, the scent of him, the taste of him, filled all her senses. Besides, it hadn't happened. She *had* met him, she was going to marry him. Nothing would stop her, nothing would come between them. Not anymore.

His hand was on her back, pressing her against him, his other arm around her shoulders, holding her tightly.... All the feelings of excitement, of danger, of exquisite expectation that she'd felt in his arms earlier that afternoon down at the creek came back to her. His mouth, familiar now, sought the deep, sweet secrets of hers, testing, questing, and she answered him fully. Their mouths matched, fused and then...with a loud groan, Boone broke away and held her tightly against his shoulder, so tightly it hurt.

"Lucie! We've got to—" He stopped, breathing heavily. Lucie felt his heart pounding under her cheek, his voice a deep rumble in his chest. "We've got to quit this—this fooling around right now, or I'm going to end up making love to you right here on the kitchen table."

She laughed softly, an ancient exultant sound, the utterly feminine sound of a woman who knows she's well desired, and he growled and bit playfully at the soft skin of her throat. "To tell you the truth, nothing would suit me better, sunshine, except that the crew's going to walk in any minute for supper and I'm pretty sure that's not what they're expecting to find on the table."

"Later?" She smiled up at him impishly, and he bent down to place a quick, hard kiss on her mouth.

"Later."

Later, Jane was back, and, of course, Boone hadn't really meant what he'd said literally, Lucie thought with a smile. But there was no more pretense of separate bedrooms, and that night Lucie lay in the half dark, in Boone's bed, and watched as the big orange harvest moon rose from behind the jagged peaks outside Boone's curtainless window. The moon rose slowly, swollen and sedate, heavy with the secrets of the planet, with the secrets of the seasons, with the secrets of birth and renewal and death, with the secrets of lovers, old and new.

Lucie whispered her own secrets, the secrets of her childhood to her lover, of how she'd yearned for the kind of love she knew other children had, of how she'd yearned for the companionship of the sister she'd never known, of how she'd yearned for a family that belonged to her, that cared for her. Boone said little. He listened, and held her, and sometimes he turned to her and kissed her and made love to her in silence, the rough urgency of his hands, the deep sweet kisses that told her that he'd never drink her fill, the way his powerful body moved over hers, claiming her, exciting her, offering her his strength, his silent pledge to protect her forever, and in the end, bringing her pure and perfect fulfillment.

She lay watching the moon, sated to the skin with his tenderness, with his passion, her tears staining the pillow slip long after Boone had finally fallen asleep. It was too wonderful, it was too perfect; how could she ever deserve such happiness? How could she possibly contain it, keep it? Yet, it seemed to belong to her, for each time she awoke, she reached out and he was there beside her. And each time he awoke, she was there.

The center of her happiness held…for nearly a week. They were days of smiles and secret glances and tumbled nights of passion and, for a while, one blended into another in her contentment. Somehow, Lucie managed to block out, to mask the reality of what she must do in another week or so, what awaited her back in Concord, what she must eventually tell Boone. A thousand times she wished she'd told him, a thousand times she'd nearly worked up her nerve to tell him, and a thousand times, at the very last moment, she weakened, afraid to jeopardize happiness today for what must be only the possibility of happiness tomorrow. Suddenly, what had brought her here—her desire to run away from her problems at Four Elms, her disappearance in the night, telling no one, her need to outwit and outmaneuver her scheming uncle, her determination to secure her inheritance despite her uncle's machinations, her need to avenge her mother—suddenly it all seemed…it seemed childish, and foolish and even a little sordid. Winning, that's all the game was about. Somehow she'd been drawn into playing their game after all, by their rules. Somehow everything that had gone before, all of it, her entire past life as a Douglass, seemed so mercenary, so very much a product of calculation and determination to succeed at any cost, acceptance of any challenger's agenda, no matter how poisoned, as long as the possibility existed of winning in the end. Winning what?

What she'd found, what she valued more than anything in the world—her love for Boone, her love for Mattie—couldn't be bought...at any price. It could only flourish freely, die freely. When it came right down to it, she was afraid of what Boone might think of her. She was afraid that her motives would not stand up to the scrutiny of the kind of man he was, a man of honor. Doing the right thing was part of the very fabric that made up a man like Boone. Doing the right thing didn't take thinking about, it didn't take planning, it didn't take strategy. Lucie was afraid her conduct would not stand up to the simple test of an honest man, and she didn't trust Boone's feelings for her enough to risk losing what they'd forged together. Not yet. She needed more time, dear Lord, more time...time to make him love her, truly love her as she loved him.

He'd never said he loved her. She'd kept her feelings to herself, hard as it was. No one as tender and loving as Boone was with her could feel mere indifference, she knew that, but she also knew that Boone regarded their liaison as one of convenience, of good sense, of measured judgment, of solid possibilities. After all, he knew nothing about her, about who she'd been all her life. But, yet, no one knew the real Lucie Crane better than he did. He'd gotten used to her, her ways, he'd said. And she'd gotten used to him, more than any woman every had, he'd said. Not the most romantic of proposals, she knew that. Still, *that* was the basis of their relationship, what they knew, what they had to build upon.

Love was...love was nothing. Love was not what he wanted, it was what he feared. If it was going to work between them—and Lucie prayed desperately every day that it would—it would be built on the simple, solid basis of them together, man and woman, two human beings who cared for each other, who cared about the land, the ranch, the Harlow tradition here; it would be built on nothing else. Love didn't come into it.

But their future was doomed, inexorably doomed. Lucie knew it for the truth as each precious day slipped by. She felt it in her bones, and knowing it sickened her, right to her soul. It terrified her. She knew it would be utterly her own fault, if it failed—when it failed. She should have told him everything long ago. Each passing day made it harder. Yet she couldn't bring herself to confess now, to beg his forgiveness. She was paralyzed with indecision, with fear.

And one evening, when Ho Pickens had come over to gossip and pick up the afghan Mattie had knitted for him— he had tears in his eyes when he took it—the entire matter was taken out of her hands, in the most unexpected way.

Lucie and Boone had been sitting companionably in the family room watching a public television program on a dry-land grazing project that Boone had been involved with the summer before, long before she'd arrived. This side of her lover fascinated her, the side that was deeply committed to improving ranching practices in his beloved valley, the side that was committed to the environment, committed to saving the Sawtooths in all their glory for future generations. If anything, it made her love him more, if that was possible. Boone was committed to more than himself, his own ranch, his own livelihood. He cared about others, about the community, about the future. It was part of his life and always had been.

The knock at the door startled her, and she watched as Boone got up, with a smile for her, to answer it. "Ho, probably. I was expecting him tonight to pick up some papers I promised him."

"Well, well…ain't this cozy?" It was Ho Pickens, all right. As usual, he was rubbing his gnarled hands together,

Lucie never quite knew whether it was from some private sort of glee he carried around with him, or if he was always cold. It was getting a little nippy in the evenings, now that it was late September. Boone had mentioned perhaps lighting a fire in the fireplace that evening, but he'd agreed with a grin when she'd said she'd rather just snuggle up to him.

But Ho's actions reminded Lucie of the afghan. She got up to get it from where it had lain on top of an old trunk in the corner, neatly folded, ever since Mattie had left for her last trip to the hospital.

"Here, Ho." Lucie held out the colorful throw to the man who would soon be her neighbor. "Mattie wanted you to have this. She knitted it herself."

"She did!" Ho took the afghan in his hands and turned it over reverently. "For me?" That's when Lucie'd seen the tears in his eyes. He cleared his throat and blinked a few times quickly.

Boone stepped forward. "I got those papers you were after, Ho. I'll just get them for you, they're in my office somewhere." And he left the room.

Ho took a seat, feeling for it almost blindly, shaking his head. "Gosh darn it, Miss Lucie. Gosh darn it, anyway. You're the best thing ever happened to that boy, y'know. Especially after what happened with his ma all them years ago. Thought he'd never put it behind him." Ho shook his head again, looking at the afghan that he'd put down next to himself on the sofa. He stroked the surface of the bright throw with one work-gnarled hand. "Mattie went to all that trouble to knit this for me?"

He seemed quite touched by Mattie's gesture. He also had the most irritating habit of changing the subject at random. Usually, Lucie had discovered, just when she was getting interested in what he was saying. "She said you needed something to cover your knees when you watched television."

Ho laughed…more of a silent extended wheeze, really. Lucie watched him for a moment, hesitated, then, with a quick indrawn breath, asked quietly, "What about Boone's mother, Ho?"

"Oh, heck, now there was a real genuine lady. Yessirree. Came from one of them top-drawer Philadelphia families back East. Rich folks. Very la-de-da." He made a gesture of dismissal. "Don't mean a whole lot of us folks out West, y'know, but them as comes from that kind of highfalutin' background always think it impresses folks more'n it does." He winked at her, as though letting her in on a big secret. "Mind you, I don't think that was true in the case of Sarah Harlow. She never acted like she was too good for anybody. No, sir! A wonderful lady and right handsome, too. Hmm." Lucie thought for a moment that Ho had lost his train of thought, but after a moment's appreciative reflection, he continued.

"Naw, she loved Boone's daddy, all right, was crazy about him even though he didn't have a whole lot of time for her. Too busy with his pictures and whatnot." He sighed noisily. "Didn't seem to work out, though. Too bad. It was pretty rough around here for a time. The Harlows was havin' to scratch pretty hard back then, not what she was used to. She just couldn't take the winters, I guess, and bein' alone, mostly, raisin' them four kids—*I* don't know." Ho shook his head and looked up at Lucie suddenly as though maybe she might put forward a theory as to what it was that made a woman unable to stick it.

Lucie looked at Ho steadily. "Uh, do you—" She swallowed, her throat dry. She shouldn't really be pumping Ho; it was none of her business. "That was an awful long time ago. Do you think that's really what put Boone off marrying?"

"Put him off!" Ho slapped his knee and snorted. Lucie winced, praying Boone wouldn't hear and wonder what was going on downstairs. "Why you couldn't drag that boy hog-tied anywhere near a single woman for years! Didn't believe it *would* work, didn't believe it *could* work. Not after his mama pined away and died here when he was just a boy carryin' a man's load on his shoulders, not after Becky McNeill dragged Carson off the ranch like she did a coupla years back. Said it wasn't fair to the young ladies, might git their hopes up 'n' he warn't the marrying kind—no way—had nothin' to offer 'em. I can see that it mighta raised their hopes, too—he's a mighty fine-looking buckaroo, he is, but gosh darn it—" He stopped what he was saying abruptly and leaned forward, his eyes twinkling.

"Ya know somethin', Miss Lucie. You're the first woman he's ever taken a real second look at—that *we* know of anyway, up here in the valley. That teacher down at Twin Falls don't count none. Can ya believe it? And now yer gettin' married. Lordy! And to think if I hadn't hollered at him to stop and pick you up that day comin' back from Ket-chum—" He grinned, absolutely bursting with pleasure at the ever-growing role he'd played in their courtship.

"How would you like some popcorn?" Lucie jumped up, desperate suddenly for something to do. "And a cup of hot chocolate?"

"Well, now, I'd hate to overstay my welcome and inter-rupt you lovebirds—"

"You wouldn't be interrupting anything." Lucie felt her cheeks flush with embarrassment. No doubt she and Boone were the subject of quite a bit of speculation in the valley. "Please stay."

"Well, then, the hot chocolate sounds awful good, I don't know whether the popcorn'd agreed with my upper plate."

Lucie hurried out to the kitchen, cheeks burning. She shouldn't have asked Ho about Boone's mother; it wasn't right. She should have asked Boone if she wanted to know anything. But she was glad she hadn't. His mother was from

Philadelphia, from a wealthy family. She'd obviously pined for her life back East and eventually died here and was buried here. Boone had shown her his mother's grave the day they'd buried Mattie. Sarah Livingstone Harlow.

What would he say when he found out about *her* family? Would he think history was bound to repeat itself? Would he think she was cut from the same cloth: a pampered rich girl who'd never fit in on a rough-and-ready Western ranch? Lord, what a mess! If only she'd had the strength to tell him before, if she'd had the courage....

When Lucie returned with a tray of hot chocolate and a big bowl of popcorn, Ho and Boone were standing together, watching the small screen. Boone had obviously rewound the program he'd taped and was going to give the cassette to Ho. But just before he stopped the machine, he flipped to a news channel.

To Lucie's absolute horror, she saw a newsreader introducing a story from New Hampshire, and then she saw a rather hazy, old black-and-white photo of herself in the background, holding a horse's bridle and the words penetrated her mind like a dental drill.

"And now our final story. An heiress from New Hampshire has gone missing. Her guardian suspects she may have been kidnapped, but so far there have been no ransom demands. More details after this message—"

"Oh!"

"Watch it there, Miss Lucie—" Ho hopped to one side, surprising her with his agility.

Lucie managed to set down her load, saving the hot chocolate, but the bowl of popcorn went flying, and one mug toppled off the tray at the last moment. "Oh my goodness, I'm sorry—" She held her hands to her hot cheeks. She couldn't believe it! Now look what she'd done! Uncle Charles was looking for her, he'd talked to the press—

"Sit down, Lucie...I'll get a cloth." Was it her imagi-

nation, or had Boone given her a very strange look? Lucie
sank to her knees, mindlessly gathering the popcorn off the
carpet and stuffing it back into the bowl. She grabbed the
remote control and turned off the set when she heard
Boone's footsteps returning. Thank heavens! At least he
hadn't heard the rest of the news item, perhaps he hadn't
noticed anything at all....

"Here ya go—hardly any dog hairs or nothing! Now, if
it hadda been *my* place—" Ho smiled and winked at her as
he gathered up a last handful and she felt like bursting into
tears. Boone returned with a cloth and a few minutes later
they were sitting down again.

Lucie racked her brain, had she imagined it all? Had there
really been an item on her disappearance on the news program? Boone hadn't looked at her again, he was talking with
Ho, about the program he'd taped, about the papers on dry-
land grazing he'd loaned Ho, on the prospects for an exten-
sion of the grazing season in the high country, about the
obligations they had as ranchers to make sure overgrazing
didn't damage the delicate ecology in the area. He seemed
perfectly normal, the way he always was. Lucie held her
hands up slightly, realized they were still trembling and in
a few minutes, she excused herself and went upstairs. It was
late anyway, she'd let Boone entertain their guest...not that
Ho Pickens needed any entertaining. She needed to be alone,
to think.

A television program! She'd never dreamed in a million
years that something like that might give her away. She bit
her lip. Had Boone noticed? That was the big question. Lucie shut her eyes and prayed, prayed hard, that he hadn't.
This is it, she swore to herself silently, this is the final push
she needed, long overdue. She *had* to tell him; she had to
tell him everything. She'd tell him tomorrow. Tomorrow
was another day.

* * *

Boone got up early and left the ranch house before Lucie got up to prepare breakfast for the men. That was unlike him. Most mornings she woke when he bent to kiss her as he left the room, or, still in bed beside her, when he pulled her into his arms for a warm morning embrace, an embrace that so often turned into something more.

But not that morning. When she awoke, he'd already left. Lucie mulled over just how she'd present Boone with the facts when he got back from wherever he'd gone. She went over it in her mind, again and again.

He didn't return for lunch. By half past two, Lucie felt she was a nervous wreck. One thing she had to do, and did, was call her uncle. Her uncle's private secretary put her through immediately.

"Lucie? For God's sake, what kind of a stupid trick have you pulled this time? Where are you?"

"Never mind. I'm fine. I'm not kidnapped or whatever all that nonsense was about on the news last night. You knew that. I'm—"

"Where are you?"

"I'm not telling you."

"Why not?"

"You know perfectly well why not. I don't want you to know. I want to spend some time by myself. I'm not coming back to Concord until my birthday. I'm sick and tired of being hounded by the kind of men you want me to see and I'm sick and tired of being spied on every moment of my life by one of your hired goons—"

"Lucie, Lucie.... Don't be silly, girl. All I've got are your best interests at heart. You know that. Rich girls in your position are the target of every good-looking con man in the country. Goons?" Her uncle laughed, that confident, overbearing laugh that she hated. "What in the world are you talking about?"

"You know *exactly* what I'm talking about! Every friend

I've ever managed to find on my own, without your per-
mission, you've ruined, male or female. Don't pretend you
don't know what I'm talking about. I'm talking about *ruined,* about contracts that are suddenly withdrawn, jobs that
suddenly vanish, credit that banks suddenly aren't keen to
extend. You're not going to ruin—'' She bit her lips. There
was no point in going into every grievance she'd ever had
with her uncle now. And she wouldn't mention Boone's
name. She shouldn't keep her uncle on the line like this,
either. She didn't trust him. ''Anyway. I'm fine. I'll be back
next week, on my birthday, not a minute before. And I want
you to call off this missing-heiress search nonsense...
please! Goodbye!''

She should have felt some satisfaction; she'd been wanting to tell her uncle a few home truths for a long time. But
the satisfaction was short-lived. What she wanted was to
have Boone come back. What she wanted was to have it all
over with and have Boone forgive her and hold her and say
none of that mattered, that he cared about her and that he
still wanted to marry her.

Next week! Was her birthday really next week? She shuddered. How could she have deceived herself for so long!
There was so little time left....

But Boone wasn't back when she put supper on the table
for the crew that evening. And he wasn't back by the time
she cleared the table to load the dishwasher and clean up.
By now, what Lucie felt was fear—cold, pure fear. It wasn't
like Boone to leave without telling her where he was going,
when he'd be back. Maybe something had happened to him,
maybe that old clunker that he drove had finally broken
down for good. Maybe—

She heard the sound of Balzac barking a welcome, of the
truck coming noisily up the drive. At last! She put down
the tea towel she was carrying and reached behind her to

untie her apron. She'd heard Boone's footsteps on the step outside. Then the screen door opened and he stepped inside.

He looked drawn and pale and tired. He stared at her for a long, long moment. Then, when Lucie nearly wept with tension, he turned and casually took off his hat and, as always, tossed it onto the hat rack with his usual easy grace. Lucie clung to the image of that movement, to the ordinariness of it. Then he looked at her again, and her heart went to her throat.

"I've been doing a little research, Miss Lucie Crane *Douglass*—"

She gasped.

"And I think you've got a little explaining to do."

Chapter Fourteen

"I know." She barely heard her own reply. She tried to swallow…couldn't.

Boone continued to stare at her, his jaw hard, his gaze black and unflinching.

"I—I can explain, Boone. I—" She stopped and this time she did manage to swallow, but the fear stayed lodged in her throat, holding back the words she wanted to say. She looked at Boone, searching for some sign of softness, of understanding, but saw none. This was a stranger; this wasn't the man who knew her better, who knew her more intimately than any other man on earth. He hadn't even come farther into the room; he had just jammed his hands in the pockets of his jeans and leaned back against the door frame, shoulders hunched. He was waiting for her explanation. His posture was a parody of a man at ease. Every line of his body screamed at her…tightness, stiffness… *outrage.*

"Well?"

"I—I don't know where to start, Boone," she began. "I—I'm sorry it happened like this—you don't know how sorry I am!" She realized she was clenching her apron with whitened knuckles and slowly reached to set it back on the counter. Why didn't he come in? Why didn't he sit down?

"So you say," he breathed, so quietly that she barely heard, but she did hear, and when she did, she reddened, and whirled to face him again.

He continued to stare at her. She lowered her eyes, unable to meet the hard demand for truth she saw there. She was ashamed of herself, that it had come to this, after all that had happened between them. Completely, utterly ashamed.

"*Are* you Lucinda Douglass?"

"Yes." She cleared her throat and repeated herself, more loudly, "Yes."

"Lucinda Douglass of Four Elms, Concord, New Hampshire?"

"Yes."

"Lucinda Douglass, sole heiress to one half of the Douglass Textile and Douglass and Hunter Manufacturing fortunes? Beloved only child of Jack and Myrta Douglass, deceased?"

She didn't reply immediately, knew her face was brick red with anguish. But she squared her shoulders, even as she flinched at the sarcasm in his voice, and she met his gaze defiantly.

"Well—*are you?*"

"*Yes!*"

There was silence for a few seconds, as Boone's gaze moved from her face to her left shoulder, down slowly, lingering on her breasts, on her waist, then returned to her face. "Funny," he said softly, "I thought you were poor little Lucie Crane, motherless child, with not a soul to help her in the world, with not a soul she could turn to for help. Wonder where I got that idea?''

She wouldn't answer. What was the point—when he was acting the way he was? Nothing she could say could make a difference, she could see that. She bit her lip, to still its trembling. Then she walked over to the counter. It took every ounce of willpower she had to pick up the cloth and continue wiping off the counter. As though nothing had happened...when everything had.

"Have you had supper, Boone?" She was proud of her control, not a shadow of what she felt evident in her voice, not a quaver. Boone didn't answer, and she turned. "Well? There's some stew left. I could heat it up in a minute if you want.''

"I ate on the way back, in Ketchum.''

Way back? Where had he been all day?

He might have read her mind. "I spent the afternoon in Twin Falls, in the main library. That's where I managed to piece together the story you've been hiding from me—hiding from us all. The librarian was *most* interested, and *most* helpful.''

The sarcasm, the bitterness, were back. Did she blame him? How could she, when she could have avoided this, all of this, if she'd only had the courage, if only she'd taken the chance, told him everything....

"How—how did you—''

"I'm not completely blind and stupid, Lucie. Although it may have seemed like it in the past couple of weeks—'' That hurt—that really hurt—and Lucie felt the pain twist like a knife in her ribs. "I got the notion it might not hurt to check things out from the item on the news last night—oh, I saw it all right.'' He grimaced. "I recognized you, even in that fancy English riding getup. You must have been—''

"I was nineteen.''

"Yeah. Well, I might have saved myself the trip. Everybody I met in Ketchum had seen the story on television and couldn't wait to congratulate me on my engagement to *a bloody heiress!*" He cursed and turned away from her to stare out the darkened window, hands still jammed deep in his pockets. "What could I say? That I didn't know? That that was the first I'd heard of it?" Lucie could just see the rim of the moon over his head. "Just what the Double H needed, everybody said...cash flow!" He cursed again and spun on his heel. *"What the hell is the meaning of this?"*

"I'm sorry, Boone. I never intended it to happen like this, I thought of telling you everything so many times—"

"Why didn't you?"

"I—I don't know," she whispered. She knew her face had gone pale again. "I—I was scared, I guess—"

"Of me?"

"Scared of what you might think of me. I—I don't know how I can ever explain everything to you now, Boone—"

"Try me."

Lucie took a deep breath, praying for calm, praying for reason to make him see that she couldn't help doing what she'd done. "I—I ran away from home at the beginning of the summer—I had to...my uncle was making my life hell—"

"How?" His voice was harsh, his eyes black, implacable, and Lucie could see a small muscle jump in his tightened jaw.

"He had people following me, spying on me everywhere I went. I—I couldn't bear it. They were private detectives he'd hired. He said it was for my own safety, but it wasn't. He just wanted to keep me under his thumb, like he'd done ever since Jack and Myrta died, since before they'd died. He wanted to find out who my friends were, where I spent my time—"

"Why, Lucie?"

"He did it because he wanted to control me, I guess, to control everything I did. He's my guardian, until I turn twenty-five. You see, my parents left me most of their money, a lot of money, but they set it up so that it wasn't really mine until I turned twenty-five. Or earlier, if I married a man my uncle approved of—" Lucie risked a quick glance at Boone. She was frightened by the coldness she saw on his face.

"Why, Lucie? Didn't they trust you?"

"No. They never did, ever. I—I think it was because of my mother. My mother fell in love with a man the family didn't approve of and they threw her out. They never spoke to her again, never gave her any money. Even when she had two small children and my father had run out on her. He was a dreamer, Boone, a drifter. He never really supported her, not properly. Then, when she died—" Lucie's voice wavered for a moment and she paused, then continued, "They took me, they adopted me, and my sister vanished and I never knew what became of her. I wasn't even sure that I had a sister. Until—until now. Until Bonnie found her."

She looked at Boone. Was it her imagination, or had she seen a flicker of her own pain in those dark eyes?

But she must have been wrong—"So that part was true, at least. Does your uncle know you've been looking for her?"

"No! He knows nothing...I don't want him to know anything. I've been very careful. He knows why I'm hiding, of course, that I want to be left alone. Never in my whole life have I ever been free to do what I wanted, free to make my own decisions, to go where I wanted—*never.* Don't you understand, Boone? That's why this last couple of months here in Idaho have been—" Lucie caught herself. She wouldn't make an emotional appeal to Boone. She didn't dare. The facts had to stand on their own. "My uncle knows

I won't come back until my birthday. Until everything is legally mine, until—"

"That matters a great deal to you." It was more a quiet statement than a question.

"Yes." She looked at him, failed to read any sympathy for her position on that stern face. "Yes, it does. I—I suppose you think that's petty and mean. But it matters. It's mine, it belongs to me. It helps to make up for what they've done to me, the lies, what they did for my mother. It's the principle involved. Don't you see? I'm not just doing it for myself, I'm doing it to—to—"

"To avenge your mother."

She looked at him, her gaze lost for a moment in his, the beginnings of hope in her eyes. Was it possible that he might understand, really understand...?

Boone looked at her for a long, long moment and then he walked toward her, away from the black square of the window behind him. Her heart began to pound. She heard each step as his boot heels struck the linoleum—right, left, right, and remembered thinking later how odd that sound was, that Boone usually automatically took off his boots outside the kitchen door, how this time he hadn't. He stopped in front of her, but his voice, when he spoke, was as harsh as it had been before.

"So that's why you wouldn't marry me last week, when I wanted you to. When you said it didn't make any difference, that we were husband and wife in every way but the eyes of the law."

Lucie knew her answer was critical, but Boone was demanding the truth and he deserved the truth. And truth was all she had left to give him, truth that she should have given him long ago.... "Yes. That's why."

He cursed under his breath and turned away from her, but before he turned, Lucie saw the swift shard of pain that pierced the blackness of his eyes. It gave her hope, the smallest glimmer of hope. He began to pace, up and down the kitchen, frowning, not looking at her. Tension mounted in the bright, cheerful room. She felt it, thick and heavy. The clock ticked on, loud in the unnatural silence—*tick, tick, tick*—until she felt she wanted to scream. It was all wrong—the room, the time of day, the sequence of events that had led to this moment. She wanted to wipe out everything, to push time back until yesterday morning when she'd woken in his arms, when he'd kissed her, all sexy and unshaven, his eyes warm still with sleep, when he'd smiled at her. Then, if she could wind time back, she'd tell him, no matter what. She'd tell him everything, and trust and believe in his feelings for her. He *must* have feelings for her!

"When's your birthday?" He was standing in front of her again.

"Thursday."

"Next week?"

"Yes." Five more days. Five too-short days.

"Why, Lucie? Why didn't you tell me all this, before?"

"Boone, I—I—" She slicked her dry lips, then began again. "Boone, I didn't want to burden you with my problems. They weren't your concern and—and I knew you were busy with the ranch, and your worries about Mattie. I was afraid you'd feel responsible for me, that you should do something…that maybe you'd try and talk me into going back. I couldn't do that…don't you see?" She looked up at him, pleading with him to understand, to say that he understood.

"You didn't trust me," he said flatly.

"Don't say it like that, so—so hard…I didn't mean it like that—"

"But it's the truth. You didn't trust me. You didn't trust Mattie."

She covered her face with her hands, took a deep breath,

a gulp of air, then, with an immense effort of will, lowered her hands. She saw the muscle tense in the side of his jaw again, his face hard with indifference. "Don't you see why I did what I did? What I *had* to—"

"No." The interjection fell like a stone into the midst of her words—quiet, merciless, cold. He turned away from her again. He walked slowly toward the door, then turned back. "What about us? What about this little game you've been playing with me, Lucie?"

"It's not a game!"

"No?" He smiled, but there was no humor in his face. He shrugged. "You mean the heiress from New Hampshire really intended to go through with it, to marry the hard-rock rancher from Idaho? That it wasn't just a way to amuse herself until she went home again? A summer affair, here and gone, just a bit of harmless fun?"

"No!"

He reached for his hat. Where was he going? He couldn't leave now; it was late. They hadn't finished talking—

"Maybe the rich little girl from New Hampshire had never had a cowboy in her bed before. Was that it? Maybe she thought it might be something different—"

"*Boone!*" She covered her ears for a few seconds. "*Don't say things like that!*" Then, weeping with rage at what he'd said, at what was happening to her, to them, she grabbed the apron she'd taken off earlier and flung it at him. It hit him, harmlessly in the chest and fell to the floor. She stared at it, at him, aghast.

"Ah, Lucie." He smiled, but again there was no humor in his smile, just a sadness she glimpsed behind the blackness in his eyes. "I'll miss you. As I said once, I've kind of gotten used to you—"

"What do you mean? What do you mean—you'll miss me?" Her words were little more than a hoarse whisper. He was leaving; he was walking out of her life. He couldn't!

"Surely you know that there's nothing more to be said, Lucie Crane," he said softly. He settled his hat firmly on his head. "You'll be gone in a few days and I can handle any questions that come up here."

"You asked me to marry you," she whispered. Her blood was pounding through her veins, first hot, then cold, then hot again. She had to do this, she had to—

"I did."

"And I said yes, I'd marry you." She saw the surprise on his face. "I thought the Harlows were men of their word. I thought when they made a promise it meant something—"

"They are—I am. But hell, you can't be serious, Lucie. You don't want to carry on with this charade any more than I do. I'm giving you an easy out, Lucie. Take it."

"I don't want out," she said. Her voice was stronger, she stood straighter. Her eyes sought his, held his. "I intend to hold you to your word, Boone Harlow. You said you'd marry me. Damn it! *I intend to marry you.*"

Boone cursed and slammed the frame of the door with his fist. Lucie saw him wince, knew it must have hurt. His face, when he turned to her, was ashen beneath his tan, tight with anger. "*Why*, Lucie? In God's name, why are you doing this to me? To us? You know how we ended up in this situation in the first place. You know why—"

"I know what you thought, Boone, but it wasn't like that for me—" She took a step toward him. "Look—I'm different. I—I'm not like your mother. Yes, I'm from a wealthy family, yes, I'm from the East, yes, I've led a pampered, sheltered life. But I'm not like her." At her mention of his mother, Boone's face had flushed, his jaw had tightened. "I'm strong, I'm—I'm happy here, I know what I want, I—"

"*Tell me why, Lucie,*" he interrupted, and his voice was harsh, thick with emotion. "Just tell me why you're doing this."

Lucie wrapped her arms around herself to stop her trembling. She raised her chin and looked Boone straight in the eye. "I want you to marry me, I want to hold you to your promise…because I—I love you, Boone."

Boone reached for the handle of the door with a loud curse. He opened it. Then he turned to her and she was shocked to see his expression, the way his eyes glittered, the way his nostrils flared with anger. "My mother's got nothing to do with this. Nothing! But even if she did, she may have been many things, Lucie," he said quietly, "but she wasn't a liar."

Then he was gone.

Boone didn't come back that night, and he didn't come to her the next night, although she knew he'd slept in the house somewhere because the shower had been used in the morning when she went to use it. She was reminded of her first morning at the Double H, reminded of the thrill she'd felt at finding the Sawtooth Valley, at finding paradise, a place she'd only dreamed of finding, remembered the excitement she'd felt in Boone's presence that first day. That afternoon, she moved her things out of Boone's room, back into the one with the white lace curtains, where she'd slept most of the summer.

Thursday was her birthday. Thursday she had to leave.

She saw Boone several times before she left. Three times she served the evening meal and he was among the other hands, and once she saw him with his back to the doorway of his room as she passed, the room they'd once shared, staring out at the Sawtooth range, hard and bright, behind the ranch house.

The morning after he'd come back from Twin Falls, she'd found a thick pile of crisp bills on the kitchen table, the sugar bowl anchoring them, and a note. "Your summer wages," it had said. She'd wanted to burst into tears at the sight. Money! As though she could, after all this, take his money!

But she had to. She had to gather up the mound of bills with a trembling hand and stuff it into her jeans pocket without even looking at it, without counting it. She knew if she didn't, there'd be hell to pay. Boone would make her take it, somehow, and she didn't want—couldn't bear—the thought of more anger between them, more terrible words. It was clear enough: he hated her, he despised her for her duplicity, for her betrayal. He could never forgive her. He wanted her gone, away from the Double H, out of his life, as soon as possible.

Once, when she put down a bowl of salad on the table with the men all seated around, she made a point of putting it next to Boone, kept her left hand on the bowl for an extra couple of seconds, hoped he'd see that she hadn't taken off his mother's ring, her engagement ring. Boone noticed, all right, and gave her a level look that brought the blood to her face and sent her scurrying back to the kitchen, ashamed.

Was this what she'd come to? A spoiled, spiteful brat who wanted to triumph over this man, to get her own way, no matter what? This man she'd professed to love? Lucie wept, then, great, gulping sobs that wouldn't quit. But she didn't take off the ring.

Tuesday evening she packed her bag with clothes and cookbooks, stuffing the knitting needles and case Mattie had left her into the side of her backpack. She'd treasure them, as she treasured her memories of the old woman who'd shown her the way to love. Who'd shown her the path to loving herself.

And, then, when the call came late that night—she took it because she hadn't seen Boone since that afternoon when he'd stared out his window, and she had no idea where he was—she collapsed again. Her uncle had traced her earlier call—hadn't she known he would?—and had phoned to say he intended to send the company's plane to bring her home again. *Home.* At that word, Lucie's defenses shattered and she sobbed into the receiver. "Yes, yes...please, bring me home again."

That was that. Next morning she called a taxi from Ketchum, telling the skeptical cabbie that she'd gladly pay him double if he'd come all the way out to the Double H. She had a plane to catch in Hailey. While she waited, she walked from one window to the other of the big, rambling ranch house, the ranch house that, only last week, she'd thought would become her home, the place she'd raise her children, hers and Boone's, the place she'd finally find the happiness she'd longed for all her life. Home free. That's what she'd thought when she'd found this valley. What a fool she was!

As she said her goodbyes to the house, to the brooding portraits of long-dead Harlows in the parlor, to the tarnished rodeo trophies on the mantel, to the knitted evidence of Mattie's industry everywhere—cushions and throws—to the faded wallpaper in the stairwell, she kept hoping and fearing that she'd hear a familiar tread, the familiar sound of hard leather heels on wooden floors. Perhaps Boone would tell her he'd changed his mind, he wanted her to come back. Perhaps he'd just say goodbye and wish her well.

But he never came. And, with ten minutes to go before the taxi arrived, she ripped a few pages out of her diary and scribbled a note to leave on the kitchen table.

Then, in a cloud of dust, the taxi arrived. She hugged Balzac goodbye, the tears spilling over and wetting the fur of his neck. He licked her face enthusiastically and thumped his tail, his big brown eyes sad. Then she was gone, and she steeled herself not to look back at what might have been.

Boone watched her leave from his vantage point halfway up the flank of the mountain. He'd seen the plume of dust approaching the ranch far below and, frowning, had got up from the foot of a sun-baked boulder, where he'd been sitting staring out over the valley as he ate the lunch he'd packed for himself that morning before she'd even woken to make breakfast for the men. He rummaged in his saddlebag for his field glasses, then returned to the boulder and hunkered down, balancing his elbows on his knees to steady himself.

Tom's Taxi. From Ketchum. His immediate frown at the presence of the the taxi forty miles from town eased as he realized what was happening. She was leaving. As for the taxi, she could afford to pay anything the cabbie asked to take her back to town. He felt a moment's pique beneath the pain. He would have taken her, if only she'd asked him.

But, of course, she wouldn't ask. He knew that. Pride. They both had plenty of that. And he hadn't given her much of a chance in the past few days. The knowledge that he'd gone so far out of his way to avoid her annoyed him. He hated the way he'd felt these past few days: unsettled, ornery with the men, irritable as hell. He'd thought he felt that way because she'd betrayed him as she had. He couldn't forgive that. But he was beginning to realize that his feelings weren't just the result of pure, cold anger at the way she'd treated him. But that was crazy! What else *could* be bothering him? Whatever it was, he didn't want to think about it. He was through thinking about Lucie Crane.

She was leaving.

He set down the field glasses on a flat rock next to him and picked up the rest of his sandwich. He finished it, slowly, deliberately, but he knew that if anyone had asked him later what he'd eaten for lunch, he wouldn't have been able to answer. Then he picked up the waxed paper the sandwich had been wrapped in, shook off the crumbs and carefully folded the paper and pushed it into his hip pocket to dispose of later back at the ranch. It was a lifelong habit, something his father had taught them all—leave the world the way you found it...or better, if you can.

He picked up the field glasses again to watch as Lucie left the house, feeling all the time that he shouldn't be doing this, that he was spying on her. He felt his jaw clench, his belly tighten, as he saw her walk out into the sunshine, her pack slung loosely over one shoulder, her body slim and straight, her red-gold hair aflame, even from this distance. He felt a quick sharp ache, just under his heart, as he thought of how she'd looked, so many mornings, that bright silken hair spread on the pillow beneath him, those blue eyes sinking deep into his, losing themselves in his eyes, even as he lost himself in hers.

When he saw her bend to haul the dog into her arms, to bury her face against his grizzled ruff, he set the glasses down with a loud curse. He forced himself not to pick them up again, just to watch her leave in the far distance, a speck of a woman in a larger speck of a red-and-white taxicab. He forced himself to relax, to let the tension ease from his throat and chest and shoulders, to loosen the tendons in his legs that had tightened in instant response to the fact that she was leaving. That he was powerless to stop her. That, he told himself over and over, he didn't *want* to stop her.

Damnation! He got to his feet suddenly and walked over to Bogart. The quickest way to forget her was to keep his mind on his work, on what he had to do, on reality. He'd lost touch these past few weeks, he admitted that. But it wasn't going to happen again.

"Whoa, boy," he soothed the horse automatically. Bogart snorted a soft grass-scented response. They understood each other, the big bay gelding and him. He knew horses, he knew cows, he knew broken-down machinery. What he didn't know was women.

Boone put his left foot into the stirrup and swung up

lightly and easily. He set off up the canyon he'd been working this morning for strays. He and some of the hands had
flushed it out earlier this week, but the cows and calves
they'd brought down didn't add up. There had to be a few
strays they hadn't caught, unless he'd lost some this year to
the cougars that stayed in the high country, or to the occa-
sional grizzly that ventured to the lower slopes looking for
an easy meal. He hoped not—his profit margin was slim
enough. That kind of bad luck was extra, the kind he didn't
need.

Boone straightened in the saddle and flexed the tight muscles in his shoulders. Then he smiled grimly to himself.
Mattie would have insisted he stick around to say goodbye
to the girl, would have said it was only right. Perhaps he
was a coward, perhaps it was a coward's way, but just now
the prospect of a skirmish with a Sawtooth grizzly interested
him a whole lot more than what he maybe should have
done—stuck around to say goodbye to Lucie Crane.

Keep busy—that was the key. But it didn't always work
that way.

The next day was her birthday, and all day long he wondered about her. Twenty-five. He never would have guessed
it that first day he'd picked her up. Seventeen, he'd thought
at first, maybe eighteen…certainly no older than J.J. But
when he got to know her better, he realized he'd misjudged
her. There were things about her that were incredibly naive—such as the time he'd discovered she didn't even know
how to brew coffee or how to load a dishwasher—but there
were things about her that weren't naive at all…the hurt
she'd suffered as an unwanted and neglected child, the way
she'd dealt with it, risen above it, the strength of courage
that had brought her to the Sawtooths one early summer
day. Brought her to the Sawtooths…and to him.

Thoughts like that made Boone angry. As angry as he'd

been that day when he'd come down from the hills to find her note to him on the table. He'd snatched it up and scanned it rapidly, as though he couldn't take in her words fast enough. And then he'd crumpled it into a ball and thrown it in the cold kitchen wood stove when he'd come to her words of love, to her words of thankfulness for all he'd done for her. *Done for her!* With a bellow of rage, Boone had thrown it away, then, that night, he had crept down the stairs to take the ball of paper out of the cold firebox and smooth it and read it again.

Then, aghast this time at his own weakness, a weakness that had settled deeper and deeper into his soul, into all the lonely corners of his spirit as he lay in that big bed he'd shared with her so many nights, this time he struck a match and set the paper afire. He watched until it burned down to his fingers, then dropped it into the stove.

That was that. He'd made a mistake, that's all. He'd misjudged her, misjudged himself. He wasn't going to ruin his life over it; he was going to learn from it. It'd be a cold day in hell before he got interested in another woman, no matter what Ho and Lyle and Alice managed to cook up. There wouldn't be anyone after Lucie, because he didn't want anyone after Lucie. What he didn't consider, what he didn't dare name to himself, was that if he couldn't have Lucie Crane, he didn't want anyone at all.

Thank God they'd planned to start fall roundup Monday morning, if the weather held. A couple of days of hard riding, chasing the cutting cows, sleeping under the stars, getting cold and hungry and tired, living on beans and bacon and campfire coffee, listening to cowboy yarns...he was looking forward to it. The company of men. Once, a couple of weeks ago, he'd considered inviting Lucie along. Fall roundup was special. It was a ritual of ranching life that never changed. It took good men and good cowponies to flush out the cattle from the hills, just as it always had.

Technology didn't change that. He'd thought she might like to see it for herself. But that's when he'd thought of her as his future wife, when he'd thought she'd like to see what he did, what his work was like, what her life would be like married to him. But now...hell! If nothing else would put Lucie out of his mind, the rigors of fall roundup would.

Saturday evening the phone rang. It was J.J. Not, Boone told himself, that he was expecting anyone else. J.J. told him first that he'd sold several of his poems to a prestigious literary quarterly—not much, but a start, J.J. said proudly—then that he'd sold three of their father's pictures, that a gallery in Seattle had told him they'd take all they could get their hands on, that Western art was red-hot in the current art market. J.J. couldn't stop laughing when he told him, and nor could Boone keep a grin off his face. If only Mattie had lived to see it! How she'd have laughed at the irony of it all.

"So the old man's finally earning his keep," Boone said. "High time." He thought of the stack of pictures up in the attic. Maybe now...

"Yeah. Can you believe it, Boone? After all the work you've had to do to get the ranch back on its feet, after Dad let everything run to hell like he did?" J.J. was obviously ecstatic. "I'll send you back that money you sent me for my tuition, as soon as the gallery pays me—"

"No need to do that, J.J. Save it for next term," Boone said gruffly. "You might need it." He hadn't realized until now how much J.J. had wanted to contribute to his own keep. He hadn't realized until now that J.J. might feel better about wanting to be a poet when he knew his family didn't approve—at least Mattie hadn't—if he was the one paying for it. A man would. It showed him that J.J. was growing up...maybe had grown up when Boone hadn't been looking. It made him feel old.

"No way, Boone! I want to send it back. You've been

carrying the whole family on your shoulders for years. I know you could use the money for the ranch—fix up that old baler or something. Buy yourself a new truck.'' J.J. had laughed again and asked him to pass on the good news to Jane…

…Which he'd done. He'd had an awkward moment or two when Jane asked to speak to Lucie.

"She's not here, Jane,'' he'd finally said. The plain simple truth was best. It was always best.

"Where is she?''

"She's gone back. Back home. She's, uh—turns out she's that New Hampshire heiress that's gone missing awhile back. Maybe you heard about her, Lucinda Douglass—''

"What?''

"Yeah.''

There was silence for a moment, then Jane continued. "Did you ask her to leave, Boone?''

"Uh, not really. She told me she'd always intended to go back anyway, she had stuff to clear up there. I think this was just a bit of a lark for her. It doesn't matter all that much.'' Lord, it hurt to say it! He cleared his throat. "Look, Jane, it's really none of your business, and I don't really want to discuss Lucie with—''

"It wasn't a lark…not for her. I'd stake my life on it. Know what, Boone? You're crazier than I thought you were if you let her go like that, if you believe something like that.''

"Maybe I am, sis.'' Boone frowned at the darkened square of the kitchen window and took a deep breath. In the far distance he could hear the sad *yip, yip, yip* of a coyote's lonely cry. "Maybe I am.''

Chapter Fifteen

Boone continued to sit at the kitchen table after he'd hung up the telephone. He didn't bother to turn on the lights. He just rocked back in the hard wooden chair, wondering about that lonely coyote out in the sage somewhere, feeling a deep regret inside that maybe Jane was right—maybe he was a little crazy. Maybe he'd already spent too much of his life in his own company. Ah, hell, he thought, pushing his fingers irritably through his hair and leaning back farther...that's just the way he was made. Couldn't be helped.

Then his mind turned to J.J.'s plans to send back his tuition. The very idea of having a few extra dollars that weren't already earmarked for a dozen projects was amazingly pleasant to consider. Let's see... Boone calculated just how those dollars would translate into bales of fencing wire, wages for an extra hand over the winter to rebuild a couple of hay shelters. The house could sure use a coat of paint, maybe he ought to make a down payment on a new baler....

No, he'd make do with the old one. Now that he'd bought that old John Deere carcass from the Babbses he'd be in spare parts for years.

He thought of the day he'd bought it. He remembered Lucie's laugh, the light in her eyes, the way she'd blinked in the bright sunshine, the way she'd held out her hand to him, as regally as though she really were a fairy princess. He'd thought of the way she'd fallen into his arms, and the way he'd held her, tight and close and allowed himself to fill his lungs with her scent, the scent of her hair, her skin. Then he recalled the way he'd put her away from him, the way he'd asserted control over the wild impulse he'd had, to kiss her, to touch her intimately, to pull her down into the long grass and make her his, right there and then—damn!

Boone got up from the table abruptly and headed for the stairs. He had some paperwork to catch up on. Sitting about mooning over a woman who'd never been the woman he'd thought she was, who'd been someone else altogether, someone else all along, was no way to get on with his life.

The next day, Boone cleared up some of the jobs he'd been meaning to do for weeks. He moved his office back downstairs to the room Mattie had been in. He cleaned the saddle he intended to use and checked the equipment and supplies he was taking on the roundup. While he was cleaning his saddle, he decided he might as well take care of the old Hermès saddle of his mother's and put it back in storage. Maybe Jane would get sentimental one of these days and want it, perhaps to pass on to one of her daughters someday. As he worked at the neglected leather, rubbing in neat's-foot oil and restoring the hardware to its original brightness, he thought of all that saddle represented. It was an English riding saddle—no horn and a low cantle—and not much good in the rough country out West. The stirrup irons were strong but delicate; they had no protective cover to guard a rider's feet from thick brush or to stop a rider's foot from slipping through the stirrup, a potentially dangerous situation if the rider was ever unseated. It was a deceptively simple piece of equipment, beautiful in its way, with smooth, clean, fluid lines, a fifth the weight of his own saddle, a brilliantly crafted example of the European saddle-maker's art.

But it didn't suit the needs of a Western rider. As his mother hadn't suited the demands of a rough-and-tumble ranching life after the genteel, ordered existence of her youth. It shook him, really, to realize how close he'd come to ending up with the same kind of woman, making the same kind of mistake. It was uncanny how similar Lucie's life had been to the one he vaguely recalled his mother talking about, dreaming of, on the bad days. The days she'd wished she'd never set eyes on the state of Idaho. Still, she'd loved his father.... He remembered them together the rare times his father spent a few days at home, remembered them touching, standing close together, smiling at each other. They'd loved each other. He couldn't deny that...didn't want to deny it. He was glad for them but at the same time he knew their lives had been hell. That kind of hell wasn't for him.

Lucie'd said she was different, that she knew what she wanted. Lucie Crane didn't know what she was talking about. Boone grimaced as he lifted the now-gleaming saddle onto the highest bar in the tack room. There! He brushed his hands on his jeans. It was safe up there, out of the way of the saddles and bridles he and the hands used every day. Still...he saw the soft glow of the fine dark leather, felt the suppleness beneath his hands, for a long time after he'd turned out the light and closed the door. And he knew he'd see it in the dark corners of his mind for a long, long time....

Fall roundup would cleanse him, heal him. The magic of the mountains, the crisp air, the chill, would lift his spirit, would nourish him as it always had. Tomorrow, before dawn, he'd be riding out with some of his own hands and with a few of his neighbors to hunt for the cows that had grazed all summer in the high country. To find them and bring them down and cut his own out and bring the Double H herd down to its own home pasture for the winter.

Home. Why didn't that simple word give him the good feeling, the full heart, the sense of deep satisfaction that it always had? When had alone started to feel like plain damn lonely?

Lucie fidgeted with her fitted coral-colored jacket in the mirror, pulling it down snugly over her slim, short, matching skirt. She patted her hair, six inches shorter now and swept up into a firm but feminine knot at her nape, then she dipped her head slightly to one side and studied her reflection critically. She hesitated for a few seconds, then impatiently removed her earrings and reached for another pair, plain mabe pearls. Yes. Couturier suit and fake pearls. It suited her mood.

She was meeting Bonnie for lunch and ordinarily she would have just worn jeans and a comfortable jacket or a cotton skirt...what she was beginning to think of as her Idaho style—loose, relaxed, easy. She frowned at her image in the glass. Idaho. Since her return to Concord nearly two weeks ago, not an hour passed that she didn't think of Idaho and the Sawtooth Valley...and Boone. Her heart squeezed with pain as she saw him...smiling slightly, silent, as always, his eyes intent on her, watching her, reading her innermost dreams...and she deliberately forced his image from her mind, as she'd done so many times. She couldn't bear it.

After lunch with Bonnie, she planned to meet with her lawyers, the team that was handling the transfer of Douglass holdings and property to her. Thus, the little Chanel afternoon suit. It didn't matter anymore. She wasn't trying to make a statement with her clothes, as she'd once done, as a form of rebellion to Uncle Charles and her parents and the rest of the family. That kind of behavior was childish; she knew that now. The lawyers expected to see a resolute, competent, conservatively dressed New England heiress…that's what they'd get.

Since she'd arrived back in New Hampshire, tearstained and travel-weary, aching for nothing more than a hot bath and a long uninterrupted sleep in her own bed again, Lucie had come to realize that the few months in Idaho had changed her. Had changed her forever.

She felt stronger, she felt more confident, she felt much, much older. She knew who she was now. The ache in her heart at losing Boone never left her and she knew it never would. But she surprised herself at how coolly and competently she had dealt with her Uncle Charles. And she'd been surprised at how her new determination seemed to facilitate her goals, in a way that her pleading and sulking and nagging never had. Her uncle had been practically agreeable, and, once he knew that she didn't intend to take an active hand in the affairs of the family firm, positively helpful.

It was his greed, she knew, that had led him to spy on her, to interfere in her friendships. He was so desperately afraid that she'd end up under the influence of someone he didn't approve of, someone he couldn't control, someone whose interests might jeopardize the profitability of the family firm. That's why he'd inundated her with young men he knew he could influence, hoping she'd marry one of them and he could keep on overseeing the affairs of his very rich young niece, sure that the status quo would continue. It would have made her laugh, really, if it hadn't been so painful, when she thought of how mystified he'd always been that none of the men he introduced had interested her in the slightest.

Now she knew she could count on that same greed to serve her purposes. She was retaining ownership of her family's shares in the company, but she was leaving the helm to Uncle Charles. She knew she could count on his greed to keep Douglass and Hunter profitable. His gratitude, once he learned of her plans, positively sickened her. After all he'd been involved with, even back in the days before she'd been born, when her mother had been tossed out without a penny, after everything was said and done—even giving him credit for perhaps having the best, if misguided, motives— her Uncle Charles still thoroughly nauseated her. She wanted as little to do with him as possible. Except, what *was* she to do now, to do with the rest of her life...?

"Yoo hoo!"

Lucie made her way through the crowded restaurant to the window table where she'd spied her friend, waving wildly. Bonnie hadn't changed a bit since college. She was petite, brown-eyed, brown-haired...just about the last stereotype anyone might have of a private investigator. Maybe that's why she was so successful: no one noticed her—until it was too late.

"Bonnie! Oh, it's so good to see you." Lucie hugged her friend, oblivious to the stares from neighboring tables. Since Lucie's return, her face had been splashed in all the newspapers, her uncle had been quoted pooh-poohing the return of his niece who'd just "taken a little private holiday" and scotching rumors the press had uncovered about the existence of a certain Idaho rancher. Lucie had been horrified to see the very possibility of Boone's existence bandied about like that. Thank God he need never know! That kind of invasion of his privacy would hurt him, hurt him terribly, she knew, and it was then she had realized, perhaps for the very first time, just how unlikely a pair they really were, how absolutely separate their worlds were. Had Boone seen that right away? Had he been right when he'd said they had nothing more to say to each other? She didn't believe it; she *wouldn't* believe it!

"So...tell me all about it. Everything!" Bonnie leaned forward, her brown eyes dancing. "You look great, Lucie, really great. Have you put on a few pounds? Suits you. You were getting too skinny. Did you call your sister in California yet? Tell me about this rancher!"

"You, too? Mattie always said I was too skinny." Lucie laughed and told her friend that, yes, she had called Eva, and that they had laughed and cried for hours on the phone. Eva had told her how their father had been a rambler, an irresponsible charmer who'd shown up at school one day just after their mother had died, while Lucie was being cared for by a neighbor, and had whisked her away to live with him, riding the rails, moving from town to town, from odd job to odd job. It had been an exciting life for a child, Eva told her, and her memories of it to this day were still of all the fun they'd had. She told Lucie how their father had tried, at first, to regain custody of Lucie, too, but that the vast Douglass wealth and the threat of litigation had, in the end, intimidated him. That, and the fact that he had probably realized, Eva believed, that his youngest would have a far better life—at least materially—than he could offer her. On the other hand, his threats to go public with his story stopped the Douglasses from trying to regain Eva, as well. Eva told her how their father had always regretted being unable to care for his youngest daughter, and that piece of information, true or not, was something Lucie clung to. Somehow it eased the deep, dull ache she'd always felt at being rejected by her natural father. She'd never even known who he was. At least now he was a shadowy figure in her imagination, a figure who gained strength and substance as Eva related details from her memory. She told Bonnie she'd made plans to go to California to visit her sister and her sister's family soon.

"And she's expecting another baby—in two more months. Isn't that exciting?" She smiled at her friend, aware at the same time of feeling a deep and terrible ache at her own loss, guilt at knowing she envied her sister's happiness. "So I've finally got the family I wanted, Bonnie. My sister, a niece and nephew, another on the way. I can never thank you enough for what you've done for me."

Bonnie patted her hand and said dryly, "Just doing what I do best, dear. The question is this, Lucie. Eva's family isn't the family you wanted, is it? Not really, wonderful as that is. You can't fool me, you know. I'm your best friend. Now what happened to that rancher, Lucie? The man you told me about who'd asked you to marry him...*twice?*"

"Well..." Of course, Lucie couldn't lie to her friend. Nor would she. Her fingers automatically went to the place where Boone's engagement ring had circled the third finger of her left hand. Her hand was bare now, the ring on a thin gold chain about her neck, hidden beneath her blouse. "It's all off now. I've—we've changed our minds. These things happen. But it's true...he did ask me to marry him twice—" She tried to laugh, succeeded, barely. "Sounds kind of crazy, doesn't it? The first time wasn't for real, though. It was just because his grandmother insisted and I—I thought she might get better if her mind was at ease over Boone—"

"His name is Boone?"

"Yes. Boone Harlow. Actually it's D. Boone Harlow..." Her mind wandered slightly and she frowned. She never had known what the *D* stood for.

"Nice name. God, Lucie. I can see him now. Tall?"

"Yes."

"Dark?"

"Yes."

"Handsome?"

Lucie smiled, a private, secret smile. *Handsomer, truer, stronger than I ever knew a man could be.* "Yes. I think so anyway, but you'd probably think he looked a little too rough around the edges."

"Sure I would. And I suppose he carries a saddle around and big coils of rope over his shoulder and wears those sexy beat-up leather chaps—"

Lucie laughed. "Not *all* the time."

"Lucie, girl, you must be *crazy*—what are you doing back here? There's no men here, there's just a bunch of oversensitive, overdressed overachievers that you can barely trust with your unlisted phone number, let alone lean on the way a woman needs to lean on a man sometimes—"

Bonnie was teasing her, she knew that, and yet she knew that what her friend said was true: Boone was worth fighting for—Jane had told her that. She knew he was; of course, she knew he was—but what else could she have done? She'd left him the note, hadn't she? She knew how he must be feeling—she'd betrayed him. Trust wasn't earned, it was given freely, it was part of loving. Betrayal was a knife in your back in the middle of the night; betrayal poisoned your soul. No one knew the pain of betrayal more than Lucie Crane Douglass did.

Bonnie didn't pry. Once Lucie had told her friend that it was off and had given her a few of the details, Bonnie backed away. Still, something she had said in passing made Lucie think. All through the long meeting with the lawyers, she was preoccupied. She had dinner by herself at a favorite restaurant, a student hangout where eccentricities were the norm and no one bothered the young woman in the Chanel suit. Then on the way back to Four Elms she had the bad luck to get stuck in traffic and had plenty more time to mull over Bonnie's remark.

Bonnie had said that Boone wouldn't have reacted the

way he did if he didn't love her. Well, she didn't believe that. She knew Boone didn't love her, she knew how he felt about love. He'd reacted the way he had because she'd let him down, plain and simple. Still he must have cared...must have cared a little or why would he have been as angry and upset as he was? What he considered to be her lack of trust in him must have hurt him or he wouldn't have said the things he did, and...if he hurt, then that meant he cared, too.

It wasn't much, but it was a start. It was a place to begin again. To try to pick up the pieces...maybe. She knew she couldn't live with herself if she didn't try. Maybe she ought to go back to Idaho as soon as she could, before she went out to California. Maybe she ought to try and see if she and Boone had something worth fixing. If he'd listen to her this time. He'd had nearly two weeks to think about it.

What did she have to lose? Lucie took a deep breath. *Nothing. She had nothing to lose.* Only her pride, and her pride wasn't worth much these days anyway. And she had everything—*everything*—to gain. If he didn't want her, told her to leave again, well...so be it. Was she a quitter? No. Was she a fighter? Absolutely! She felt her New England spine stiffen; she held her head a little higher, a little straighter.

By the time she turned into the long driveway that led to Four Elms she was actually feeling a little better. It was scary, sure, the very thought of going back to the Sawtooth Valley. Everything was different now. But the alternative was the absolute certainty of a future without the man she loved: exactly what she faced now. She had to make one last effort.

She parked her car around the back of the house and headed for the side entrance, then remembered that she'd left her gloves on the seat and went back. As she bent to pick them up from the floor on the passenger side, where they'd fallen, Lucie had a strange sense of déjà vu, as though she'd done just this in another time, another way. But that was silly. She straightened and stretched.

Lord, she was tired! She looked at the rambling old mansion outlined against the night sky, and shivered. Ugh! Four Elms wasn't a home; it was a centerpiece of New Hampshire pride that stretched over a half-dozen generations. More a museum than a home. Always had been, for as long as she could remember.

Lucie went round the side of the house. To her surprise, Mr. Pip came hurrying to meet her. He and his wife had been fixtures at Four Elms for as long as anyone could remember. "Mr. Pip" dated from the days when Lucie couldn't pronounce his proper name—Phillips—any other way.

"Thought you'd have gone to bed, Mr. Pip," she said. Lucie had never stood on ceremony and there'd never been any question of having doors opened and closed for her. She'd even have preferred to get her own meals these days, if Mrs. Pip would have allowed it.

"Oh, no, Miss Lucie, I, er—"

Lucie thought the old man looked uncharacteristically awkward. Her eyes narrowed. "What is it, Mr. Pip?"

"Ah, well, you see, there's a, er, a *gentleman* come to see you. I showed him into the study an hour ago. He's there now. He said he'd wait—"

"A gentleman?" Lucie felt her heart skip a beat and her palms were suddenly clammy. It seemed sacrilegious, somehow, to wipe them on the skirt of the Chanel suit, but she did anyway.

"I tried to stop him, Miss Lucie. I told him you weren't home at the present, but—well, he was very insistent—"

"Did he say who he was?"

"A Mr. Harlow, I believe he said, from Idaho."

Boone! Boone was here in this house—right now! Lucie

knew she'd paled, because she'd seen the look of concern on the face of Mr. Pip.

"Do you know him, Miss Lucie?"

"Yes. Yes—I do." Her voice was little more than a hoarse whisper.

"You don't look well, if I may say so, my dear. Shall I call the police and have him thrown out?"

"Oh, no!" Lucie put her hand on Mr. Pip's arms. It felt so thin and old beneath her palm. "No. Actually, I—I know him very well, Mr. Pip, and I—I'm delighted that he's here. It's just that it's such a surprise. That's all. I had no idea he was coming."

She smiled and the elderly manservant gave her a somewhat bewildered smile back. She patted his arm. "I'm fine. Thanks for telling me." Impulsively she placed a kiss on his withered cheek. He patted her hand in return, and she watched as he made his way slowly up the back stairs.

Boone was here! Lucie put her palms to her cheeks, which were hot now. She wanted to rush in to see him, she wanted to duck into the powder room to see if she looked all right, if her hair was a mess, she wanted to rush back outside and get back in her car and drive somewhere far away and very dark, to hide, to give herself time to think. To figure out what she'd say to him.

Boone was here at Four Elms. Why had he come?

In the end, she went straight to the study and paused only a few long painful seconds before opening the door quietly and stepping inside.

He was standing with his back to her, half turned toward the fireplace, which was blazing. Mr. Pip—or someone— must have lit the fire to fight the cool autumnal gloom. Boone was leaning on one arm propped on the mantel as he stared down into the dancing flames. Lucie didn't think he'd heard her come in.

She cleared her throat nervously and he straightened and turned toward her.

"Boone—" she began, then stopped as he walked slowly toward her, looking very tall and very rugged and so, so very beautiful that he took her breath away. Her heart twisted and squeezed and she shut her eyes briefly to stop the pain. How she'd missed him! How had she ever thought, even for a moment, that she could live without him? When she opened her eyes he was standing in front of her, his hands thrust casually into the pockets of his trousers—a very presentable-looking jacket and trousers, too, only slightly Western in cut, she noticed with the one very small part of her brain that did not seem to be affected by his presence—

"Hello, Lucie." His voice was deep and dark and quiet, exactly as she'd remembered it. It sent shivers down her spine. His eyes were direct, as always, on hers. Clear, intense—she felt she'd drown in them if she didn't wrench her own away.

She cleared her throat again and took a small step to one side, her hands fluttering in the direction of a chair.

"Well! Isn't this a surprise—" Her voice was cracking, she knew, and she prayed for control, not to make a fool of herself. So far he'd given no indication of why he was here, why he'd come all this way....

"I'll admit I am impressed, Miss Lucie—" The soft sound of the name he'd called her most often brought quick tears momentarily to her eyes. She blinked them back. "This is very grand." He looked admiringly around the room, dark-paneled in cherrywood, furnished with leather club chairs, a highly polished seldom-used antique partners desk, gilt-framed oils on the wall—seascapes, still lifes, family portraits. "Your home is much grander than I'd expected."

His eyes held hers, and there was an alertness, a narrowness, a coolness that she hadn't seen at first.

"It's a—it's a mausoleum," she said. Her voice was still strained, but it sounded slightly firmer. She was glad.

He grinned, and Lucie felt her heart squeeze unbearably again. "Yeah. Maybe that's it. Somehow I can't imagine you as a little girl here, running around corners, hair flying, chasing the cat—"

"Is that what you think I was like as a girl?" She smiled, her heart feeling suddenly, unaccountable, immensely lighter.

"I do." His eyes held hers for a second too long, then he turned and walked casually back toward the center of the room. She followed him.

"I never had a cat, Boone. Mother thought they'd bring dead things into the house and disease. And I was never allowed a dog. Too much mess, she said. Losing hair, drooling all over everything—"

"No pets?"

"A goldfish I loved dearly. And a chipmunk down in the garden, that I'd tamed. He'd eat out of my hand—"

Suddenly Boone was close, too close. She looked up at him, and he took his hands out of his pockets and put them on her shoulders. She could feel the strength of his hands, the warmth, through the thin wool crepe of her jacket. "Ah. You have quite a talent for that, Miss Lucie."

She frowned slightly, so aware of his touch, of his nearness, that she could barely think. Talent?

He smiled. "A very special talent. For having things eat out of your hand. Chipmunks, dogs, men...me."

Him? She looked at him again, her mouth trembling. She didn't trust herself to speak.

"Me." He looked at her, almost sternly, for a very long time, but he made no move to draw her closer. "Lucie," he went on, very softly. "I came here for one reason, one reason only. I'm going to tell you why, and I don't want you to interrupt me, not until I've said what I came to say.

"I'll admit, when I saw where you lived, when I saw the reality of what you'd told me, that your family was very wealthy, that you, having inherited everything, were very rich—I'll admit I had second thoughts. I'll admit the notion struck me that I'd probably be a lot better off turning that rental car right around and heading back to the airport. Back to the Sawtooth Valley, where I belong.

"And maybe I should have. But—" He stopped and Lucie saw him take a deep breath. His fingers were tight on her shoulders, now, so tight it nearly hurt. But she wouldn't have said anything, not if the house had fallen down around them. "But I didn't. Because I hadn't done what I'd come to do."

He took one hand off her shoulder and moved it up so that his fingers slid under her hair at her nape and his thumb brushed her cheek lightly. He looked down at his hand, at her cheek, at her mouth. He was frowning slightly, and Lucie didn't even dare to breathe.

"When you left the Double H, I—I'd never felt so lonely in my life. Not when my brother left, not when Mattie died. You'd only been there a short while, one short summer, but I realized you'd changed something in my life, Lucie, something in me. I knew I'd never be the same." His voice was huskier, thick with emotion, and Lucie knew her own tears had spilled over to run down her cheeks. "I didn't know what it was. I thought it didn't matter, thought that I'd get over it. I thought I'd be happy with what had made me happy before—with riding, with chasing cows, with putting in a hard day's work, just like I'd always done. But it didn't happen.

"I felt this great big hole in me, Lucie. I thought when I went up into the mountains on the fall roundup, the mountains would heal that empty place in me the way they always had. But it didn't happen this time, Lucie, and when I came back down to the Double H, going into that dark, empty ranch house was the hardest thing I ever had to make myself do. And—and I knew then that whatever it was, it *did* matter, and that it wasn't going to go away. I knew I had to come after you and tell you how I felt, and…and maybe bring you back again.''

"Boone—"

"Hush!" He put his thumb lightly against her mouth. "Let me finish." She felt her lips trembling against the hardness of his thumb. She met his gaze again, his eyes burning into hers, intense with a light she'd only glimpsed before. She tried to swallow back the tears.

"I'm sorry I treated you the way I did. I know you didn't mean to hurt me, that you don't have a hurtful bone in your body. I was hurting, and I just lashed out at you and—and hell! I can't justify my behavior, but I want you to know I regret taking such a damned superior line. As if I was the only one who'd ever had to make a tough decision—"

"Boone. Please, I—"

"I'm not finished. Listen, Lucie—I asked you to marry me the first time because, well, because Mattie wanted it— you know the reasons for that. I asked you the second time because I thought maybe there was a chance of things working out between us and it seemed the easiest way out of a mixed-up situation." Lucie tried to speak, but again he silenced her. "I never thought I'd ever ask a woman to marry me three times. But that's what I want—I want you to be my wife, Lucie Crane. I still want to marry you, if you'll still have me."

"Oh, Boone—"

"This time is different, Lucie. I'm asking you this time because I love you." She couldn't stand it anymore. She bent her head to rest her forehead against his chest, and felt him cradle her head with his hands. Then he tilted her head slightly, so that she had to look up at him again. "It's taken me a long time, but I've finally figured it out. I love you.

And I don't think I can stand living by myself anymore, without you—''

"Boone—'' She wanted to laugh through her tears. She'd never heard him talk so much at one time in his entire life!

"I'll understand if you don't feel the same way, after—after everything that's happened. I'm sorry about how I treated you, the things I said, but I can't say I'd have done it any differently, considering. And hell! All this would be tough to leave behind—'' He waved briefly around the lavishly furnished room.

"Boone—''

"Hmm?''

He looked so serious, so sober, so well worth loving. *Boone Harlow loved her!* All she felt was joy, joy, joy…joy that was bigger than she could bear. She knew the tears were streaming down her face, knew her hair was a mess, and didn't give a damn about any of it.

"Boone Harlow,'' she whispered, "just shut up and kiss me.''

And he did. He bent his head and his mouth claimed hers, hard and hot and demanding. There was nothing apologetic about his kiss, nor would she have wanted it. It had been so long…so long! He was her lover again, her dark and silent lover, the man who'd touched her heart as no other man ever had, as no other man ever would. She was ready for him—more than ready—and she met his every demand with her own, tasting, exploring, reacquainting herself with his scent, with the texture of his mouth, with the feel of his body, so strange, so familiar, so hard and strong against hers. He kissed her until she felt herself go limp against him, her body trembling against his, her mind swamped with pleasure.

Boone finally wrenched his mouth from hers with a loud groan and held her tightly in his arms, his face buried in her neck, in her hair. Then he raised his head and looked down at her. He was smiling, and his eyes were black as midnight. "Does that—does that mean what I think it means?" His breathing was as rough and ragged as her own. "Does that mean you'll marry me, Miss Lucie?"

"Yes, yes, *yes!*"

"Right away?"

"Yes!"

"Tomorrow?"

"If we possibly can," she whispered. She wiped her eyes against his shirt and heard the deep rumble of his laughter. "Oh, Boone. Please don't ask me to marry you again—I don't think I could stand it."

"I won't." He laughed. "This is the last time. I promise."

She leaned back in his arms, slowly studying each tiny, well-remembered feature of the man who'd come back to her, who'd come back to her out of her deepest dreams. She remembered a scrap of poetry, knew now what it meant. *Drink to me only with thine eyes.* "I love you so much. I always have, you know—"

"Not always."

"Yes. As long as I can remember, since way before Mattie died."

"Hell. I knew I was in deep trouble the day Ho talked me into stopping to pick you up. Ho knew it. Everybody else seemed to know it." Boone looked down at her and smiled. Lucie couldn't stop smiling. "But I'd convinced myself that it was just a bad case of—well, lust. I'd never looked at a woman before and known so quickly that I wanted her, the way it happened with you. It scared me, Lucie."

"What about that teacher in Twin Falls?" she teased, reaching up to twine her fingers in his dark hair, to pull gently. "The one Mattie took me for that first day?"

"Yeah. I cared about her." Lucie looked at him, in mock

outrage. "While it lasted. But we both knew it wasn't the stuff that dreams are made out of. She's married now. She's happy."

"Boone?" The talk of dreams had touched her heart.

"Hmm?"

She looked up at him, sideways. "Is this really true—that we're really getting married, that you really love me, that—that I'm going to come back to Idaho with you and someday we'll have a family. Together. Is this—is this happy ever after? For real?"

"True. All of it. I love you and you're going to be a rancher's wife and we're going to have babies together—lots of them. The sooner the better, if I have anything to say about it." He gave her a hard, quick kiss full on the lips. "And, yes, we're going to live happily ever after, sunshine. We already are."

He grinned suddenly and swung her around and around, with a wild whoop, just the sort of whoop he probably used on his cows, she thought. She shrieked and clung to his neck, and just as he stopped and set her down, she saw the study door open slightly and, behind it, the astonished face of Mr. Pip.

The dear! He was just checking to see that she was all right; he was worried about her being in here alone with this wild man from Idaho. Lucie put her finger to her lips and winked and smiled. And Mr. Pip broke into the most amazing smile, a smile that lit up his whole face, and he nodded and returned her wink and backed silently away, closing the door firmly as he went.

Was she all right? Lucie reached up again, to pull Boone down to her, and as his lips met hers, as she felt his arms tighten around her, she knew she'd never been more all right in her entire life.

"Boone?" Lucie lay, completely happy, in Boone's arms next morning, admiring the sun's beams dancing on her

ring, newly repositioned on her left hand. Boone had taken
it from the gold chain on her neck and placed it on her
finger when they'd come upstairs to her room the night before, laughing, stopping to kiss at every couple of steps.
He'd finally swept her up into his arms and carried her the
remaining dozen steps, growling his impatience into her ear.
Then, safe inside her thoroughly feminine room, he'd silently taken her clothes off, then his, and had made thor-
ough, satisfying, passionate love to her in her four-poster,
amid the tangles of eyelet and lace and rose-patterned linen.

They'd made a baby. She knew in her woman's heart that
they had.

Now the sun was streaming through the sheers at her
chintz-curtained window looking out onto the garden, and
she thought of the contrast between that window and the
one in Boone's bedroom back home. The ranch was already
home to her, in a way Four Elms had never been. Still, it
was fitting that they begin their lives together here. Fitting
that they make love in this bed that had been in the Douglass
family for generations, fitting that they conceive a child
here. Four Elms and her New England legacy would be as
much a part of their children's lives as the Double H and
the wide-open spaces of the Sawtooth Valley. Lucie felt
limp and lazy, and completely happy. She was absolutely
certain in her own mind that, yes, this was happily ever
after.

"Hmm?"

She turned to him, kissed his shoulder softly, lightly.
"Boone? You never told me—what does the *D* stand for in
your name?"

She felt him tense slightly, then relax, and when she
looked at him she was surprised to see the rather pained
expression on his face. "Daniel."

"What!" Lucie clapped her hand over her mouth, stifling a shriek of laughter.

"Yeah. I told you, my father was a bit of an eccentric and he was the one who named us." Boone grinned, a little sheepishly. "Dad was crazy about the old wild West. Actually, I didn't get off so badly."

"Carson?"

"Kit."

"You're kidding!"

"No. Jane's actually Calamity Jane Harlow, if you can believe it. Don't ever tell her I told you."

"What about J.J.?" Lucie felt her eyes widen more and more in utter astonishment. Just what kind of a family was she marrying into?

"Let's just say his teachers used to call him Jesse."

"Jesse James! But he was a train robber!"

"Dad wasn't fussy. He just liked grand gestures—action, adventures, dreams." Boone turned on his side toward her, supporting himself on one elbow. He looked sleepy and sexy and one hundred percent man. Her man. The father of her children.

"We're going to name our first daughter Mattie, regardless of your family tradition," she announced.

"Mattie'd be proud."

"I wished she'd lived to see us married, Boone," Lucie said softly. "She wanted it so much."

"I think she knew. Don't you?" He stroked her cheek lightly with one finger, and she knew she'd never seen more love in a man's eyes. For her. And knew that she never would.

"Mrs. Daniel Boone Harlow," she whispered, and she knew her heart was shining from her eyes.

"Still figure I'm worth marrying, sunshine?"

"You bet I do!" And she threw her arms around his neck and pulled him down against her, laughing, to kiss her all over again.

Epilogue

They were married a week later, as soon as they could manage it under the laws of the state of New Hampshire.

Boone figured it was a good idea to get married by a magistrate in Concord, because he wanted to avoid a large wedding and he knew there'd be a terrific fuss if they were married in the Sawtooth Valley. He needn't have wasted any time thinking about that—there was a terrific party anyway awaiting him and Lucie when they returned to Idaho.

Lucie figured it was a good idea to get married before a magistrate in Concord because she didn't want to take the chance of anything else going awry, nor did she want to be asked to marry the man for the fourth time!

She decided to lease Four Elms at no cost to the Concord Historical Society, which had tried to convince the Douglass family for years to open the mansion to the public on a seasonal basis. Lucie didn't care if they opened it every day of the year. Uncle Charles was horrified at the thought of the public tramping through the family mansion. Perhaps, Lucie speculated, he'd had ideas of taking it over himself. The staff was given the option of continuing on with the historical society or taking an early pension. Some of the gardeners stayed on; Mr. and Mrs. Pip retired.

Lucie was sad to say goodbye to them; theirs were the only kind faces that she remembered from the many painful years at Four Elms.

As for the money...

"Boone," Lucie said one day, perhaps the third or fourth day after Boone arrived in Concord, "you aren't going to be one of those silly men who won't let his wife spend any of her money on the family ranch, are you?" She was very worried that Boone might turn out to be *exactly* that kind of man.

Boone had been silent for several moments, apparently giving the matter his complete attention. "I know a lot of men would feel that way, Lucie," he'd said, finally. "They'd think it was a question of pride. I have my pride, too. I'm pretty sure you know about that." He smiled at her, then, that slow, sexy smile she loved to see. "But that isn't the way I define it. You can spend your money how you want. The ranch is free and clear now, the bank's paid off and I intend to build it up gradually starting next year. Naturally I see ranching as something I know quite a lot about and you know hardly anything about and I don't expect you to interfere in that—"

"Naturally."

"So whatever else you'd care to do, you're free to do it, as far as I'm concerned."

"Thank goodness!"

"Any particular reason you're asking?"

"N-no, not really," Lucie said mysteriously. But of course there was. When they got back to the Double H, he surprised her with the new pickup he'd bought with the proceeds from some of his father's paintings. Being a practical man, Boone had discarded the idea of a new car, a pickup being far more useful around the ranch. Lucie surprised Boone with her wedding gift: A brand-new, state-of-the-art, shiny red baler. When he saw that piece of machinery sitting in the machine shed, purchased and delivered with the help of Lyle and Ho, Boone knew any doubts he might have been harboring about his new bride—just might have—had vanished: she understood him perfectly.

They honeymooned at the Double H, and a month later, Lucie made the long-awaited trip to California with her husband.

There, surrounded by the love of her sister and her sister's husband and their two young children, Lucie didn't think she could bear the immensity of her newfound happiness. The second night at her sister's, she turned to Boone the minute they'd closed the door to the guest bedroom, and, to his dismay, burst into tears.

Hormones, he thought, taking her in his arms. Or maybe her soft heart. She was the softest-hearted woman he'd ever met. How he loved her....

"All my life, I've wanted to find my sister," she sobbed, "and now I've not only found Eva and her family, but I've got you, and our baby and—and—"

She put her hand on her still-flat belly, where her unborn baby, hers and Boone's, conceived as she'd hoped that first night in New Hampshire, lay in peace. Her sister's third was due any day. Boone noted her gesture, and placed his hand, large and warm, over hers. His other arm tightened around her shoulders and he smiled down at his wife.

"That should make you happy, darling."

"It does. That's why I'm crying—it's because I feel so happy. Don't you see?"

Wisely Boone just nodded and tightened his arms around his wife and didn't say a word. But he continued smiling down at her, and after a moment or so, she began to smile back through her tears.

"Did you ever think, Boone, that things would turn out like this?" She sniffed loudly, completely earnest now. "I've got the family I always wanted and—"

"And don't forget Ho, and Lyle, and Alice, and Jane and my brothers. And everybody else in the Sawtooth Valley. They're family, too, you know. The kind you can count on."

"I wouldn't dare!" she said, laughing. "But what I mean is, my father was a drifter, your father was a dreamer and— and here's the two of us... I can't wait to go back home again, can you?"

"No." Boone hugged her tightly and closed his eyes as he felt her bury her wet face against his shirt, as he felt her heart beat strongly against his. "It takes all kinds of dreams to make a world, sunshine. All kinds."

* * * * *

A LETTER FROM THE AUTHOR

Dear Reader,

Situations where a man and a woman marry for reasons other than love—marriages of convenience—have always fascinated me. A visit to Idaho's magnificent Sawtooth Valley gave me the perfect setting for a story of two people coming together for practical reasons that had nothing to do with love. In Boone's case, he'd given up on true love but was willing to take a chance on Lucie, the young hitchhiker he'd hired as a cook for the Double H and the last woman to ever fit into a rough ranching life in the middle of nowhere. Lucie yearned for a home, and that's exactly what Boone offered.

A chance meeting with a Sawtooth Valley cowboy who, as he told me, "lived alone," got me thinking about how hard it might be for a man tied to the land here in God's country to find someone to share that life.

The landscape was my starting point; the chance remark of the cowboy gave me my inspiration. I hope you enjoy the story of Lucie Crane and Boone Harlow.

Judith Bowen

SILHOUETTE *Romance*

Escape to a place where a kiss is still a kiss...
Feel the breathless connection...
Fall in love as though it were
the very first time...
Experience the power of love!

Come to where favorite authors—such as
**Diana Palmer, Stella Bagwell,
Marie Ferrarella** and many more—
deliver heart-warming romance and genuine
emotion, time after time after time....

Silhouette Romance—
stories straight from the heart!

Silhouette®

Where love comes alive™

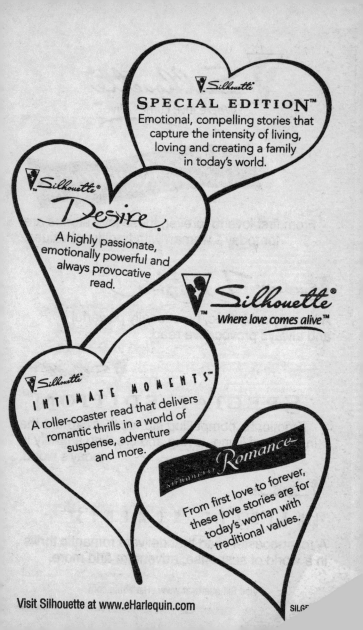

V. *Silhouette*

SPECIAL EDITION™

Emotional, compelling stories that
capture the intensity of living,
loving and creating a family
in today's world.

V. *Silhouette*®

Desire

A highly passionate,
emotionally powerful and
always provocative
read.

V. *Silhouette*®

Where love comes alive™

V. *Silhouette*

INTIMATE MOMENTS™

A roller-coaster read that delivers
romantic thrills in a world of
suspense, adventure
and more.

Silhouette *Romance*

From first love to forever,
these love stories are for
today's woman with
traditional values.

Visit Silhouette at www.eHarlequin.com

SILGE

Where love comes alive™

From first love to forever, these love stories are
for today's woman with traditional values.

A highly passionate, emotionally powerful
and always provocative read.

Silhouette®

SPECIAL EDITION™

Emotional, compelling stories that capture the
intensity of living, loving and creating a family in
today's world.

INTIMATE MOMENTS™

A roller-coaster read that delivers romantic thrills
in a world of suspense, adventure and more.

Visit Silhouette at www.eHarlequin.com

SDIR2